# Also by Susanna Shore

## The Reed Files
The Perfect Scam

## P.I. Tracy Hayes
Tracy Hayes, Apprentice P.I.
Tracy Hayes, P.I. and Proud
Tracy Hayes, P.I. to the Rescue
Tracy Hayes, P.I. with the Eye
Tracy Hayes, from P.I. with Love
Tracy Hayes, Tenacious P.I.
Tracy Hayes, Valentine of a P.I.
Tracy Hayes, P.I. on the Scent
Tracy Hayes, Unstoppable P.I.
Tracy Hayes, P.I. for the Win

## Thrillers
Personal
The Assassin

## House of Magic
Hexing the Ex
Saved by the Spell
Third Spell's the Charm

## Two-Natured London
The Wolf's Call
Warrior's Heart
A Wolf of Her Own
Her Warrior for Eternity
A Warrior for a Wolf
Magic under the Witching Moon
Moonlight, Magic and Mistletoes
Crimson Warrior
Magic on the Highland Moor
Wolf Moon
Magic for the Highland Wolf

# THE PERFECT
# SCAM

## THE REED FILES: BOOK ONE

## SUSANNA SHORE

CRIMSON HOUSE BOOKS

Book Design: A. K. S. Keinänen
Cover Design: A. K. S. Keinänen

ISBN 978-952-7061-59-6 (paperback edition)
ISBN 978-952-7061-58-9 (e-book edition)

www.susannashore.com

# 1

## ELIOT

WHEN YOU FAKE YOUR OWN DEATH to escape a life of crime—and its consequences—you should take a few things into consideration. They're sort of self-evident, but you'd be surprised how many people ignore the basic safety measures that will keep the law and—most importantly—the mafia boss you double-crossed from finding you.

Rule number one: you must cut all connections with your past, no matter how important to you.

It's painful, I know. I watched footage of my mother at my funeral that a relative had posted on Facebook, and it was heartbreaking. If I hadn't been hiding in the Canadian wilderness at the time with no transportation, I would have returned home right then.

I would have begged for her forgiveness. I still wanted to. She would've boxed my ears and then made me my favorite pasta.

The Feds would've arrested me before I finished the meal. For wasting their time with my death if for nothing else, although if my former boss were ever arrested, he'd take me down with him if I were around.

Fortunately, the forced delay had made me come to my senses and I was still a free man, if not entirely happy for hurting Mom. I was her only son.

Rule number two is more flexible, but you can't ignore it either: you must have enough identities to burn, with top quality documentation and believable backstories to go with them. It takes money, connections, and time to arrange those, but I had all three.

I'd begun to plan my exit two years before I finally went through with it. Even then, I wasn't nearly as prepared as I'd wanted to be.

Since my teens, I'd been a proud member of a New Jersey crime organization that imported and distributed drugs and ran a casino in Atlantic City to launder the gains of the drug business. I'd risen steadily from an enforcer to my boss's right-hand man, helping him to spread our business to Brooklyn, and eventually ending up running a casino hotel for him there.

But when he wanted to expand our businesses to human trafficking, I'd openly disagreed with him. That's a death sentence in a crime organization, no matter how trusted you are. He'd asked me to fall in line or put my affairs in order, and so I'd had to leave sooner than I'd anticipated.

I'd been ready.

Parents choosing the name of their firstborn couldn't have spent more time on baby name sites than I did when I selected names that felt like me. I spent hours creating backstories for them with high school and college diplomas—neither of which I had—and credible CVs consisting mostly of white-collar desk jobs. I painstakingly built social media presences for each identity—and then a tech nerd I'd befriended did the same with an algorithm that made it appear like those people had been posting for years.

He also created genuine paper trails for each assumed CV and acquired the best IDs I'd ever seen, genuine government-issued documentation, for fake identities. I don't know how he hacked into the various systems to create them, but there were government databases in many countries stating I was a natural or naturalized resident of that country. I even paid taxes in some of them.

Taxes are important. Many a mafia boss has been brought down by the taxman when no other charges have stuck.

If you don't have a hacker genius among your friends—and hacker geniuses are difficult to come by—choose large schools and companies for your backstories. You can always claim they've lost your files if anyone goes to check, but in small towns everyone knows each other. It'll be more suspicious when they don't know you.

During the first seven months after my death, I went through three lesser identities—those without fake backstories—as I made my way to where I was today and settled on the current one: Eliot Reed. He was by far my favorite. I hoped I could be him for the rest of my life, but I was ready to leave him and my present life in the blink of an eye.

That's rule number three: never get attached to what you have and who you're with, because you never know when you might need to make a hasty exit. Just because I'd been lucky so far was no reason to get complacent and settle down too comfortably.

Which leads to rule number four: have several escape plans and contingency locations ready. I have safety deposit boxes around the world with hard currency and new identities, as well as perfectly legal bank accounts in some major countries, with automated regular activity that keep the authorities from flagging them. A shell company I own pays them "salary," and then the accounts pay "bills" to other accounts of mine.

It had taken me years to establish those, some of them highly illegally, but since the crime boss I'd worked for had an efficient money laundering system in place, of which I'd been in charge towards the end, it hadn't been too difficult to stash away clean money of my own on the side.

Some of it had been my boss's money, one of the reasons I'd needed to leave.

If I lived a peaceful, inconspicuous life, that money would see me into my old age with ease, and I was only thirty-four. Well, Eliot Reed was thirty-*two*, as there was no need to stick with my biological age. And since the laundered money was now perfectly legal, if you weren't too fussy about the origin, I could invest it and even live in luxury. Provided I didn't draw attention to myself.

That's rule number five: lay low.

I knew even before I left that I would have difficulties with this one. I'm a social creature. I like people. I like parties. I like luxury items. And I love women and good food.

I didn't even consider living in some remote village in a South American jungle or a fishing community in Thailand. I'd go stir-crazy in a month. The two months I'd spent in Canadian forests as part of a logging crew while I waited for things to cool down after my explosive death were the longest of my life. The only way I was able to get through it without crying uncle was by taking it as a chance to finalize the changes in my appearance and counting the days to when I could leave.

I'd chosen large cities for my hideouts. You'd be surprised how alone and anonymous you can be in them. Transactions are handled through lawyers—always different, obviously—and in no time at all you'll have a nice condo, or the equivalent in that country, in a good neighborhood. If you pretend to live a regular nine-to-five life and don't bother your neighbors, you might as well not exist as far as they're concerned.

I wasn't a recluse. I'd established a couple of businesses to justify my lifestyle without inventing rich parents that I'd have to find a way to prove. They took off, to my surprise, which had led to business meetings and lunches. I dated a few times—a man can go only so long without the company of a woman—and I went to sport events and clubs where I could be a nameless face in the crowd. But I have no friends, coworkers, or permanent lovers. I don't know my neighbors and they don't know me.

Imagine my surprise, then, when I found myself invited to a rooftop party organized by the man who owned the penthouse of the building where I lived.

I was even more surprised to find myself attending.

THE PENTHOUSE IN QUESTION was in Lyon, in South-Eastern France, where I'd settled sort of accidentally on purpose. I didn't even know it existed before I came to Europe, but it suited me perfectly.

I tried to avoid capitals and major tourist hubs, but I needed a large city with a thriving business scene to explain why I was there. Lyon, with a population of about half a million within its city limits and two million in its metropolitan area, was the third largest city in France and a major center for banking and specialized tech industries like pharmaceutics, and a thriving hub for video game industries and tech startups, the latter of which I'd begun to dabble in.

It was also the location of Interpol headquarters, but I figured they would never think I'd moved right under their noses. And it kept me on my toes, so that I wouldn't get too comfortable.

I'd first heard of the city from Elizabeth Harris, a woman I'd dated when I lived in Frankfurt, another banking hub, in Germany, to have a believable alibi. Or a backstory, if you prefer that word; someone I could refer to with ease to make it look like I had a normal past before coming to Lyon.

She was a Brit in her late thirties who worked for a huge international banking firm and was relocated every year or so. I'd chosen her especially knowing she would leave soon—I'd been hanging around in bars where bankers spent their evenings and eavesdropped on her conversation with her friends—and then chatted her up. She was a nice woman and I'd had a pleasant time with her, but when the time for her transfer came, neither of us was heartbroken when I didn't follow.

She'd hoped to be transferred to Lyon, but instead she'd been moved to Singapore. I wouldn't have minded living in Singapore—you could definitely disappear there—but instead I'd looked into Lyon and liked what I saw.

I arrived in early March and spent two weeks scouting locations. The old town was on a narrow strip of land between two major rivers, the Rhône and the Saône, which combined at the southern tip to form a peninsula—

like Manhattan, but a fraction of its size. And like Manhattan, most of the city was spread beyond the rivers.

Unlike Manhattan, it had a thriving countryside with famous vineyards and other agriculture right outside the metropolitan area on the surrounding hills.

The city oozed history from the Roman era onwards, with ruins to prove it, but what spoke to me most was an area called Confluence at the southern end of the old town. It was an erstwhile industrial area that had been razed and was being transformed into a modern hub of small tech startups, with new, sought-after apartment buildings in the mix that didn't have to conform to the architectural rules of the historical neighborhoods.

It reminded me of Red Hook, Brooklyn, the old harbor and industrial area by the East River where I'd run a hotel and casino converted from an old warehouse. Confluence had similar conversions, like the railway station slash mall, and it was constantly buzzing too, with new buildings rising everywhere, but on a smaller scale.

Everything was smaller here.

I'd lucked out and managed to rent a fully furnished third-floor apartment in an eight-story building that had probably represented the peak of architectural whimsy a decade ago with its green metal walls and irregular balcony placements, but it already managed to look old-fashioned. Inside, it was nice and modern.

It was located at a cul-de-sac by the Saône, the western of the rivers, and I had a view toward the hills of the fifth arrondissement across it from my balcony. Not that I'd spent much time on it so far, but it was early May, spring had sprung, and the sun was warming the south-facing balcony nicely. I might start having my morning coffee there.

I had rented an office in a new building full of similar small businesses by the Confluence railway station less than a ten-minute walk from my home. I didn't really need it, I had an office at home, but it gave purpose and structure to my days.

And it kept my neighbors from getting suspicious.

I left for work every morning, had breakfast at one of the cafés by the quay outside the railway station, and spent the day handling my businesses. On my way home, I ate at one of the restaurants in the mall or ventured to the old town for the excellent cuisine Lyon was famous for, and then returned home to watch TV like a normal person.

I'd become a businessman sort of accidentally. But I liked it, I was good at it, and it gave me something to do. However, I hadn't kept as low a profile as I thought.

# 2

## ELIOT

I DIDN'T KNOW ANYONE AT THE PARTY, not even the host. But it had been a while since I'd done anything sociable and I needed human company. I was excited to attend, even.

I was wearing a new suit I hadn't been able to use yet. It was off the rack—I had the figure for it now—but it was Armani, and it made me feel like my old self for the first time in a year.

In my previous life, I'd loved managing a hotel and casino for my crime boss, ambling among the guests and attending to the high rollers. It was hands down the best job I'd had in my lifelong career in crime. If I could return to it without drawing attention to myself, I would in a heartbeat.

In lieu of it, an event with nameless wealthy people who were solely concerned about themselves was a safe way to be among people. That didn't mean I hadn't run a thorough check of my host, Dominique Fabre.

He was in his late forties and had made his fortune with a series of technology startups which he had sold one after another with ever increasing sums. Currently he was busy helping other startups to the next level. The party tonight was for such companies and their potential investors, and select people living in the building. I'd been invited as the latter.

Or so I thought.

"I took the liberty of checking you out," Fabre said affably as he shook my hand, the words guaranteed to make me break out in a cold sweat.

"Oh?" I managed to say, hopefully indicating mild interest instead of an acute onslaught of panic, but I was locating the exits for a hasty retreat.

The penthouse was a two-tier cube on top of our long, rectangular building. There were three similar penthouses sticking out of the roof like studs on a Lego brick, and his was the closest to the river.

The upper story of the cube was smaller, and the garden where the party was being held spread outside it on the roof of the lower tier. A small foyer with an elevator and a stairwell from the lobby gave access to the garden and to Fabre's apartment. Only one door led to the foyer, and Fabre was standing between me and it.

Before I managed to act on my first impulse and jump over the brick railing lining the roof garden, Fabre continued with his fairly good English. Everyone spoke English to me the moment they realized I wasn't local. I could speak French, I'd learned for my job as hotel manager, but what had delighted hotel guests in America made the locals here roll their eyes.

"Yes, I noticed you've been investing in technology companies recently. I have just the ticket that might interest you."

Not waiting for my answer, he took me by my arm—not something the old me had ever had to endure—and led me across the garden to a group of three men who were trying to hide their nervousness behind champagne glasses. The moment Fabre introduced me, they launched into a well-practiced elevator pitch about their company—the first of many that night.

I'd intended to keep a low profile, have a drink or two, and then slip away unnoticed once I'd filled my need to socialize, maybe with a willing woman if I was lucky. But people were flocking to me to pitch their business ideas, and it would've gained me the wrong kind of attention if I'd fled. So I stayed, mingled, and listened to the pitches. I even found myself warming up to a couple of them.

When you've spent years looking for twisted business opportunities for laundering money, you became surprisingly good at spotting the real deals.

But not for a moment did I forget to keep an eye on new arrivals for faces I might recognize—and who might recognize me in return.

That's rule number six: keep away from anyone you've met before. There isn't a disguise so good that you couldn't be made by a random, friendly acquaintance.

Obviously, I'd made myself look as different as possible without extensive plastic surgery. I'd only had my nose fixed, as it had been very recognizable. It had been broken several times during my years as an enforcer when my crime boss had still needed me for physical intimidation. I'd been good at it.

Now the nose was an elegant Greek, straight and narrow—heh—which, considering that it had started as a very Italian nozzle, was a testament to my plastic surgeon's skills.

As a side-effect, I could breathe more easily, I didn't snore as much, and my voice had lost the nasal pitch of Jersey Italians.

The other changes had been slower to make, and took self-discipline I hadn't known I possessed until it became a matter of life and death.

Jonathan "Jonny" Moreira—the old me—had been three hundred pounds of bulging muscle and hulking frame. When he walked into a room, people noticed—and feared.

The look was deliberate and had taken years to build. In my adolescence, I'd been a short and scrawny runt of the litter with curly red hair and the inability to keep my mouth shut. I got beaten up a lot.

I began to pump iron until I was strong enough to fight back—and then I kept pumping. To appear taller, I wore platform shoes or hidden heels that I kept using even after I grew six inches during the summer that I turned nineteen, adding an inch to my sudden six two to make me a six three. Or, since I was in France now, the home of metric system, transforming my one meter eighty-eight centimeters to one ninety-one.

At the peak of my enforcer career, I was a barrel-chested behemoth, with a neck that began widening from my ears and a heavy jaw to match, and biceps that made my tailor weep when he tried to fit sleeves around them. With my broken nose and permanently glowering thick brows, I only had to enter a room and people cowered.

I won't bore you with details of my transformation, which began two years before I faked my death, but it required leaving the weights alone, regulating my intake of protein, and starting jogging and yoga.

It went as well as you can imagine at first. You try lugging around three hundred pounds of muscle—or a hundred and forty kilos in local—but as my muscle mass started to diminish, running became easier.

Incidentally, it's much easier to lose muscle than fat, so the change was faster than I'd feared. The difficulty was to hide it from people and involved wearing football padding under my suit, among other things.

Now, three years after I began the transformation, Eliot Reed—the current me—who didn't wear heels, was one meter eighty-eight with the lean, long-muscled, and tight body of a soccer player. I had a normal neck between nice, wide shoulders, and my jaw didn't look like I could chew nails anymore. The structure of my face had become more sculptured too as I lost weight. Who knew I had cheekbones?

Tired of being bullied for the red hair, I'd dyed it black since I was fifteen, and had kept it tightly combed back with pomade to prevent it from curling. I shaved it off the day before I died. As it grew back, I'd been surprised to discover that it wasn't red anymore. It was dark chestnut brown with a hint of gray creeping in that aggravated me to no end. I was only thirty-four—sorry, thirty-two.

A hairstylist took care of those. He added strategically placed highlights too, which made the hair look a lighter shade of chestnut that suited me well.

My current hairstyle was longer than I was comfortable with. The front hair fell softly from a side partition over my forehead, which the stylist assured me became me before asking me out. It was layered to slightly shorter at the back and it had begun to curl lightly again, now that I didn't try to beat it into submission with pomade.

I declined the date invitation, by the way. I wasn't as opposed to the idea of dating men as a stereotypical Jersey mafia enforcer should be, but I'd never tried it and I wasn't about to start experimenting now. But I took it as a proof that my transformation was working.

My eyes were no longer the dark brown of my adult years either. No magic involved there. I had a girlfriend when I was about twenty who didn't like my green-gray eyes and convinced me to wear brown contacts instead. I'd gotten used to the look by the time we broke up and I'd kept using them.

With the straight nose, trimmed brows, and strategically grown facial hair—tightly-trimmed sideburns that narrowed my face further—I didn't look like a Jersey goon of Italian origin anymore. I looked like any stylish Frenchman of my age. My face startled me every time I spotted my reflection, but I blended in. I doubt even my mother would've recognized me.

Well, she probably would, but AI facial recognition systems on borders wouldn't. Six two was a marked difference from six three for algorithms, and a three-hundred-pound guy didn't walk like a wiry one-eighty. I'd had to practice walking anew after losing weight.

But it wasn't the software I was trying to fool here.

OTHER GUESTS WEREN'T the only people on my radar. I kept an eye on the wait staff too, in case they'd worked at my hotel before. There was a small army of them serving the eighty or so guests that had gathered on the roof, offering finger foods and excellent Beaujolais the area was famous for.

I found myself keeping an eye on them like I were still a hotel manager. I noticed their efficiency and politeness with approval, as well as the speed with which they whisked the empty glasses away. I even found myself frowning at one waitress when the empty glasses began to accumulate on the low wall around the garden, sending her hastily to collect them.

It was an effort to shake myself out of the habit and start enjoying the party as a guest. The pitches didn't completely hold my attention though. I was looking for company for the night too.

Unfortunately for me, there were more men than women present, and the few women were older than the men and most of them were married. And while all women are attractive and French women doubly so, none of them were interesting enough to bother with.

I was ready to give up and head home when a woman crossed my line of sight with unhurried steps. Judging by the empty tray she carried under her arm, she belonged to the wait staff. Her light gait gave natural sway to her hips and made the ponytail of her long blond hair bounce.

She was taller than most women here, and some of the men too, even though she was wearing sneakers—which probably helped with the easy walk. But she wasn't slouching to appear smaller; she was holding her head high.

Her long legs were sheathed in black leggings, and she wore a wraparound tunic that hid everything, unlike the other waitresses who wore LBDs with plunging necklines and makeup that was guaranteed to draw male attention—if the man managed to pull his eyes off the cleavage first.

I watched her cross the roof to the staging area, my head tilting in appreciation. She disappeared behind the screens that separated it from the party and a sudden urge to ask her name quickened me unlike any woman had since my death.

I excused myself, to knowing chuckles of the men with me, put down my glass and went after her. But I was only halfway cross the roof when I saw her enter the foyer. Was she leaving already?

I lengthened my steps to catch her, but I wasn't fast enough. The foyer was empty, and the digital display above the elevator door was counting down. Driven by a need, I almost ran down the stairs, only to halt before I pushed open the door to the stairwell. She'd be long gone before I reached the lobby.

Disproportionally disappointed for my bad luck, I turned to head back to the party, only to halt with a puzzled frown. The door to Fabre's apartment opposite to the elevator was slightly open. Had one of the guests wandered where they shouldn't?

It was none of my business. I didn't want to walk in on the guests having sex on the host's bed, or witness someone making off with Fabre's valuables. The last thing I wanted was to get involved in criminal endeavors.

That was rule number seven, one you should never break if you are on the run. Keep away from a life of crime. You've made it out. Don't go back, even vicariously.

And yet, I found myself glancing around and looking for cameras. There weren't any, which was foolish of Fabre. Satisfied that no one would see me, I pushed the door open with my elbow and entered the apartment.

IT WAS DARK AND QUIET inside, and I hoped that whoever had forgotten to close the door had already left. I stood still, straining my ears while my eyes adjusted to the dim light that the full moon and the garden lights shone through the large windows.

The upper floor was one open space that doubled as a library and a family room. It was empty. Stairs led down on my right, but it looked dark there too.

I should leave before Fabre popped in and found me here.

But a noise downstairs made me tense. Before I had considered the action through, I was heading down the stairs as quietly as I could. I'd been surprisingly good at it when I was twice the size. Now I barely made a sound.

At the bottom, a hallway led to left and right with rooms on both sides. It was dark, but a door was open at the far end on the right, letting in ambient light from outside that helped me to walk there without tripping.

I paused outside the open door and peeked in. The sight made adrenaline surge through my body.

A form in black stood in front of a wall-safe, silhouetted against the window where one curtain had been pulled aside to give them just enough light to work by. They'd managed to open the safe and were moving the contents to a bag hanging over their shoulder with efficient movements.

My hand went inside my suit jacket where I'd been accustomed to carrying a piece on a shoulder holster, but it met with emptiness. Weapon laws were strict around here, and I was a legitimate businessman who had no need for a gun. I didn't even own one anymore.

But I had the element of surprise on my side. As the burglar made to close the safe door, I rushed across the floor. A soft Persian rug silenced my approach, but I must've made a sound anyway, because as I reached for the thief they stepped aside, twirled around, and kicked me in the gut with enough force that it robbed me off my breath.

This wasn't the first time I'd been at the receiving end of such a kick, even if I didn't have the armor of muscle anymore. It didn't floor me. I lunged after the thief, who was trying to escape, and executed a perfect tackle. I landed on them with my full weight, which even in my diminished size was enough to pin them against the floor.

The body under me felt less substantial than I'd anticipated, which gave me pause. Pushing up, I made to turn them around, and my hand met what was unmistakably a breast.

The thief was a woman.

# 3

## ADA

"WHAT THE HELL?"

The man who had tackled me rose to his feet with sinuous grace, pulling me up too. I was winded from him landing on me and my heart was beating too hard for the fright he'd given me, but I would've run if his grip around my wrist hadn't been so tight.

"You're a woman."

I rolled my eyes, even though he couldn't see it. It was dark, for one, and night-vision goggles covered my eyes. I hated the greenish tint they gave to everything, but they were indispensable in my line of work.

His face was a white blob through them. I didn't recognize him, but he wasn't the owner of the flat, that much was certain. Fabre wasn't this tall, at least half a head taller than me, and I was one meter seventy-five. Fabre's shoulders were narrower and stooping, whereas this guy filled his suit perfectly.

"As if women couldn't be safecrackers."

I couldn't keep the comment in, but at least the balaclava covering my face muffled my voice, and I remembered to lower my voice and affect a Boston accent.

Only when he startled did I register that he had spoken English too, and he was clearly American.

Bugger.

"You're the waitress, aren't you?"

His words stunned me so completely that I didn't resist when he dragged me to the large desk by the window and lit the lamp on it. I barely had time to close my eyes before the goggles flooded my eyes with light.

*The* waitress? Not one of the waitresses?

"You are. I recognize those legs."

Surprise made me open my eyes. I closed them instantly again, but it was too late. Bright spots were dancing behind my lids and water was running from my eyes.

It took all my self-control to keep my mouth shut, even though questions were rushing through my head. How had he noticed me? People never paid attention to waiters in an event like this and I'd made sure to be unnoticeable.

Was he security? My intel had indicated there wouldn't be any, but perhaps Fabre had made a last-minute change. I'd made an error somewhere and gained his attention. Had he followed me here?

I had to flee.

My hip was propped against the desk, so I knew where I was in relation to the room, even though my eyes were firmly shut. The hand gripping my wrist gave me the man's position. I needed a weapon, but I had nothing immediately available. I never carried anything that might compromise my safety.

"Remove the goggles," the man ordered. His voice was authoritative, so he was used to being in charge. But in charge of what?

Since he seemed perfectly capable of removing them for me, I obeyed, lifting them on my forehead so that they pressed my brows down. With the balaclava, it might just be enough to distort my features so that he wouldn't recognize me later.

I blinked, trying to clear my vision. Then I studied my captor. I didn't recognize him. He hadn't been on my checklist prior to the event, so he couldn't be one of the investors. But with such an expensive suit, he wasn't security either—or a startup nerd.

Puzzled, I concentrated on his face. The sculpted jaw and defined features said France, but the voice said America. He was younger than I'd assumed, about my age, and while his trim body fit my image of high-end private security, the carefree hair and elegant sideburns didn't.

Then again, his skill in capturing me and the authority with which he was interrogating me meant he was more than a suit.

"Who are you?"

His straight brows shot up and I realized I'd asked it aloud.

"Shouldn't I be asking that?"

I let my lip curl into a sneer, even though the balaclava covered my mouth and he couldn't see it. "As if you'd believe I'd give you my real name."

He acknowledged this with a small shrug. "The police will learn it."

His free hand went to his side inside his jacket, only to come out empty. He cursed and muttered something about stupid laws. My body went cold when it hit me that he had been reaching for a weapon. Was he a cop?

I had to get out of here.

He slipped his hand in the inside pocket of his jacket, presumably to fish out a phone, but since it was the left pocket and left hand, he fumbled.

His attention on his task, I reached for the desk lamp and switched it off. His grip on my wrist slackened minutely. It was all I needed. I executed a nifty self-defense move and broke his hold.

Then I was already rolling away from him like a ninja. But not toward the hallway door like the man assumed.

As he rushed out of the room, I headed to the terrace, having opened the door before I opened the safe. I slipped through the curtains, careful not to stir them to let light in.

If there were any rules to being a successful burglar, it was this: always have your escape route ready.

I grabbed a rappel rope I'd attached earlier that night onto the wall circling the garden above. The terrace of the study was conveniently on the opposite side of the roof from the party, but if it hadn't been I would've planned a different escape route. I secured the rope into a motored winch on my belt, and with its assistance, ran up the wall as silently as possible.

I was climbing over the garden wall when I heard the man enter the balcony below. He'd returned faster than I assumed. I'd hoped he would search the flat first.

The urge to look down to see what he would do was almost irresistible. Ignoring it, I pulled out a bag that I'd hidden behind a large pot of a palm earlier. No one would come to this side of the building, it was closed off from the guests, but I didn't have time to waste.

With the practiced moves of numerous similar operations, I removed the goggles, gloves, balaclava, and the long blond wig underneath, and stuffed them into a black plastic bin liner. My trainers and leggings came off next, along with the sports bra that had kept my breasts squished to near invisibility.

Not that it had helped. The man had instantly realized I was a woman. The memory of his large hand landing on my breast made my face burn.

I took out a dress of some stretchy material that looked festive in a dim light and didn't wrinkle when stuffed into a bag and pulled it on hastily. It reached to my ankles, hiding my legs, which I hadn't realized were so recognizable before, and cut under the breasts with inbuilt support that gave me a good cleavage even without a bra underneath. No one would pay attention to my face now.

I didn't have time to take off the chocolate brown contact lenses like I'd planned. The man had seen my eyes, but many people had brown eyes. And they fit the dark brown curly wig that I pulled on.

High-heeled sandals were next, after which I applied red lipstick generously, before clipping on earrings and fluffing out the wig. I checked my face with a compact mirror for press marks left by the goggles, but thanks to the balaclava there weren't any.

I took out an evening bag that contained a few chosen items like keys and some money, and put the lipstick in. Then I stuffed all the incriminating evidence, including my loot, into the binbag and secured it tightly before tying the rappelling rope around it.

I hurried to the side of the roof that faced the small park in the middle of the housing complex, the only place where Fabre's roof garden aligned with the wall of the rest of the building. Peeking down, I made sure no one was watching. Using the rope, I glided the binbag down into the park. When I felt it hit the ground behind the hedges, I dropped the rope down too.

The park was gated and closed for the night. With any luck, no one would find the bag before I did.

With no more time to waste, I rounded the roof to where the party was. Taking another peek to see that no one was paying attention to me, I slipped out of my hiding place and into the party.

I took a glass of wine from a passing waitress who didn't bat an eye in recognition even though we'd worked side by side the whole evening. A couple of steps brought me near a group of men who were talking loudly, relaxed now that their pitches were done. They didn't pay attention to me, but to other guests it would look like I was part of their group.

My heart still beating too fast for my narrow escape, I took a sip from my glass just as the man I'd escaped from entered the roof from the foyer. He must've searched the flat and called the police. I had to be grateful for his delay, but with the police on their way I would have to leave immediately.

He scanned the roof with the sharp eye of someone accustomed to doing it. I held my breath when his gaze brushed past me, fighting not to look directly at him. Frowning, he headed to the staff staging area. He knew I'd been a waitress here. It was only a matter of time before one of the staff pointed at me, no matter how good my disguise.

It took all my self-control not to run to the foyer, the only way out. I waited until a group of people near me headed there and followed in their wake.

The lift car wasn't in the foyer; I'd sent it down before slipping into Fabre's flat—not that it had fooled the man.

The wait for it to arrive made sweat trickle down my spine. My muscles were tense for expecting a detaining hand to land on my shoulder at any moment.

When the car finally arrived, I entered first, but stayed by the door to be the first to exit. Someone pushed the button to the lobby and the doors began to close. I sighed in relief.

Too early.

A large hand blocked the door sensor and the doors opened again. The man I didn't want to see entered the car and took post right next to me. Even in my heels, he was much taller than me, standing straight and like he owned the place.

"Thank you for hearing our pitch, Mr. Reed," one of the men in the lift gushed in passable English. "I hope you liked it. We'll be happy to give more information if you need."

My heart stopped, and not merely because the man turned to the talker, his gaze taking me in and discarding me on his way, but because of the name.

My name.


SHOCK MADE ME MISS the rest of the conversation, until one of the men nudged me. "How about you, Mademoiselle?" he asked in French. "Would you like to go to Azar with us?"

It was a club near here, located in a huge warehouse, and a favorite of mine. But even if I'd been at liberty to go, I wouldn't have gone with them. I shook my head.

"I need to go to release my babysitter."

Thanks to my French mother, my French had been good even before I moved to Lyon, and after four years living here it was damn near perfect. My fast-beating heart made my voice breathy and higher than normal, a natural disguise, as I'd been too addlebrained to alter my voice.

The bloke who had asked the question sneered, like I had known he would. "Word of advice: men don't like to hear that a hot woman has a child."

He was saved from my reaction when the doors opened and I could escape to the lobby. But the men were even more eager to leave and they pushed past me, forcing me to stay behind. I gritted my teeth and let them go first. It was best they weren't outside waiting when I got there.

Finally able to exit, I walked with purposeful steps half across the lobby, when Mr. Reed's voice right behind me made my step falter.

"There's no child, is there?" His French was good, but it had a clear American accent.

I glanced briefly at him, unwilling to let him have a good look at my face. "Then you should know that it was used for brushing those men off."

"In that case, may I offer you a ride home?"

I paused and faced him properly, ready to explain to him—in no uncertain terms—that I hadn't brushed the other men off so that I could go home with him. But genuine concern in his eyes made me hold my tongue—as did their remarkable color. They were gray with a sheen of green, like mother of pearl or seafoam.

I blinked. "Thank you, but I have a car."

Good thing it was true, because he nodded. "Allow me to walk you there, then."

What was his angle? Did he suspect me and was trying to keep me here until the police arrived? And what was holding them anyway? Shouldn't they be arriving with sirens blaring by now?

But the woman I was pretending to be would welcome the escort, so I nodded. He walked me across the lobby and opened the door for me. I exited without a glance at him.

The men from the lift were gone and the street was empty. It was quiet in this neighborhood even during the day. At this time of night, with my senses heightened and adrenaline coursing through my veins, the silent street seemed ominous.

"I don't remember seeing you at the party," Mr. Reed said.

Good.

"I arrived late. My team handled most of the pitches already."

"That was careless of you."

I shrugged. "Served the jerks right." I was imagining the blokes from the lift.

He laughed. "Not an exclusive work environment, is it?"

I shrugged again, the way the French did, with the entire body. I'd had to practice it and now it came naturally. "It has its good points."

"What was your pitch about?"

Shit. I tried to remember the snippets I'd overheard while I carried trays around. "The sunglasses with camera in their frames that connects to the phone." I only barely managed not to make it sound like a question.

He made a dismissive brush with his hand. "It won't succeed. Facebook has already done it."

"But ours is better, and it isn't exclusive to a social media platform." I don't know why I was defending it, other than that a dedicated worker would.

Fortunately, we arrived at my car before he could launch into a deeper discussion, because that was literally everything I'd managed to hear of that pitch.

"This is me," I said, digging into my evening purse for the car key. I'd remembered to put it there this time, instead of stashing it with the rest in the hidden equipment. That had been a long walk home. "Thank you for seeing me safely here."

He offered me a hand. "My pleasure. May I know your name? I'm Eliot Reed."

Again, the name made me miss a beat, and he smiled. "I promise I'm not a stalker."

I smiled too, hopefully looking charmed instead of franticly struggling to remember the name I'd used with the car share app.

"Sandrine."

He took my hand and bowed over it, looking me in the eyes. It was effective, I had to give him that.

"Just Sandrine?"

"Just Sandrine." I removed my hand from his and opened the car door, slipping in. "Thank you for your help."

He didn't try to detain me longer but just closed the door for me. I switched the engine on, put the car in gear, and pulled away with a wave of my hand. I managed to drive to the end of the short street before glancing in the rearview mirror. He was standing in the middle of the street, hands in the pockets of his trousers, looking after me.

I didn't remember to use the blinker when I turned at the corner.

# 4

## ADA

I EXPECTED TO HEAR SIRENS AT any moment as I drove north through the old town. I wasn't paying attention to where I was going, but it was impossible to drive to random directions in Lyon, as most streets were one way only. I didn't register my surroundings until I was about to turn to Quai de la Pêcherie, a boulevard by the Saône, on which my flat was.

Leading the cops straight to my home was one way to get caught.

I turned east instead and crossed the Rhône by Pont Lafayette. I drove to a parking garage by Gare de Lyon Part-Dieu railway station, not far from the river, and chose a spot as far from the cameras as possible.

Before exiting the car, I needed another quick change, so I retrieved the large tote bag I'd hidden in the footwell on the passenger side, where I had another set of disguises.

It's not easy to pull on tight black jeans in a car, especially with legs as long as mine, but thanks to years of gymnastics when I was a child, I was flexible. A black turtleneck was easier to put on. The night was chilly, so it wouldn't draw attention, even paired with a black trench coat and knee-high boots.

I removed the curly wig and replaced it with an auburn bob with a fringe that reached my eyes—annoying but necessary. The red lipstick and brown contacts had to come off too. I blinked to moisten my eyes, staring at the pale blues in the rearview mirror.

Nothing to write home about, those, unlike the seafoam grays of Eliot Reed.

Damn, but that name irked me. How dare he have the same name? It wasn't even the name I'd been born with, but my married name, and it still vexed me. I was annoyed with myself too, for letting it shake me enough to almost make mistakes, as if I were a rookie on my first job.

Was he a relative of Danny's come to town to find me?

Cold settled in my bones with that thought and I was able to finish my transformation. I pulled out a black silk scarf from the bag and wrapped it artistically over my head and around my throat. Très chic. And it shielded my face from cameras.

Satisfied with my look, I stuffed my belongings into the bag. Then I put on soft, feminine leather gloves that wouldn't look odd even in this weather, and wiped the steering wheel and everything I could possibly have touched with a tissue soaked in hand sanitizer.

Exiting the car, I checked that I hadn't left hairs or other evidence in the car and then wiped the door handle and the key, before locking the car. I went to drop the key into the lockbox near the exit and even remembered to inform the car share app where the car was. It wouldn't do to get caught for failing to return a car.

Satisfied that everything was in order, I headed to the nearest tram stop. The trams would stop operating at midnight, but I still had time. People who had arrived on train or were leaving the concert hall nearby were filling the stop, making it easier for me to go unnoticed.

It was a twenty-minute ride back to where I had come from. To my amazement, there were still no police cars outside Fabre's building, and the soft glow of lights on the roof garden indicated the party was going strong.

*Incroyable.*

I exited the tram at the Confluence railway station with a bunch of people who headed briskly across the quay. I trailed after three young women who were chatting happily about the concert they'd just seen, as if I wanted to keep close for safety.

They entered one of the weird looking blocks of flats of the housing complex by the quay, on the opposite side of the park from Fabre's penthouse. I hastened my steps, catching the door just as it was about to close. I had my lockpicks, but someone might notice me using them. I waited for the women to disappear up the stairs before slipping in.

I took a moment to catch my breath—figuratively—and tug the scarf back in place to hide my face from the security camera. I crossed the lobby to a hallway at the back that led to the gated park in the middle of the complex. No alarms on the back door, and there was a helpful wedge of wood by it meant for keeping the door from closing.

Only a couple of dim lights illuminated the park. It was quiet and I could hear low sounds from Fabre's rooftop garden where the party continued uninterrupted.

Keeping under the trees lining the path, I crossed the park and fetched the binbag I'd dropped behind the bushes. I stashed it inside the large tote and returned the way I came. In no time at all I was entering the Confluence railway station and exiting it a moment later through the entrance of the hotel at the other end. A taxi was waiting for random nighttime customers outside, and I climbed in.

"Lyon-Saint Exupéry, *s'il vous plaît.*"

It was a half an hour drive to the airport at the eastern edge of the metropolitan area, the traffic nonexistent at that time of night. He left me outside terminal 2 and drove off before I'd entered the building.

It was well past one o'clock in the morning and the terminal was quiet but not empty. No one paid attention to me as I took the escalator one level down and headed to the loo. I removed the wig and made a few changes to my clothing before heading to the car park on the same level, looking like my regular self. I paid the parking fee, collected my car, and was on my way home in no time at all.

It might seem excessive to take so many safety measures, but I was operating in my hometown tonight. I could leave absolutely no traces. And it wasn't solely the police that worried me anymore.

It was Eliot Reed.

BY MONDAY MORNING, I was fully recovered from the excitement on Saturday night. I'd had a quiet Sunday removing the traces of my activities. I'd washed the clothes I'd worn and cleaned the shoes, stored the rope and night vision goggles to their appointed drawers, and the wigs on Styrofoam heads in the hidden closet in my flat. I checked that the car I'd used had no red flags attached to it.

I'd emptied Fabre's safe completely, not having had time to sort through the contents, and my loot held some surprises. I was now in possession of the deeds to his penthouse and other property, as well as his diplomas from the Sorbonne I didn't know what to do with. Hopefully he had everything in digitalized form too, because he wasn't getting them back any time soon.

There were also four identical sets of diamond and ruby necklaces with matching earrings and bracelets. Fabre wasn't married, had never been, so I couldn't understand what he would do with one set, let alone four. They weren't very good quality, so they couldn't be an investment. But I could sell them for a few quid.

Compared with the ten million I'd made the last time I opened a private safe, it was almost insulting, but it wasn't the payload I'd gone there for. That was a small external drive I'd been commissioned to steal and was itching to get my hands into.

I didn't usually care about the contents of whatever devices I was asked to take, but this was an exception. Unfortunately, the device was heavily encrypted, and I didn't have the skills to crack those. I needed help.

Luckily, I knew just the girl.

The May morning was bright, so I chose a light gray pantsuit, off-the-rack but good quality. A powder pink chiffon blouse with a floppy bow softened the starkness of the suit and gave to understand that while I took my job seriously, I wasn't persnickety. The black leather ballerina shoes with white polka dots added a bit of whimsy.

My day job persona was as much a performance as my disguises.

I kept my strawberry blond hair short, both because the pixie cut looked good on me and because it was easier to wear wigs over it. Work makeup was understated, basically just black mascara, and the rims of my glasses were wine red. I actually needed glasses, though not so badly I couldn't go without. But they fit my role.

I looked what I was: a thirty-two-year-old woman with a well, but not too well-paying, white-collar job. Accountant maybe, or a lawyer.

Or an analyst at Interpol.

My tote was large. It could've fit a laptop, but we weren't allowed to take them home. The external drive was hidden inside a folder with some random papers.

Basically, the bag held my lunch and jiu-jitsu gear. I'd promised to help my friend to teach a self-defense class for housewives and other random safety conscious people that afternoon.

The morning commute was the normal hassle; the five kilometers took about the same time if I'd walked instead of taking the bus. I spent the time staring at my phone like everyone else, reading the news. There had been nothing about the burglary yesterday, but I couldn't relax yet. It just hadn't caught the interest of reporters yet.

Interpol headquarters was located in the sixth arrondissement in northeast Lyon by the Rhône, where the river bent east. Or since it flowed from the east, bent south to flow by the old town.

Incidentally, if you thought the sixth arrondissement was anywhere near the fifth, you'd be wrong. The sixth was north of the third on the east side of the Rhône, and the fifth was south of the ninth on the west side of the Saône. Easy.

The building was a huge glass cube with concrete buttresses that emulated the Gothic cathedrals the town was famous for. It was slightly outdated inside, but functional.

Security was tight, but the guards searched for weapons and explosives, not hidden external drives. I showed the middle-aged man on duty my Interpol ID, and he scrutinized it like every morning, before allowing me to walk through the metal detectors.

"Have a good day, Mademoiselle Reed."

"You too, Philippe."

I didn't head to my desk on the third floor but took a lift to the basement, where the cyber team had their lair, growing larger every year. As I'd hoped, the person I wanted to see was here already. She was always here.

Laïla Diab was a local woman who had been recruited by Interpol when she was studying at EPITA, a private *grande école*, a college specializing in computer science that only accepted the most exceptional students.

Laïla was most assuredly exceptional.

At twenty-five, she was the best cyber expert we had, probably in the entirety of Interpol. One wouldn't know it by looking at her though, and there were many otherwise intelligent people working here who constantly overlooked her and took their problems to lesser experts.

We'd started at Interpol at the same time four years ago, and during the introduction period we'd become friends. Our colleagues found our friendship amusing, mostly because of our twenty-five-centimeter height difference. I was tall, lean, and athletic; Laïla was short, tiny, and wiry.

She had a black belt in jiu-jitsu though and could easily take down people bigger than me. She was also the friend I'd promised to help that afternoon.

That wasn't why I was here this morning. "*Salut*, Laïla," I greeted her, leaning down to press my cheek against hers.

She perked. "Morning, Ada." Then she glanced at her wristwatch. "It is morning?"

I rolled my eyes as I plopped down in a chair next to her desk. "Yes, it's morning. Have you been here the whole night?"

"Cybercrime isn't bound by a clock."

She yawned and stretched her hands above her head. The loose sleeves of her shirt fell to her shoulders, revealing full-sleeve tattoos on both arms. I was pretty sure her Algerian grandparents were horrified by them, as well as the piercings down the lobes of her ears, one eyebrow, nostril, and lower lip.

Then again, my very British and French grandparents would be horrified too if I looked like her. Her family let her be. Mine wouldn't have.

"Are you here to send me home?"

I should, but I needed her help. I took out the external drive from my bag. "I need to get into this, but it's heavily protected."

Her brown eyes lit in excitement. "How heavily?"

"I didn't dare to look."

"Is this connected with one of your cases?"

I nodded. It wasn't even a lie—just not to any criminal investigations I was conducting.

"Do you have a reference number for the case?"

She might look like a punk Tinkerbell, but she was a by-the-book girl at heart.

I consulted a notebook and gave her the number of a case I was working on. Then, because I wasn't a total bastard I said: "It can wait. Go get some sleep. We have that self-defense class this afternoon."

"Yes, mother."

Laughing, I left her to it and headed to my desk. I had work to do.

MY FIRST ORDER OF BUSINESS after logging on to the Interpol network was to check the local police reports, but there wasn't a single burglary listed among the crimes over the weekend. I couldn't fathom it. Had Eliot Reed not called the police after all? Or had he told Fabre first and Fabre had decided not to involve the police?

I didn't find that a likely explanation. Apart from the external drive, which he didn't have to tell the police about, there had been nothing odd or incriminating among the items I'd taken from the safe.

Abandoning the puzzle, I searched for Eliot Reed instead. Nothing caught my attention. He was thirty-two and a dual citizen of US and Italy. He'd grown up in the United States, New York to be precise, where he had owned a private security firm.

Ha! I'd been right about that.

He'd sold it for good money and had then moved to Europe about six months ago. He'd moved to Lyon in March and started businesses that concentrated on funding small tech startups. That would explain why Fabre had invited him.

But it didn't reveal why he had moved to Europe in the first place. I checked his social media sites. He posted on Facebook sporadically, but even so it was clear that there was a gap in posts for about a year, as if he'd removed traces about his relocation.

"What do you think of that?" I asked Richard Svenson, a Swede whose desk was next to mine. He'd worked in other Interpol locations before and had only transferred here about six months ago. His French was atrocious, so we used English instead.

The name was pronounced with double k, by the way, not with ch like in English, which had taken some getting used to. Rikkard.

He listened to my explanation and smiled. "Isn't it self-evident? A woman."

I pulled back. "There's no woman in these posts. Well, except this Elizabeth Harris he dated in Frankfurt."

By the looks of her, she suited a businessman perfectly.

"Not anymore. He clearly came here with or because of a woman. Then they broke up and he removed all posts involving her."

That made sense, even if he hadn't struck me as a man who followed his heart across an ocean. "Then why hasn't he removed this Elizabeth? They're still Facebook friends even."

"She's a meaningless rebound girlfriend. The other saddened or angered him so hard he had to remove all traces of her."

"Huh."

But I could relate. When my husband disappeared on me, a glimpse of his face had been enough to enrage me. The only reason I hadn't deleted the posts with his photos was because I was supposed to be a grieving widow, not a jilted wife—or a double-crossed partner in crime.

Though it had been over four years already. How long was I expected to grieve?

"Is he connected with a case?" Richard asked, and I shook my head.

"No, I'm just…"

"Stalking a good looking guy you met over the weekend?" His eyes were twinkling, but since it was a better explanation than what I had to offer, I nodded.

"Something like that."

"Well, I hope something comes of it. He looks like a catch."

I tilted my head and studied the latest photo my search had brought up, posted by one of the startups that had been pitching to him at the party on Saturday. Eliot had moved his head at the last moment and it was a tad blurry, but perfectly recognizable.

"I guess, if wealth and good looks are all you want from a relationship…"

He laughed. "Just because he has those doesn't mean he wouldn't have other good qualities too."

Like the ability to catch safecrackers…

Abandoning the search, I concentrated on my work. Most people think that Interpol is a law-enforcement organization, but that's not true. We analyze data from all over the world, making connections across borders that help local police to enforce law in their countries. We also liaise between law enforcement of different countries if they have to operate on a foreign turf.

Any criminal activity that left a trace, or anything that might help catching criminals, like airport surveillance, was researched and analyzed here. We had fields we specialized in; mine was mostly organized crime.

It was interesting and more peaceful than my previous job at the Metropolitan Police in London. I never had to arrest anyone, I wasn't as stressed, and I was never threatened by criminals. On the other hand, I never saw the results of my efforts either.

I wasn't so busy that I would have forgotten the self-defense class. Laïla was bound to forget if she was deep into cracking a problem, so I sent her a message as a reminder. I received a thumbs-up emoji in return.

Before logging off, I checked the local police reports one more time. Fabre's name was the first to pop up. I clicked the link and my heart stopped.

It wasn't about burglary. It was about a murder.

Fabre was dead.

# 5

## ELIOT

RULE NUMBER EIGHT OF FAKING YOUR death to escape life of crime: keep away from the police and law enforcement officials of any kind. Try not to so much as get a parking ticket if you can avoid it. The fewer reasons the police have for checking you out, the better.

When the burglar had escaped—and I still had no idea how she had done it—I'd switched on lights in Fabre's study and scrutinized the place. I'd closed the door to the empty safe and wiped it clean of prints. I'd wiped every possible surface on the desk I might have touched, including the lamp the burglar had touched last. I'd closed the balcony door. I suspected she'd fled through there, even though I hadn't been able to detect her in the dark park. She must have rappelled down lightning-fast and hidden in the shadows so her movement wouldn't give her away.

After returning to the roof garden, I hadn't contacted Fabre. There was no reasonable explanation I could give him for my involvement, and it would only put me on the police's radar. I'd checked the female guests and the staff, just in case she'd returned to the party, but she hadn't been there. None of the women leaving the party had large enough bags that could contain the loot either.

After seeing Sandrine to her car, I'd stayed on the dark street and watched from the shadows the guests, and then the caterers, leave. The guy who brought down the trash bags dumped them unceremoniously into the large trash receptacle. If the stolen items were in them, he wasn't aware of it.

I contemplated waiting to see if the woman came to rummage the trash, but eventually I had to give up. I returned to the roof garden, where the party had wound down. I went through the entire roof with the help of the flashlight in my phone, even the closed off sections, but I hadn't seen anything that might be considered evidence.

Satisfied, I went home. I spent the Sunday puzzling over the burglary and the woman, but whatever she had taken, it hadn't been so important that Fabre alerted the police. No one came to talk to me of it anyway.

I checked the license plate of Sandrine's car, but she had acquired it through a car share, and I couldn't get into their client information. She didn't remind me of the burglar as such, she'd been softer and curvier, but she was the only one tall enough to be her. How she could've returned to the party so fast and without the loot though…

By Monday morning, I'd resolved to put the incident behind me. I prepared to leave for work as normal, though a tad later than usually. I was the boss. I could make my own schedules.

I was fantasizing about what I would have for breakfast at my favorite café—a tie between an almond croissant, which I could eat only so often if I wanted to maintain my current trim figure, and an omelet—when there was a knock on my door.

My entire body tensed. I recognized that knock. Only the police knocked with such authority.

The need to flee made my knees buckle, but I steeled them and went to open the door. Two men stood in the hallway. The younger was in his early forties, a handsome white man with curling, fashionably cut hair going gray, and a suit that looked tailored. The other was in his fifties, of Algerian origin, and short, with black hair and an olive complexion darker than mine.

"Monsieur Reed?" the older one asked. "I'm Detective Gagne. This is Detective Bellamy."

He showed a police ID and I gave it a cursory glance. I had no reason to suspect he wouldn't be the real deal, but it was good to know he wasn't from immigration—or the FBI.

"Yes. How may I help you?" I asked in French.

"It's a delicate matter," the other man, Bellamy, said. "May we come in?"

Since I was a law-abiding person with nothing to hide, I stepped aside, and led them down a short hallway to a space that doubled as a living room and kitchen, the two separated by a bar counter.

My eyes skimmed the room, but there was nothing odd or out of place there. The house had come fully furnished and the seating group with a sofa and two armchairs were both comfortable and very French.

"Please, take a seat. May I offer you anything?"

Both declined, which I took as a bad sign, but I sat calmly on one of the armchairs as the men chose the sofa. They looked grave, much more serious than a burglary would merit, but I didn't want to speculate. It would only make me nervous and more likely to make mistakes.

"We understand you attended a party held by one Dominique Fabre on Saturday?" Gagne said in French. I probably took too long to answer, because he lifted his brows and switched language. "Would you like we speak English?"

Since his English was better than my French, I nodded. "Thank you. Yes, I attended his party."

"Do you know him well?"

"Not at all. I met him first time at the party. He invited a few people from this building. Randomly, I had assumed."

"But it wasn't?" Bellamy asked, his English more broken but understandable.

"It turned out he had learned I've been investing in tech startups recently, and since the event was about finding backers for such companies, he'd included me."

"Are you well known in those circles?"

I shrugged. "I didn't know I was. I've only been here for two months, but they're small circles."

The men nodded. "You're American, yes?"

"Yes, though I have a dual Italian citizenship. I've been using the Italian passport here." It made things easier, all around, not just on border crossings.

So far the questions had been general, but I decided to push matters a little. "Is Monsieur Fabre under investigation? Should I not have attended his event?"

The men glanced at each other and then Gagne spoke. "Monsieur Fabre is dead."

My mouth went slack. If he'd hit me with a two-by-four, he couldn't have stunned me more thoroughly. I struggled to form a coherent thought.

"Dead?" My voice squealed to my embarrassment. It wasn't like I was unfamiliar with the concept. I cleared my throat. "Natural causes?"

"If you consider bullet through the head natural causes, then yes."

In my previous line of work, that was considered a perfectly natural way to die, yet I couldn't merge my life before with the one I'd been living this past year.

"Own hand?"

"No."

The curt answer got through the shock. Fabre had been killed? By whom? And why? Was it the burglar?

I cast that notion aside immediately.

"Was it … during the party?"

Bellamy shook his head. "We're not sure. That's why we're interviewing everyone attending it. Fabre had a list of people he had invited on his desk," he added, as if I needed an explanation for how he had found me. "It was easiest to start with you since you live in the same building."

Gagne leaned closer. "He was found last evening by his housekeeper in his study."

"The party was on the roof," I said feebly, my mind racing. "Was there a struggle? Was anything stolen?"

"No, and we don't know yet." Gagne tilted his head. "Those are very specific questions."

I startled, but I'd schooled myself well on my backstory, and the answer came easily. "I used to own a private security firm."

"Ah."

It could mean anything, but I decided to leave be.

"Did you see or hear anything interesting?"

Did I ever. "No. I left the party before midnight, and I didn't see Fabre after. He didn't contact me either."

"Should he have?"

I shrugged. "He could've called to ask if I was interested in any of the startups he introduced to me. But in truth, I didn't expect him to, at least not before today."

"And you didn't see anyone suspicious around?"

"No. But I wasn't here yesterday."

"May I ask where you were?"

It was none of his business, but since I had nothing to hide, I told the truth. "I attended the Mass at Notre Dame de Fourvière and spent the rest of the day playing tourist around the neighborhood there."

"There are churches closer."

Only if the Mass had mattered to me. "But none as grand. And I wanted to see the Roman ruins."

I'd had a great day. I'd returned home late, tired and a little sunburnt, but wonderfully relaxed. I'd been just one of the tourists. No one knew me there and no one paid attention to me the whole day.

The men nodded and rose as if on a signal. "Thank you for your time. We just wanted to let you know that there's going to be a police presence in the building for a few days. And if we come up with more pertinent questions, we'll be back."

"I'll be here every evening, but I have an office nearby." I dug into my pocket and gave Gagne my business card.

I saw the men out and closed the door, leaning my forehead heavily against it. I barely resisted banging it on it.

Fuck. I'd done my best to avoid the police and now this?

With a queasy lurch, I tried to recall if I'd cleaned the office as well as I thought, or if I'd touched any other surfaces in the house that I'd forgotten to wipe. But there was nothing I could do about it now.

Sighing, I pushed myself up and headed to work.

I'D NEVER NEEDED MY afternoon yoga session as badly as I needed it today. There was a gym at the building next to my office, which I'd joined the first thing after I rented the office. I made good use of it too.

The afternoon class was full of pensioners, middle-aged housewives, and new mothers on maternity leave. I was the odd man out, but no one made a number of it. Some of the old ladies stayed after the class to have smoothies with me and flirt shamelessly. It was the closest equivalent of friendships I had here. I loved it.

But the yoga didn't help. I put every effort in concentrating on the moves and my breathing, but my mind kept churning the news the entire session, like it had the whole day.

Why was Fabre killed? Was it a coincidence or did it have something to do with the burglary?

Of course it was because of the burglary. There had been something in the safe that was worth killing him for. But what could it be? Had the woman known what she was stealing, or had she taken it by accident?

Would the killer go after her next?

I was sweaty after the class, but I didn't have any answers and I wasn't calm either. I needed something more tiring.

Showered and dressed up, I paused at the gym reception and read the notice board to see what else they offered. Kickboxing sounded exactly like what I needed, but there were no classes today.

"What's this self-defense class about?" I asked the guy behind the reception desk, and he lit up.

"It's a basic course for women and those who want to have a bit of self-confidence when facing risky situations, but it's basically a thorough introduction to jiu-jitsu and has always been popular. At least half of every class continue to our starter class to jiu-jitsu."

It probably wouldn't be what I needed right now, but I nodded. "Who is teaching it?"

"Laïla Diab and her colleague from Interpol."

My face went blank and he grinned. "They're not cops. They're analysts. Laïla is a cybercrime expert of some sort. But she has a black belt in jiu-jitsu, and she knows what she's doing. Would you like to attend?"

"Is there room? And are men allowed, if it's for women?"

"There are a lot of men too, though usually on the older side. You'll fit right in. It starts in half an hour and there's room for one more."

I glanced down at myself. "Do I need special clothing?"

"Sweatpants and a T-shirt are fine. Shoes and socks are never worn at a dojo, so you don't need those."

I made a quick decision. "I'll attend. But I'll need a new set of clothing. Mine are already sweaty from yoga."

He grinned. "No problem. We have everything on sale here."

Half an hour later, in fresh clothes and fortified by a smoothie at the gym café, I entered the dojo on the top floor of the building. It was a fair-sized room with mirrors on one wall and tatami covering the entire floor.

There were twenty of us, some of them familiar faces from yoga. A woman in her sixties I'd met there stood next to me, practically vibrating with excitement. She was small and round, with purple hair in a perm and black eyes that were twinkling as she looked at me.

"You don't look like you need this class."

I shrugged. "You never know what life throws at you. Just because I'm tall and strapping now doesn't mean I'll always be. It's good to be prepared."

She giggled. "Isn't that the truth."

A woman in white jiu-jitsu suit—I couldn't remember what it was called—and a black belt wrapped around her waist entered the dojo and bowed to the room. She was so tiny I couldn't believe she was the teacher, but you didn't get a black belt for nothing.

Her hair was buzzed near the skull, and as she walked, the lapels of her coat parted to show colorful tattoos edging toward her throat.

She was followed by another woman in similar gear. She was tall and walked with the self-confidence and ease of a person who knew what she was doing. Her hair was reddish blond and elegantly short, and her face was familiar, though I struggled to remember where I'd seen her before. I didn't know any cops here, even if Interpol agents weren't law enforcement officers. And I hadn't met many people anyway. But the nagging feeling that I should know her almost made me miss the introductions.

"I'm Sensei Diab and this is Sensei Reed," the tiny woman said, and my mind cleared. I'd done a thorough research of people named Reed when I assumed the name. I must have come across her then.

The class proceeded at a brisk pace. There was a short warm-up, which I didn't really need, having come from yoga, but which I enjoyed, nonetheless. I liked stretching my new muscles, seeing where I could push my body.

"Okay, does anyone know what's the best form of self-defense?" Sensei Diab asked. I almost said "Shooting first" but managed to keep my mouth shot.

"Running," she answered after no one made any suggestions. "No matter what we teach you here, if you're in a threatening situation, run. That being said, there are a few tricks we can teach you."

She scanned the room. Her gaze landed on me and she smiled, delighted and a little challenging. "Would you be so kind as to help me demonstrate? It won't hurt. Much."

That didn't sound promising, but I wasn't afraid of pain, so I smiled and stepped up to the front. She was even smaller close up, reaching barely to my chest. Some people snickered, but I braced myself for being royally hurt. Nothing would drive her message home better than beating the living daylights out of a man my size.

Beating up opponents bigger than me was how I'd made my name as an enforcer. I hadn't always won.

She took my right hand gently into hers—and I dropped on my knees. I had no idea what happened, but it wasn't over. She was holding my thumb in some sort of vise that put painful pressure on my joints. I could've tried to resist, but I feared my thumb would come off if I did.

Then she switched her hold, bending my wrist and elbow in a way that caused even greater pressure on my joints, and made me walk around as if on leash. I could only obey.

I had to learn these moves.

She proceeded to teach us just that. We paired up. I was with the old lady, who almost ripped my thumb off in her eagerness to get me on my knees. But when it was my turn, I couldn't bring myself to apply any force. She glowered at me.

"How am I supposed to learn if you don't take this seriously?"

I apologized, but before I could try again, Sensei Reed, who had been circling the room, keeping an eye on our techniques, interrupted me.

"Let me show you." Her French was so good that despite her looks and name I had to assume she was native. Her voice was low and calm and didn't remind me of anyone.

She took my partner's hand and made her go onto her knees with similar ease as I'd been. "You see, no force is necessary. You apply small pressure at first, and then increase it until she can't take it anymore. Of course, in real situation, there's no need to wait for the pain threshold to come up. Go for full pressure."

She watched me perform the move. I tried to be as gentle as possible—I'd never liked hurting women even when I was still an enforcer—but I still grimaced apologetically when my partner went to her knees.

Sensei Reed nodded and moved on.

We practiced another move with different partners. Mine was a middle-aged woman who was so intimidated by me that I had to coax her to cause me pain. I tried not to think of what her backstory might be, but I feared it had to do with domestic abuse. She froze like a deer in headlights after successfully subduing me, as if fearing my retribution. I smiled approvingly, and tried to be extra gentle with her, but it didn't help much.

Sensei Diab clapped her hands together. "Okay, one more technique before we end for today. We'll practice it better next week. If the big fellow could help demonstrate again…?"

That was me. But it was Sensei Reed who was teaching this time. Standing face to face, looking at her straight in her light blue eyes, I had the uncanny sensation again of having met her before, but she didn't react to me the same way.

"Take a good grip on my wrist."

I did and she winced in pain, so I slackened my grip. She shook her head. "Take a proper hold."

I tightened it again, but I didn't use full force. She lifted her brows, indicating she knew it, but let it slide. Instead, she demonstrated how you could break such a hold on your wrist, even against a stronger opponent. It wasn't painful, but it was effective. So effective that she could've broken my hold even if I'd held tighter—which I knew for a fact.

I knew this move. The burglar had released herself from my hold with it.

My body tense, I studied her face as she spoke to the class. Was she the burglar? Was that why she seemed so familiar? But apart from the height, I couldn't tell.

Then the loose sleeves of her jacket hiked up as she gestured with her arms, and I could see bruises around her wrist. No wonder she had winced when I squeezed her. And I bet my hand fit the bruises perfectly.

Because I had caused them.

# 6

## ADA

I HAVE NO IDEA HOW I GOT THROUGH the class. The shock of seeing Eliot Reed had shaken me like nothing since my husband's betrayal.

I hadn't paid attention to the people attending when I entered the dojo. When Laïla had asked him to help her demonstrate the technique, it had been too late to run.

What was he doing here? Everyone else was either old or physically weaker. He was neither. Moreover, I'd witnessed him act with swift authority in a difficult situation, so he didn't need a boost to his self-confidence either.

He had to know who I was. Why else would he be in my class? Was he connected with Danny? Had my husband sent him? But to what end? He's the one who left.

I'd never come even remotely close to being discovered before. I wanted to flee, or throw up, or both at the same time.

Quiet contemplation during the warmup brought clarity. He couldn't have known I would be here. My name wasn't on the class description. It had to be coincidence after all.

I'd managed to gather my wits by the time I needed to help him with a technique, and I'd been perfectly calm when Laïla asked him to help me demonstrate one.

And then he took a grip of the exact spot he'd squeezed me before. I hadn't even realized it was so sore and I hadn't been able to hide my wince. His face had remained impassive, apart from a brief apologetic grimace, but I knew he had figured out where the bruise had come from.

The class ended before I did anything stupid. I fled to the dressing room as fast as I dared, leaving Laïla to deal with the participants' eager questions. I wanted to grab my bag and rush out in my jiu-jitsu gi, but a moment's reflection made me slow down. Men dressed up fast and were always first to leave. Eliot was probably already waiting for me in the lobby.

It was agony to slow down, the adrenaline coursing through me speeding up my pulse. I took a long shower, standing under the cold water until my panic subsided, ignoring the people washing themselves around me.

Laïla was still in the dressing room when I finally emerged, reattaching all her piercings she had to remove for the class. "Took you long enough. Are you headed out or something?"

"No, just needed to work on kinks in my muscles," I said in an easy tone. "I'll have a bite somewhere and then go home. Want to join me?"

She grimaced. "I can't. My little brother is still staying with me, and I have to go home and make sure he does his homework."

She was the oldest of four siblings, the youngest of whom was giving trouble to their parents. They'd foisted him on Laïla in the hope that she understood him better and had the authority to see him through the last year of school—though how that could work when she spent more time at the office than home, I had no idea.

"Good luck with that."

"I'm not stressing about it. But it doesn't make me want to have children of my own, so the joke is on my parents." She gathered her bags and got up. "Anyway, I'll probably have the external drive encrypted soon. I'll see you tomorrow."

"See you," I said lightly, even though I wasn't sure I'd be there. If the police weren't coming for me, Eliot Reed was. "Don't bust yourself with the encryption. I can wait."

The gym lobby was empty when I finally emerged, looking calm and competent once again in my work clothes. No one was waiting for me outside either, but I was unable to relax as I headed to the tram stop by the railway station. The need to fidget and constantly check over my shoulder as I waited for the tram to arrive was almost overwhelming.

I had only a short ride to the Perrache railway station in the old town where I switched to a Metro line that would take me to the other end of the old town, closer to my home. There were enough people around at that time of early evening that I could disappear among them, but I didn't head home when I emerged back onto the street.

I walked a couple of blocks north to a plaza in front of the national opera and took a table on the terrace of a restaurant where the evening sun reached beautifully. I often dined there, as it was about midway between work and my home.

It was also next to the main police station of the first and fourth arrondissements, but that couldn't be helped.

At quarter to six, it was early for dinner—locals would start showing up after seven—but I was starving and couldn't wait. Apart from a few tourists, I had the place to myself.

I was reading the menu when I sensed someone pause across the table from me. Expecting the waiter, I glanced up—and saw Eliot Reed standing there.

"*BONSOIR*, MADEMOISELLE REED. May I join you?" He waited politely for me to nod, which I eventually managed, before taking a seat. "I didn't have a chance to introduce myself in the class. I'm Eliot Reed."

He offered a hand over the table and I shook it automatically. I couldn't fathom how he could be here. Had he followed me, or was it a coincidence? I hadn't spotted him, but I had tried not to be paranoid.

"Ada Reed."

"Ada. Beautiful name. Are you by any chance Boston Reeds?" he asked, switching to English.

"Boston?" The random location threw me, until I remembered using that accent with him in Fabre's study.

My body went cold. He knew.

My voice was calm, but I was squeezing my hands into tight fists under the table. "No, I'm from London— England," I added, in case there were towns with that name in the States.

He picked up a menu and skimmed it. "Pity. I was hoping we might be related."

"Are you from there?" I managed to ask, my voice catching a little.

"No, New York. But you never know where you find family."

He put a slight emphasis on family. He was here because of Danny then, though I couldn't remember him having any family in New York. Had he known I was Danny's wife already in Fabre's study?

I hoped my smile looked more relaxed than it felt. "We wouldn't be related either way. My husband was Reed."

He glanced at my empty ring-finger and lifted a brow in inquiry. "Was?"

"He's ... dead."

Genuine compassion flashed in his eyes. "I'm sorry."

Surely he knew Danny was *allegedly* dead if he was here because of him? Or had I got this wrong?

"It was over four years ago."

"Still, it is a loss."

He didn't know the half of it.

Mercifully, the waiter showed up, ending the uncomfortable conversation. His face lit up when he spotted Eliot. "Monsieur Reed, how good to see you. The usual?"

Eliot smiled and glanced at me. "Unless the lady has something to suggest?"

I hadn't read a word of the menu, but I'd dined there often enough to know I liked everything. "I'm absolutely happy with whatever you're having."

"Chicken tajine?"

"That's fine." It wasn't as good as what Laïla's mother made, but I wouldn't be able to taste anything anyway.

"Algerian food isn't a thing in New York," he said conversationally when the waiter had left with our orders. "I've developed quite a taste for it since moving here."

"There are better restaurants for it than this one." The restaurant was good, but it wasn't specialized in Algerian food.

"Have you lived here long enough to find the best places?"

I smiled, relaxing despite myself. "Four years. And Laïla—Sensei Diab—has introduced me to her favorite places."

"Suppose you wouldn't be willing to show them to me?" His smile was charming and hopeful—and I couldn't understand it at all. Had I read the situation wrong? Was he here simply to ask me out? In which case, what did I think of that?

I was legally a widow, so technically I could even marry again if I wanted to. But I hadn't really dated since Danny left, and I wasn't interested in it with someone who might be holding a Sword of Damocles over my head.

"Of course," I said, as calmly as I could. "But I'm currently busy at work, so maybe I should give you the names instead and you can check them out yourself?"

If he was disappointed for being brushed off, he didn't show it. "Anything interesting you're working on? I was told you work for Interpol."

It irritated me that he was in charge of this conversation, constantly forcing me to react, but I didn't know how to turn the tables when he was so affably polite. "Yes. But we're not the police. I'm an analyst."

"Have you ever been a police officer?"

Did I imagine the sharpness in his voice?

"I used to work at the Metropolitan Police in London. I joined after law school when the idea of corporate law made me sick, and courtrooms didn't feel satisfying enough. Moreover, the wages of junior criminal barristers are a disgrace."

I had no idea why I was volunteering such information. Did I hope it would make me seem less suspicious?

"You wanted to catch the bad guys?"

My mouth curved a little. "Something like that. But I spent most of the time there behind the desk too."

"Was your husband a cop?"

He would know, if he knew Danny, wouldn't he?

After so many years, the thought of him didn't fill me with immediate rage anymore, but the question still made me twitch. "Yes. He ... died in the line of duty."

"I'm sorry." There was the genuine compassion again. "I thought such things didn't happen all that often in Britain."

"Not often," I answered easily enough. And not to Danny either, although I'd been treated like a widow of a hero—one of the reasons I'd needed to relocate to Lyon, lest I blurted out the truth in my anger. "It was bad luck. He responded to a bank robbery that went wrong. One of the robbers triggered an explosive."

While I was opening the vault. I still didn't know how Danny had managed to fake his heroic death and get away with the money while the rest of our team were busy fleeing without a penny.

He grimaced. "Were there many casualties?"

"Just Danny and the idiot who blew him up." Though I'd occasionally wondered if that other victim had been Joe after all. Maybe they'd been in it together and his was a random body too. It had been a lot of money for one man to carry easily.

"I can see how that would make you want to relocate."

I nodded and seized the opportunity to turn the interrogation to him. "Have you been here long?"

"Since March. I lived in Frankfurt before."

"And how did an American decide to move to Europe? It's not the usual location, is it."

He spread his arms as if to say he couldn't understand it either, showing off a trim torso that looked as good in a slim-fit button-up shirt as it had in a technical T-shirt that had hugged his chest.

I shook myself, disgusted. He was the enemy. I should not spend a moment watching him for anything other than the sleight of hand he was about to pull to bust me.

"I followed a woman here. And then she decided to move back to the States—with a guy she worked with."

"That blows." Not exactly the height of sympathy, but I was miffed that Richard had guessed correctly when I hadn't even come to think of it.

"Yeah … I decided I needed an ocean between us and stayed. A woman I dated later recommended Lyon and here I am. I like it here."

The waiter arrived with the food, and for a few moments we were busy enjoying the first bites. It was good enough, and I was hungry. Then Eliot lowered his utensils and gave me a sheepish look, a sentiment I was sure he didn't often express.

"I confess, I had an ulterior motive when I sat down here with you."

I STRUGGLED TO FORCE the food down, my throat refusing to work. "Oh?"

This was it. He would either tell me he wanted to ask me out or that he knew who I was and threatened to go to the police.

I had no idea how to react to either, so I reached for my glass and took a sip.

He continued to eat, as if nothing was amiss. "My neighbor was killed over the weekend."

I inhaled the wine in surprise and had to cough to clear my airways. "What?"

He studied me worriedly, until he was sure I could breathe again. "His name was Dominique Fabre, and I'm more curious about the case than I should be. I was hoping you'd be able to offer me insight?"

I blinked, trying to wrap my mind around his request. "We're not the police. We don't participate in local investigations."

"But you do have access to the data, yes?"

I made to deny it, but we did have access. "It wouldn't be appropriate to look into an active case."

"I wouldn't want you to do anything illegal," he assured me, but I couldn't help thinking he'd emphasized the last word. "But I'd like to learn more about Fabre."

I found myself intrigued despite myself. "What about him?"

"I thought he was a perfectly normal businessman. But according to the detectives who interviewed me this morning, he was basically executed."

I paled. "Why did they interview you?"

"I attended a party at his place. But he was alive when I left." He hesitated, then ate a mouthful. I forced myself to eat too.

"I ... intercepted a burglar that night."

"What?" I was really showing off my conversational skills here, but he kept throwing these stunners at me that took me by surprise despite knowing to expect them.

"It was accidental," he said with a small shrug. Then his gaze met mine and held. "But whatever it was they stole is the key to this."

I couldn't have drawn my eyes away if I tried. He knew. I didn't know how, and I didn't understand why he was telling this to me instead of the police, but he knew.

Then his words registered. I was responsible for Fabre's death, if indirectly. I don't know why it hadn't even occurred to me after reading about his death, but now it was self-evident.

I had to say something. "Do you think the burglar came back to kill him?"

A slow smile spread on his face, his extraordinary eyes challenging. "How did you know the burglar got away?"

I'd lived double and triple lives for a long time. I was good at controlling my face, keeping the lies straight and filing away my criminal life even from myself. But I struggled to come up with an appropriate answer.

"I presumed. I'm sorry. Did you capture him?"

He studied me. "Why did you presume?"

"You said that whatever was stolen caused the death. If he'd been captured, he couldn't have stolen it."

He tilted his head in acknowledgement. "Logical. So how about checking Fabre for me?"

My mind was racing. I would most certainly have to make a more thorough check of him. And I had to get into that external drive.

"I can do that. But I won't give you any information that might compromise the murder investigation."

"No need. And thank you."

I nodded, struggling to calm my frantically beating heart. We finished the dinner in silence. When the waiter brought the check, Eliot picked it up.

"May I pay? It's the least I can do for intruding on your dinner."

I honestly didn't care if he paid, so I nodded. I couldn't wait to flee, and I didn't want him to follow. But we left together, walking side by side across the plaza toward the metro station.

"You never told me what it is you analyze at Interpol," he said out of the blue.

"Oh. Organized crime, mostly."

He startled, visibly enough for me to notice. "That sounds interesting. Anything particular?"

"Human trafficking at the moment."

His face turned into a tight mask. "Good."

His reaction seemed personal somehow, but before I had a chance to probe—it was my turn—I spotted a bus approaching down the street.

"That's me," I said, picking up the pace. I could've walked home, it wasn't far, but then he would've insisted on walking with me.

He kept easily up and we reached the bus stop before the bus did. I smiled and offered him my hand. "Thank you for the dinner. I'll let you know if I find anything interesting."

He fished out a business card and gave it to me as I took my place in the queue. "Take this. And if you don't find anything, we'll see on Monday."

I got on the bus. As it drove away, I saw him staring after it until it turned the corner. Even knowing he wasn't following me, I couldn't settle down until I was in my flat with the door locked and bolted. Because he was right: the key to Fabre's death was on the hard drive I'd stolen.

And my client wanted it.

# 7

## ADA

HERE'S THE THING ABOUT BEING AN expert safecracker: I seldom rob private safes for myself, and clients don't send me after baubles or cash. The big heists movies are made about are team efforts and I don't do teams anymore. Not after Danny's betrayal.

The commissioned work is handled through a network that preserves my anonymity as well as the clients'. I have no way to tell who my clients are, and they never tell me why they want the items. But almost always, it is about information.

I'd stolen documents and USB sticks, hard drives and photographs. I never asked what they were for, and I never stayed around for long enough to see if there were consequences of my actions.

This was my hometown. I should've known better than to take the job. But the pay was just too good. And I'm not talking about money.

Well, not solely.

What had lured me into taking the job was getting solid information on the current—or last known—whereabouts of my husband, Danny Reed. He could be dead for real by now—that tends to happen to criminals who betray their teams—but if there was a chance I could find him, I would.

And then I would kill him.

The client didn't know that I wanted the information; it would've given my identity away in a heartbeat. I'd gone by a different moniker when I worked with Danny, but if the safecracker currently known as the Hummingbird, me, started showing interest in the Hand, a bank robber of great fame, aka Danny, it would be only a matter of time before someone made a connection between the two identities. And it would be a small step from there to remember that Danny had been married, and from there to connect the Hand with me—and realize I was the Hummingbird.

My current intel had directed me to Dominic Fabre. I didn't know how he was connected, or if it was incidental, but I was certain that the information I sought was on the external drive I'd stolen. It certainly hadn't been on anything else I stole. I needed to access it before I handed it over.

But whatever else was on that drive, Fabre wasn't killed because of Danny's whereabouts.

I hadn't asked why the client wanted it. I'd assumed I was participating in industrial espionage, like so often was the case. Fabre had had several money-making startup ideas, and the chance to steal one from him had to be tempting.

But no one killed a man for a few ideas either, not even lucrative ones.

I briefly entertained the possibility that his death was unrelated to my actions. Maybe he'd owed money to his drug dealer, who'd come to collect. But he was wealthy, and the timing was too much of a coincidence. Eliot was right. This was on me.

He was another mystery that had kept me up most of the night. Why hadn't he gone to the police with his information? The only explanation I could come up with was that he was protecting Danny, despite acting like he didn't know him.

Why hadn't he confronted me directly, then, instead of giving me these hints and sending me to solve the murder for him?

But I agreed with him on that: it was up to me to solve it. The police had no clue where to even start looking. And I couldn't tell them.


LAÏLA WAS WAITING FOR me in the lobby when I arrived for work the next morning, practically vibrating with excitement. The moment I was through security, she took me by my hand and pulled me to the lift.

"Slow down," I said, amused. "You could've just sent me a message if it's important, you know."

"This can't be handled with messages! How was your date?"

I gave her a puzzled look. "What date?"

She gestured wildly. "You know, with that guy from the class yesterday." She mistook my stunned expression as denial and her shoulders slumped.

"You didn't go? He was waiting outside the gym for you, and I said you were headed to dinner. Did I send him to the wrong restaurant?"

That would explain how Eliot had found me. "No, he found me. We had dinner."

"And?"

I shook my head, exasperated. "And nothing."

"You didn't make plans for another one?"

"No." God forbid.

"Oh, come on…"

I smiled, amused despite my annoyance. "Why do you care?"

She'd never tried to set me up with anyone before—or vice versa. I wasn't even sure if she preferred the same or the opposite sex, or if she was interested in it at all.

Romance, apparently, was a different matter.

She listed the reasons with her fingers as we exited the lift. "Because I'm your friend and I'm worried that you never date, because he was hot, and because he couldn't take his eyes off you in the class."

I hadn't noticed him staring, but I knew why he would've. He'd probably spent the entire time trying to figure out why I looked familiar. I would have to invest in better disguises from now on.

And I would never, ever accept a job in my hometown again.

"Well, next time you set me up, warn me first." We reached her desk. "So why did we come here?"

She jumped excitedly. "I got into the external drive!"

"Did you work all night?" I asked, worried, but she brushed my concern aside.

"No, that's what computers are for. And it wasn't that difficult in the end after all, just sneaky."

I pulled out a chair next to hers to have a good view of her monitor—one of them, as her desk was lined with them. "What's in it?"

"Ledgers."

"What now?"

She gave me a puzzled side-eye. "You know, bookkeeping."

"I know what ledgers are, I just don't understand why they would be on a heavily protected external drive." In a private safe and wanted by someone badly enough to hire a burglar to get them—or to kill for.

"Because they're crooked. But I don't think this is related to your human trafficking case after all. I think this is mafia shit, or drugs."

My mind was racing. The case I'd given her was a scam, but I couldn't exactly tell her so. "It could still be connected. The money they generate needs laundering too."

"Maybe you should show it to Laurent."

I made a face. Laurent Paget was the head of the organized crime division at the headquarters and specialized in money laundering. He was also a self-important prick.

"And have him hog the credit for whatever it is that this cracks?"

Laïla grinned. "So how do we proceed?"

"*I* will analyze this and see where that leads me."

"Aww, I could help."

"You already did." I took the drive and patted her on the shoulder as I rose. "Thank you. I'll let you know if I find anything interesting."

At my desk, I plugged the drive into my computer and plunged in. It contained a lot of data, but it was nothing one person couldn't handle on her own—provided she was an expert in economic crime. Which I wasn't. I might as well have been reading Chinese for all I understood what the numbers meant.

But somewhere in that data was the reason for Fabre's death, and I needed to find it.

I seriously contemplated giving it to Laurent after all. He could make sense of it. But then I would have to tell him where the drive had come from, and I didn't have a plausible explanation. I couldn't very well tell him I stole it from the safe of a murder victim.

All my colleagues were out of the question. That left one person. Eliot Reed. He was a businessman. He had to understand this stuff.

But could I risk it? He'd know for sure I was the burglar then.

As if he didn't already know…

I took out his card, which had both his phone number and an email address. Since I couldn't call him from work without my colleagues overhearing, I sent him an email.

*Do you know anyone discreet who understands money laundering? A.R.*

While I waited for him to answer, I checked all the files and folders the hard drive contained. Not everything on it was about numbers, but nothing interesting caught my attention.

Moreover, it didn't have the information I'd stolen it for: it didn't tell me where my double-crossing husband was.

Upset made my hands shake. I was about to pull the hard drive off the computer and sling it at the nearest wall when my inbox pinged.

*Yes. Me. Can you come to my place after work? E.*

I'd rather not meet him on his turf, but since I had no reason to refuse, I agreed, and he sent me his address. It was the same building where Fabre had lived, which startled me, even though he had told me they were neighbors.

That done, I pushed the issue out of my mind and concentrated on my actual work. I had been following the actions of a crime organization led by Genadi Dobrev, a Bulgarian human trafficker and drug smuggler, for months. As far as I'd been able to determine, drugs came in through Portugal from South America and people went out the same route, mostly women for sex work, but all sorts of people for forced labor too, even children.

He seldom left his fortress outside Varna, a town by the Black Sea, and I had a snowball's chance in hell of catching him—or gathering the information that would help local police there catch him—but I wasn't about to give up.

Currently, I was keeping an eye on the activities of man called Artem Melnyk, who was presumably high up in Dobrev's hierarchy, likely his field operative or right-hand man. Melnyk had a yacht in which he cruised up and down the Mediterranean from Black Sea to the Atlantic. I'd been tracking its whereabouts for patterns, among other things.

I didn't find it odd that I was fighting the law with one hand and breaking it with the other. I needed both in my life. One day, some eager Interpol analyst would track me down too, but until then I would make sure I got as many bad guys as possible.

The one man I really wanted to find kept eluding me though. How could my intel have been so wrong? And if it misled me about Danny, how could I figure out who killed Fabre?

I must have made annoyed noises, because Richard leaned closer. "Is something bothering you?"

Where to start…? "A source didn't come through with intel," I settled with, and he made sympathetic noises.

"Well, let's face it, most of our sources are criminals too. Not exactly trustworthy." Then he smiled. "I was worried your date was bad."

I pulled straight, incensed. "Did you talk with Laïla?" I would murder her.

"She was so excited about it. So how was it?"

"Not a date, for one. But we had a nice dinner."

"It's a start…"

It most assuredly wouldn't be.


I TOOK A TAXI TO ELIOT'S home that evening to avoid the hassle of several changes between busses and trams. I arrived in good time, probably earlier than he had anticipated, judging by the surprised look on his face when he opened the door for me. And he wasn't alone.

Two men in suits were standing in the entrance hallway of his flat. They studied me with as much curiosity as I did them. Eliot gestured at the men.

"These are Detectives Bellamy and Gagne. They're investigating a murder in my building." Apparently, I wasn't supposed to know about it, so I made an appropriately impressed face.

"Miss Reed is an analyst at Interpol—no relation," Eliot added with an easy smile, as the brows of the detectives shot up.

"Are you here to interview Mr. Reed?" I asked in French, as that's what Eliot had used. "I can come back later."

"No, no, Mademoiselle," Detective Bellamy said, an attractive man in his early forties. He was dressed better than detectives usually were, so he likely came from money.

"We have some photos of people that visited the building before the victim was found, taken from the surveillance footage. We'd like Monsieur Reed to take a look and see if he's seen any of them. Other residents of this building have been removed from the selection."

Eliot gestured for us to move to the living room, an elegant space with a balcony view to the park between the buildings and across the river. Since I was morbidly curious, I sat next to him on the sofa to watch the photos from the laptop Detective Bellamy placed on the low coffee table in front of us.

The photos were relatively good quality. I made a mental note to hide my face better from now on even in low-security environments. There were quite a few of them, most depicting men, and I studied each carefully. I didn't recognize anyone—moreover, I wasn't in any of them—but that didn't mean they weren't important.

"May I have access to your casefiles? I could run these through our system."

Detective Gagne lifted his brows. "Do you think this case is as high profile as that?"

"Not everything we do has to do with major crime," I answered with an easy smile. "But I was wondering if this was about collecting a drug debt. We have vast records of people involved in drug crimes."

"His housekeeper had no knowledge of a drug habit, and we didn't find any drugs in the house, but it was certainly a payback of some sort. I'll give you access, if you let us know what you find first."

"Of course."

Bellamy gave me the reference number and they rose. "Please, be careful when dealing with this person," he said, shaking Eliot's hand.

"Do you expect the killer to return?"

He made a very Gallic shrug, and I made a note how to improve my own version of it. "At this point, everything is possible."

"Was anything stolen from his house?" Eliot asked, and I held my breath.

"Nothing that we could detect, and the drawers on his desk were undisturbed. But we didn't get into the safe."

"We presume it would have been left open if the shooter had managed to open it," Detective Gagne added. "Why bother hiding a robbery if there's a dead body lying around."

Why indeed?

The detectives left and Eliot returned to the sofa. We stared at each other for few moments, as if assessing which one of us would crack first and admit more knowledge than we should. But he only sat next to me.

"Let's look at those ledgers, then."

# 8

## ELIOT

ADA'S ELEGANT BROWS CURVED UP. She was sitting at the edge of the couch, looking prim and proper in a suit and a flower-print blouse. A picture of professionalism. "I'm sorry?"

And Englishness.

"You work with an organization that specializes in analyzing data about money laundering, yet you contacted me. You therefore have laundered ledgers that for some reason you can't show to your colleagues."

Her expression didn't change. She was good, I had to give her that.

"I merely need a crash course on money laundering."

"And no one at your organization can help you?"

She grimaced. "No one I wouldn't want to strangle anyway…"

I barked a laugh; I couldn't help it. "It's not for amateurs, you know."

Her eyes flashed. "Are you a professional, then?"

*Touché.*

"I'd hate anyone to try the theory in practice," I amended.

She tilted her head, a small, amused smile tugging the corner of her mouth. It was a nice mouth and kept drawing my attention. "Thank you for the warning."

She wasn't going to admit that there were any ledgers. I could work with that.

"What would you like to know, then?"

"Theoretically?"

"Of course."

She leaned her elbows on her knees, regarding me calmly. "Let's say I've come across data that I can't legitimately attach to a case."

Like something from the safe of a murder victim? No wonder she couldn't ask her colleagues. But I just nodded, and she continued.

"It could be useful, but it gets blocked by red tape. We can't risk a case falling apart because of it. So, it gets ignored."

I nodded again, because I did understand how these things worked.

"Now, you're right, I could ask a coworker to look it over, but they're already swamped with legitimate work, and it would be difficult to justify why I need it analyzed. So, I thought I could learn myself."

She really was good at this.

"And you thought of me?"

"Well, Laïla offered to help, but she's a good person and doesn't need illicit jobs to mar her record. I checked your businesses out and figured that you have to be good at reading financial data to do what you do."

She hadn't come to me because she knew who I'd been? That was a relief.

"I am. And I know a thing or two about money laundering too. Purely theoretically, of course."

"Of course," she repeated, and not like she was humoring me. Apparently I wasn't the criminal here.

"Can I get a look at this data, or is it classified?"

She pursed her lips and straightened. "I could upload it to your computer, but then the potentially incriminating data would be in your possession, and that might lead to trouble with the law."

"I wouldn't want that to happen," I said dryly, and she nodded.

"I have everything on an external drive, but I can't leave it with you. I shouldn't have it in the first place."

I was getting intrigued. "Let's take a look."

I fetched my laptop, and she took out a portable drive from her bag and plugged it in. I clicked it open and a plethora of files opened, all identified with series of numbers that didn't seem to have anything in common with each other. Nothing as simple as one to ten, more like phone numbers.

I opened the first file and skimmed it, then did the same for a couple of more.

"What made you think this is about money laundering?"

"Laïla said so."

My mouth tugged with a smile. "Is she good at detecting patterns?"

"Yes," she said emphatically. I nodded.

"Well, she's right. On the surface, everything looks legit. The first column here is the account identification number, then there's the amounts moved from one account to another, and the last is the identification number of the account it was moved to."

"How do I know what account the numbers refer to?"

"You don't. They're just random numbers on purpose. They don't represent bank accounts, for example. Someone has the list that identifies each account, but if it's not included in these files, you have no way of knowing."

She looked miffed. "Then how do you know it's about laundering money?"

"There are repeat transactions between these accounts. If you only read one of these files, you won't necessarily suspect anything, but all of them together, it's iffy, to say the least."

"They're moving money between their own accounts?"

I nodded, pleased that she got it so fast. Then again, she did this for a living. "It goes through three or four accounts, only to return to the first, like here." I pointed at the relevant line, where the exact same sum paid earlier returned the same day, having circled through the other accounts.

"I didn't realize it would be this simple."

"It's anything but outside the numbers." I should know. I'd done it for a living.

She stared at the screen, a crease forming between her brows. "This is basically useless, isn't it?"

"Unless you have the key. Was there anything in these files that could be used as one?" Or maybe in the safe? Because if this was what she'd stolen from Fabre, it held the key to his murder.

"No, but I think I might know where to look."

My heart stopped. "Don't you even fucking think about breaking into that study again."

SILENCE FELL. "I have no idea what you're talking about."

I was done pretending. "The police are keeping an eye on the penthouse. There's no way you can get in and out without being noticed."

"I'm an Interpol analyst," she said in a clipped tone. "I don't have to sneak into anywhere."

It took me a moment to figure out what she meant. "You mean you'll insinuate yourself into the investigation?"

"I already did."

She pulled my laptop closer and opened a website. With a few clicks, she'd logged on to a secure Interpol network. From there, she accessed the database of the local police and pulled out the files of Fabre's murder investigation.

"Let's see what we can find here…"

The first file were photos of Fabre's body. I'd seen enough executions in my day to recognize it for what it was, even if wet-work had never been my line of business. Ada studied them for a moment with a professional eye, nostrils flaring in distaste.

She selected another file. The investigators had done a thorough job in going through and documenting the place, but not everything had been photographed or itemized.

"Is there nothing about the contents of his drawers…?" she muttered to herself.

"How about his phone?"

She tilted her head and clicked another file. "They have it and have even managed to get into it. They're tracing the contacts."

"Any names you recognize?"

More importantly, did it contain any names I would recognize?

"It's miles long. I'd best download it." Another click of the mouse achieved that. I held my breath, hoping she didn't realize she'd downloaded it to my computer.

"Any lists that have seemingly random names on them?"

It took her a while, and it wasn't on the phone. It was on a photo of Fabre's desk, a bit blurry but legible. She downloaded it too.

"Let's see…"

But I'd already recognized one name on the list. Blood rushed to my ears and I didn't hear what she was saying.

*Benevolence.* Such a random word could mean anything or refer to anything. But I knew what it meant.

It was a ship used for human trafficking.

My crime boss hadn't come up with the idea of branching out to human trafficking on his own. He'd been lured into it by a man named Patrick Crow.

Crow ran a crime organization that operated on a whole different level of efficiency and cruelty than my former boss. One of his fields was human trafficking. He brought in migrants from South America and Eastern Europe, promising them a bright future in the land of the free, only to whisk them off to do forced labor on farms and factories, or sex work in big cities.

He got my boss interested in it too. That's when I found the limit of what I was willing to do for him. I had to leave before my boss took the choice from me.

I cleared my throat. "Are any of these words on his phone's contacts?"

Judging by the confused look she gave me, I'd interrupted her, but she opened the file she'd downloaded. "Let's see. You read them, alphabetically if possible."

"*Arctos.*" That didn't mean anything to me. Could be a company, could be a place, but my heart jumped when she nodded, her cheeks flushing with excitement.

"Here. Should I copy the phone number?"

"It's not a phone number. It's the key to an account."

She pulled straight. "Get out of town. We found it?"

"I would seem so. Are there others? The next one is *Benevolence.*"

It was there too. I didn't know what to think. Was this a coincidence? Or had I inadvertently stumbled into Patrick Crow's businesses?

That wasn't good…

One by one, we located each word on the list from Fabre's contacts, with a number that corresponded with the ledgers on the hard drive.

"You've got your work cut out for you," I noted to Ada as lightly as I could after we'd checked the last one.

"I think I'll trace these names first, see if they refer to anything real."

"Or you could give these to the police, to justify your snooping."

Her eyes sharpened. "But they don't have the ledgers. They'll never know they refer to accounts."

I shrugged. "The murder investigation isn't really your problem. You'll point them to a direction to look. If the names refer to anything, they'll find it."

"And then I can use it…"

That was one way to look at it.

She unplugged the drive and rose. "Thank you. This was more helpful than I anticipated."

I was surprised by it too. "Would you like to stay for a dinner? I'm ordering in, so you don't have to suffer my cooking."

She smiled, less reserved than she had been since yesterday's dinner. "As tempting as that sounds, I need to be on my way."

I didn't press the matter—I disliked men who did that to women, especially when they were already on his turf—and walked her to the door. "If you have more questions, don't hesitate to contact me. And if you can, let me know how the case goes."

She promised to do so, and I closed the door firmly behind her. Then I slumped against it.

Holy hell. Had my past caught up with me after all?

ADA HADN'T REMEMBERED to delete the files she downloaded from the police, though I couldn't be sure it was deliberate.

I wished I could've told her openly what *Benevolence* referred to. It might've helped her with her human trafficking case. But even though she hadn't indicated in any way that she suspected I was anything other than what I looked, I couldn't risk it. At least, not until I had a plausible explanation for why I knew about it.

That in mind, I began a search of my own. I started with *Benevolence* to see if it could refer to anything else, and if the ship was still owned by Patrick Crow's conglomerate.

The owner had changed, to my surprise, but I would have to do a more thorough search to find if it was merely a different subsidiary of Crow's.

It sailed under the Bulgarian flag now, so it might be Crow had sold the ship after the investigation that followed it being raided by border and customs agents the day I died. I couldn't immediately trace the shipping company that owned it to a person or organization, so it likely wasn't a legit business. It wouldn't feature on those ledgers if it was.

I opened a website that kept a real-life track on all maritime traffic. *Benevolence* was currently on the Black Sea outside Bulgaria and on her way to the Bosporus. I had no way of checking what it carried, but there was hardly a container ship in the world that carried entirely legitimate cargo.

But if there was a chance that it was trafficking humans, shouldn't I try to find out?

Undecided, I searched the other names on the list, but got several hits for each. I'd have to research each of them to find connections between them.

But none of this held clues for why Fabre was killed. Had he stolen the drive and the owner wanted it back? Then who had commissioned Ada to steal it and why?

It would've been easier to speculate if I could talk about it openly with her. But I had my secrets and she had hers. And if I wanted to keep mine, it was best I didn't pry into hers.

But if there was even a remotest chance that Patrick Crow was involved in Fabre's death, I had to find out. And then I would have to determine if he was aware I was here. And then I would have to disappear. Again.

# 9

## ADA

I DIDN'T CARE IF ELIOT THOUGHT I was fleeing. I needed to leave, and I didn't have time to be polite about it.

And yes, fine, I was fleeing. He'd finally admitted to knowing I was the burglar. His vehement order that I didn't go to the study *again* had caught me by surprise, but I was certain I'd managed not to admit to anything.

He truly seemed to care that I wasn't caught. He hadn't told the police—who had been *right there*—and it couldn't be for the lack of evidence either—though he couldn't have any. It was unfathomable, but his reasons could wait. I had more important issues to deal with.

Eliot had helped me more than I could've hoped. He'd explained the ledgers and how they indicated money laundering in simple terms, and he'd made useful suggestions about how I could track the accounts. If I was a suspicious person—and I was—I would say he had done this kind of investigation for a living once. Why he couldn't tell me, I had no idea.

But I had to let that mystery wait too. Because thanks to the crime scene photos, I suddenly had leads on two of my cases.

I was able to connect the money laundering files on

the external drive to my human trafficking case. One of the keywords to the accounts had been *Arctos*, the name of Melnyk's yacht I'd been tracking for months. It couldn't be a coincidence. Now I only had to figure out how it connected with the other accounts and I would have a solid case to move to the authorities.

Piece of cake…

But what had really left me breathless, my heart beating in my throat and my hands sweating, had been a word in the contacts on Fabre's phone: *Hand*.

Such a generic word could refer to anything, really. But my intel had pointed at Fabre, and here it was, proof that my two-timing husband was still alive. How Fabre knew him, I had no way of knowing now that he was dead. But I had a phone number.

Unless it was an account identifier too. Hand hadn't been a word on the list on Fabre's desk, but there could be another list somewhere on that desk the police photographer had missed.

Despite knowing better, I contemplated going back into Fabre's study. Maybe I could suggest to the police they look for more lists when I tipped them about the one we'd found.

I had to find out for sure if Danny was involved in human trafficking. It hadn't been his style back in the day; he'd strictly been a bank robber. But people changed, and money probably came more easily in destroying human lives than in breaking into bank vaults. More difficult to get caught too.

Bile rose to my mouth and I pushed it down. I wasn't searching for Danny to reconcile with him. I wanted revenge—or the very least, retribution. This would ensure that some misplaced nostalgia wouldn't make me waver when the time came to confront him.

I was itching to plunge into my research as the taxi left me outside my building, but I wasn't given a chance. Laïla was waiting outside, leaning against the wall by the entrance door, headphones over her ears, deep in a world of her own.

She startled when I paused in front of her. "There you are," she said, delighted, pulling the headphones off. "I've been waiting for you."

"I can see that. But why? And why didn't you call me? I could've come home earlier."

I let her into the lobby of my building. I lived in one of the nineteenth century buildings by the Saône, sturdy on the inside, romantic on the outside, but not terribly practical when it came to creature comforts. There was no lift, for one, so Laïla and I had to climb to the fourth floor, where my two-bedroom flat was.

"Mom showed up to check up on Samí and it didn't go well. I had to flee before her ire turned on me."

I grimaced in sympathy. Her mother was a formidable woman, so unlike my own mild-mannered mother who kept all her complaints bottled in, whether it was about her constantly absent, now deceased safecracker husband, or me.

"Were you eating out or what kept you?" she asked as I let us into my flat.

It would've been so easy to invent an errand, but I needed her help and that required some form of truth.

"I had coffee with Eliot Reed."

"Girl!" she said in English, drawling out the word, offering me a palm to slap. I rolled my eyes and ignored the high five as I headed to my kitchenette.

"It wasn't like that."

She plopped on a chair at the small dining table outside the kitchenette and leaned her arms on the counter that separated the kitchenette from the rest of the room, her eyes rapt on me as I put the electric kettle on.

"Like hell it wasn't. Second night in a row. Tell me everything."

"There's nothing to tell. We didn't even get to have the coffee." Her eyes grew large in excitement, and I realized she could interpret it wrong, so I hastened to add: "There were two detectives in his home."

A small crease appeared between her brows, making the piercings sway. "Why?"

"There was a murder in his building. Dominic Fabre, a businessman, was shot on Sunday. The detectives showed him photos of people taken from the surveillance footage. Naturally, I wanted to take a look too."

"Anyone you recognized?" She was all business now.

"No, but I was granted access to the case files. And after the detectives left, Eliot and I did a bit of snooping around."

"Ada…" she said admonishingly. "That's illegal, letting him see an active investigation."

"I know, but the chance to do some hands-on police work for a change was too irresistible. And I can't be entirely sorry, because it was helpful."

Her eyes sharpened. "You know who killed Fabre?"

"No, but among Fabre's phone contacts was one name that connects him with my human trafficking case: *Arctos*."

"What does that mean?"

"It's the name of the yacht owned by Artem Melnyk."

She pulled back, puzzled. "Why would a yacht have a phone number?"

The kettle boiled, claiming my attention before I blurted things that I shouldn't say. I busied myself by preparing us mugs of instant coffee and carried them to the table, taking a seat too.

"Because it's not a phone number. There was a list of random words on Fabre's desk that corresponded with names on his phone with a series of numbers that seem like phone numbers. But Eliot told me that they were more likely identifiers to accounts. As in illegal, cooked accounts for laundering money."

I gave her an expectant look, hoping she would leap to the conclusion I wanted her to make about the external drive, but instead she frowned, puzzled.

"How would Eliot know about such things?"

I'd asked myself that same question, but I shrugged, taking a sip of my coffee. "He used to be in the private security business."

"And they deal with money laundering?" She shook her head, decisively. "No, that can't be it. Are you sure his background is genuine?"

I startled, almost sloshing the coffee, so I put the mug carefully on the table before I burned my fingers. "Everything checked out perfectly. Nothing raised red flags."

"As in *too* perfectly?"

I narrowed my eyes. "Where are you going with this?"

"When someone has a too smooth and perfect background, it usually means it's fabricated."

I knew it, but I also knew that perfectly normal people could have smooth backgrounds too. Besides, there was that gap in his that wouldn't exist if it was fabricated. But before I could say so, she continued, practically jumping in excitement on her chair.

"Don't you see? He's a secret agent!"

I snorted a laugh and made to deny her fanciful idea—and realized I couldn't. Not entirely. It would explain so much about him. His special skills, why he had been in Fabre's study that night, his sudden move to Europe, his fluent French, and why he hadn't told the police about the burglary.

"What would a secret agent be doing in Lyon?"

Laïla shrugged. "We're here, aren't we."

I sincerely doubted Interpol was located in Lyon because it was a hub of international crime—more the opposite. But I gave her notion serious consideration.

"Maybe he's here to investigate Fabre," I suggested. "And then someone went and killed him right under his nose."

"That sucks."

I nodded, warming up to the ridiculous idea. "He must know more than he can say. That's why he's befriending me. He wants me to investigate for him or give him official access to the case."

Which I had done…

"Oh, no, I'm sure he's genuinely interested in you," Laïla said, upset, but I waved my hand to brush her concern off.

"He said as much when he showed up at the restaurant yesterday." And I hadn't found it odd at all. Some ex-cop I was. "Do you think he's here because of my human trafficking case?"

"Do secret agents investigate such cases?" She took a sip of her coffee and made a face. Instant coffee wasn't her favorite.

"He doesn't have to be from the CIA. Maybe he's FBI, who doesn't have jurisdiction to work here."

"But that's why we exist," she pointed out. "All he has to do is ask, if he's in law enforcement."

That was true.

She lowered her mug. "Why human trafficking?"

"I told you. *Arctos* was in Fabre's contacts, which connects him with human trafficking—and drug smuggling too, actually. I want to see if the number corresponds with any of the accounts on the external drive." I'd already done it, but I couldn't tell her that.

"You didn't bring it home, did you?" I bit my lip, looking guilty, and she shook her head. "Ada…"

"I was too busy at work to study it, so I thought I'd work on it home." I didn't feel as guilty as I tried to look, but I did feel bad that she was so upset.

"What if you get caught? You should give to me."

"And let you be caught instead? Absolutely not. Besides, it's an ordinary external drive. No one will look at it twice."

"Fine, but promise me you won't try to copy the contents onto your home computer."

"I promise."

I only waited until I'd switched into soft yoga pants and a warm sweatshirt after she left to break the promise. I headed to my secret room, aka my second bedroom, and powered up the laptop there. I never used it for anything except my other line of work, but this time I was making an exception.

With Laïla's unwitting help, I'd made the laptop as secure as I could. It had a state-of-the-art firewall and security encryption, and it accessed the internet through two routers and one processing unit, switching IP addresses twice, virtually making my laptop disappear. It wasn't entirely hack proof, according to Laïla who had told me about such a system, but the hacker had to be a real pro.

Like Laïla. I would have to make sure I didn't give her a reason to try.

I plugged the external drive in, opened it and made to copy the files onto my laptop. Nothing happened. They wouldn't move.

Shit. Was there some sort of security feature that prevented the files from being copied?

I didn't have the skills to find out, or to override them, if they existed. I needed Laïla's help. But how to ask without making her suspicious? She was already upset with me for bringing the drive home in the first place.

It couldn't be helped. She was my only option. I needed to copy the files before the client wanted the drive. I wanted to make notes, highlight the accounts, and draw connections, none of which I could do on files I had to give it away sooner or later.

Sighing, I dressed up again and headed back out.

I CALLED LAÏLA FROM MY desk at work an hour later. I'd made a small detour on my way there—or a large one, through three different stores that sold external drives until I found one that was exactly like the one I'd stolen from the safe.

"Hi, are you busy?" I asked her as lightly as I could.

"*So* not busy. What's up?"

"Remember that external drive? Well, I returned to the office and tried to copy the contents to our database, but they won't copy."

"Have you tried uploading them?"

"No. Doesn't that remove the contents from the drive? It's evidence." It wasn't, but it would be after I'd done some creative archiving.

"Just one, to test. Never mind. Bring it to me."

My brows shot up. "Are you the Laïla who just made me promise not to remove it from Interpol premises?"

"Ha ha. I'm at my desk."

"Of course you are…"

Five minutes later, I was watching Laïla work on the drive, biting my lip not to disturb her with my unhelpful comments. I needed the files before I had to deliver the external drive to my client, and it couldn't be empty, so the one I'd purchased wouldn't do. And I couldn't just disappear the original drive either before Laïla had had her fun with the encryption, or she would ask questions.

Laïla clickety-clicked her keyboard and mouse, and ran encryption programs and what have you on the hard drive. She kept muttering to herself in Arabic, which she never actively used, not even with her parents, who were second generation immigrants.

"Yes!" she suddenly exclaimed, making me jump. "It's copying. And the original data is intact."

Relief washed through me. I leaned in and pecked a kiss on her cheek. "Thank you. I knew you could do it."

She preened. "You want me to take this to the evidence archives?"

God forbid. "Thanks. But I have the evidence bag on my desk. I'll take it there tomorrow."

"As long as you don't take it home." She gave me a pointed look and I tried to look sheepish.

"I don't have to take it anywhere now. I can access the files in the database from home."

"Are you headed home now?"

I nodded. "As soon as I've dealt with this." I picked up the drive and got up. I gave her a stern big sister look.

"You're heading home too, right?"

"I don't want to…" She slumped over her keyboard. "Mom's probably still there."

"At this hour? And what if she's not and Samí has snuck out of the house?"

She snorted a laugh. "He's not going anywhere until he's finished playing *Doom*. I beat him at it, and he's competitive."

With a grin and wave, I left her to her work.

At my desk, I quickly copied all the files from the Interpol database Laïla had just downloaded to the external drive I'd purchased and locked it into my drawer. Despite Laïla's good intentions, I couldn't take it to the evidence archive until it opened in the morning.

Wearing a pair of the vinyl gloves we used when handling evidence, I spent a few minutes wiping off every possible trace there could be of me, Laïla, or Eliot on the original external drive. I placed it inside a small gift box I'd purchased tonight too. It was black, with faint silver stripes in it. The delivery wouldn't be face-to-face—I never agreed to those—so I would have to leave it in a dark spot somewhere. This one wouldn't easily be spotted by outsiders, but it would look innocent enough if it were.

The evening's work paid off. At home, I logged on to the inbox I used for my illicit jobs to find a message from my client. It was a series of numbers depicting date, time, and coordinates for the drop-off, and a word: "confess."

It startled me, until I checked the coordinates. I grimaced. It was risky, but doable. And it had to be done tomorrow at midnight.

Abandoning the files for the second time that night, I began to select the perfect disguise.

# 10

## ADA

FIRST THING AT WORK NEXT MORNING, I set out to make the external drive look like legitimate evidence. It was crucial, now that I could link the ledgers in it to my human trafficking case, even if the connection was flimsy.

Criminal though I was, I'd never falsified evidence before. My spine was rigid for resisting the urge to constantly check over my shoulder as I searched for a suitable inactive case.

Our evidence archives were vast, and the evidence collected there was often unitemized. They were just boxes filled with random stuff that local law enforcement all over the world had collected during raids and arrests that they hadn't needed for their cases. When they ran out of room in their archives, it ended up with us with the hopes that we could do something with it.

Occasionally we even could.

Narrowing my search down to the Mediterranean, I went through all the drug busts in the past six months that had produced unclaimed evidence. My best option was an arrest of Bulgarian drug smugglers done by Frontex, the European Border and Coast Guard Agency. They'd conducted a random search on the smugglers' boat for illegal immigrants from Africa. Instead of humans, they'd found drugs.

Since Frontex was more interested in operative than investigative work, the evidence sans the drugs had ended up in our archives, where it had remained unitemized ever since. Our archives were chronically understaffed, and the backlog to process everything that landed at their hands was miles long.

I made a request for the evidence, and half an hour later I was told I could come and collect. To my dismay, the archivist handed me two standard cardboard boxes of the kind that archives everywhere used, and gave me a stern look over her gold-rimmed glasses.

"You know the drill. You must catalogue everything you find in there. Do you remember the cataloguing system?"

I made a face, as if the task annoyed me—which it did, beyond helping me. "Yes, I remember."

She went over the cataloguing system anyway and gave me a cheat sheet too. I was grateful for it.

I didn't have room on my desk for the task, so I claimed an empty conference room and brought the boxes and my laptop there. Then I set out to work. It would take the whole day, but I hoped the good I did would balance the scam I was about to pull.

I put on gloves, broke the seal of first box, and peeked in. Even though this wasn't my case, I held my breath, hoping it would contain something exciting, but it was full of junk haphazardly thrown in.

Sighing, I took out the first item, a cheap mobile phone that had bent and broken, photographed it, applied an archive number on it based on the system our archives used, uploaded the photo with the same reference number, wrote it down on my list with a description, and put it into its own bag with the same tag, which I then sealed. Then I picked the next item and repeated the same until the contents had turned into a pile of evidence bags on the conference table and a long list on my computer.

It was slow, tedious work. Nothing in that box was even remotely useful for any outstanding cases, let alone mine. Not that it was supposed to be, apart from the scam I was pulling. I put the phone aside anyway, just in case Laïla or a tech wizard could get something out of it. Might as well make the most of my work.

I paused for a quick lunch at the staff cafeteria before proceeding to the second box. It had two rumpled and stained sheets of paper at the top, with random words on them. I was about to simply bag and tag them, but then I remembered the paper on Fabre's desk that had proven to be so useful and digitalized them too for easy access.

The contents didn't look like keywords to ledgers though, more like random passwords, or locations on a map. The latter made sense—the boat had belonged to drug smugglers after all—but since they were nothing as simple as town names and probably required an encryption key too, I didn't waste more time with it.

Under a pile of useless junk that nevertheless had to be itemized one by one, I finally located a laptop. The battery had been removed—you couldn't store them in archives—but the power cord in mine was compatible and I was able to switch it on. The first thing it wanted was a password.

I tried some of the random words on the lists I'd scanned, but it wasn't anything as simple as that. Who would've thought that drug runners were so safety conscious?

Sighing, I picked up my phone and called Laïla. "I have a laptop and a phone I need to get into, though the latter is busted, so it might be impossible."

"Nothing is impossible," she declared. "Is it the same case as the external drive?"

"Yes." Or it would be once I finished processing the boxes.

"Bring it over."

I took a couple of minutes to cross-reference the archives tags with my human trafficking case—Laïla would check—and then picked up the phone and the laptop. I locked the conference room door so that no one would mess with the evidence still spread on the table, although they were in sealed bags now, and headed to the basement.

Laïla's eyes grew large when she saw the phone. "That's out of my league. Take it to Andy."

"Will do. What about the laptop? I have lists of random words that were in the evidence box. Would those help?"

Her mouth pursed. "They might, but they'll take the fun of the job."

"Feels like cheating?" I said with a grin, ignoring the twinge in my gut that reminded me that that was what I was doing here.

"Just give me the lists…"

I gave her the reference number to the digitized lists. "Have you had lunch today?"

But she didn't hear me anymore, her attention on the laptop. Sometimes I asked again until she registered my presence—she might forget to eat if I didn't push her—but since I was busy myself, I left her to it and went to take the phone to Andy.

I finished processing the evidence. I added the external drive to the list, with the appropriate archive number and sealed in its own bag. I remembered to add the reference to my ongoing case too. I printed out the lists of items, attached them on the boxes and resealed them.

Feeling smug, and slightly terrified, I returned the boxes to the archives. The archivist's face lit up, making me feel wretched for the scam.

"Thank you for doing this. Were the contents helpful at least?"

I shrugged. "The external drive was, but I won't know about the rest until the tech finishes getting into the laptop and phone that were in there."

I returned to my desk, eagerly anticipating the chance to finally dig into the ledgers, now that I could process them under the guise of legality. I had no idea what I'd do with the information in them—it's not like I'd miraculously become an expert on money laundering—but it was the first solid lead into my case in ages.

But before I even had a chance to power up my laptop, Laïla called. "I got into the laptop, and there's all sorts of interesting stuff here. I'll upload the contents on the server."

"Thank you! I'll get right to it."

She hesitated. "Before you do that … I noticed there wasn't a photo of the external drive among the digitalized evidence. Do you know how that could've happened?"

Shit.

"That's on me," I said as lightly as I could. Apparently I couldn't even manage a scam properly. "I got so excited about finding the drive that I forgot to take the photo. I'll get right to it."

With a sigh, I headed back to the evidence archives to be told off for my carelessness and handle the missing task. I might as well write off the day as far as research went, and head home early. I had an important night ahead of me anyway.

THE DROP-OFF SITE was in a large cathedral during midnight Mass, and there would be other people around. I couldn't hide from everyone, which would make it easier for my client—or their minion—to spot me leaving the packet. My disguise, therefore, had to be perfect.

I seldom worked in my hometown, but if I had to, I never left home dressed in a character. If there was even the remotest chance that I was connected with a crime in my disguise, I didn't want any of my neighbors remember seeing that person in my building.

That meant careful preparations to make sure I had everything I needed with me. For tonight's undertaking, I'd chosen to be an old woman, which I almost never did. It was difficult to pull off, and not solely because I was too tall to make the character believable. But for a church, it was perfect. No one paid attention to old women there, let alone suspected one to be the famous safecracker, Hummingbird.

A little after ten that evening, I walked to Célestins, the Lyon municipal theater located in a beautiful nineteenth century building by the Saône. It was a ten-minute walk from my home and five from the cathedral, making it ideal for my purposes. It wasn't easy to find a place to change clothes in at this time of evening.

The evening's play hadn't ended yet, and the lobby was empty as I crossed it to the grand staircase and located a single person loo on the first tier. It was a tight fit, but roomier than the car I'd used the previous time.

I was an expert in changing clothes in cramped spaces. It also helped that I'd been a gymnast in my early teens, before I had a growth spurt at fifteen that destroyed my balance and I had to give it up.

It had coincided with Dad making a rare appearance in our lives. Seeing how I was both nimble and directionless, he decided to train me as his apprentice, which is how I ended up becoming a cat burglar in the first place.

I took my time to change my appearance. I'd practiced for hours with the help of YouTube tutorials to be able to apply makeup that made my face look wrinkled and colorless. The only exception was the red lipstick that I applied in a way that made my lips looked thinner. A French woman wore lipstick to a theater and church, no matter how old she was, and I had to look believable.

My face wouldn't hold up to close scrutiny, but from afar and in poor light, it would do.

The wig in a bun was mostly gray, with some black streaks here and there, and wisps that I let frame my face. The glasses were black and heavy rimmed. For further measure, a black pillbox hat with a full veil would obscure my features, a wonderful vintage find that I wished I could wear somewhere as myself too.

I pulled on thick, beige stockings, and stuffed a bra that was two cup sizes larger than mine with padding. The backpack that held my regular clothes and the makeup equipment went on my back to give me a hump. It felt awful under the clothes, but it would remind me to stoop.

To add bulk to my frame, I put on several layers of underskirts and shirts over the backpack before donning a black, full-sleeved dress that a woman of certain age would wear on a special occasion.

I began to sweat instantly, which wasn't good, as it would make my makeup run sooner rather than later.

My shoes were orthopedic, worn but well-polished leather, and amazingly comfortable. Gloves were black silk and necessary, because my hands didn't look like old woman's. My handbag was large black patent leather, and vintage too. I slipped the gift box in, with an untraceable phone, some money, and my keys.

When the audience began to exit the auditorium, I added a black cardigan and an overcoat that still retained some of the elegance of its earlier days. Then I picked up a collapsible cane, exited the loo, and joined the exodus out of the theater. My steps were slow but determined. I caught a glimpse of my reflection in a mirror as I crossed the lobby, and even I was fooled by my act.

The Cathedral of Lyon, or Cathédrale Saint-Jean-Baptiste, was right across the Saône in the fifth arrondissement. The distance was maybe five hundred meters from the theater, which would take a brisk woman less than five minutes to walk. I wasn't a brisk woman now, and I wasn't in a hurry. It was still over an hour to midnight.

The cathedral was a large, beautiful sandstone building from the twelfth century, with an imposing Gothic façade. Once a month, on Wednesdays, they held a midnight Mass that was popular with locals and tourists alike. I tottered slowly and steadily there, pausing every now and then as if to catch my breath.

Already people were flocking in, and I joined the crowd, thanking the young man who held the door open for me in a frail voice. I walked through the narthex, the people letting me pass at my own pace. The huge main doors to the nave hadn't been opened in ages, and the access was through modern doors to the aisles on both its sides. I chose the one on the right.

The confessional turned out to be on the left aisle between two chapels. Only one booth, with a long queue of confessors already, but it would make my task easier.

The queue would be gone by the time Mass started at midnight, so I took a seat on the back row of chairs in the nave and settled to wait. No one bothered me.

As the service was about to begin, I pushed myself up with the help of the cane and made my way to the queue. The line had thinned considerably, and unless there were true sinners confessing their entire lives before me, my turn would come exactly at midnight.

My timing was perfect. I entered the confessional just as the Mass began. The modern organ not far from the confessional began to blast out music, drowning out the noises of the congregation—and the sound of my purse opening as I took out the gift box.

I'm not Catholic, but my mother is, and I knew the drill. As the partition between the booths opened, I went through the routine, confessing to a couple of sins a woman my age might have done—coveting my neighbors, mostly—and was absolved. While I spoke, I located a small business card, hidden behind the hanging velvet cloth at the back.

When I left the booth, the small box had taken its place.

I made my steady but tottery way to the narthex, where I paused to draw breath like an old woman would, taking a seat someone politely vacated for me.

There were some latecomers and I had to wait. The moment the place was empty, I pulled out my phone and scanned the QR code on the business card. It opened an electronic transfer form, and I added my account number on the appointed place on it. I pressed send, and the transaction was complete. I had been paid for my services.

I pushed myself up, careful to stay in character even though there were no people around. And I was glad I'd done so when a young priest hurried through the narthex and exited without pausing to hold the door for me. Patiently, I made my slow way to the door. Just as I was about to reach for the handle, someone behind me pushed the door open for me.

"*Après vous, Madame.*"

My entire body tensed as I recognized the voice. Eliot Reed.

What the bloody hell was he doing here?

# 11

## ELIOT

DESPITE MY MOTHER'S BEST EFFORTS, I'd never been what you would call a good Catholic—or even passable Christian. And I'm not talking about my previous line of work, which most assuredly would see me in hell—if I believed in it.

I'd never been able to believe in God, no matter what denomination or televangelist tried to sell him to me. I'd sat in church on Sundays when I was a child and my mother could make me, but nothing there had moved me enough to even try to believe.

After I grew so large and muscled that Mom couldn't drag me to church anymore, I hadn't set a foot in one other than for weddings and funerals. Craig Douglas, the crime boss I'd worked for, had spurned all religions and churches, so I hadn't had to pretend to be religious for him either.

However, after my death, scam though it was, I'd found myself drawn to churches. Not to religion, but to the buildings themselves. Mostly it was to admire the architecture—there are amazing old churches in Europe— and to enjoy the atmosphere of quiet contemplation. Occasionally, I even found myself dropping two euros to a box by an altar and lighting a candle for the memory of the absent dead. It was always Jonathan Moreira that I thought of then.

I guess I missed my old self.

I hadn't lied to the detectives when I'd told them I'd been in a church on Sunday. But I hadn't attended the service. I'd wandered around the building with other tourists, admiring the imposing architecture, barely paying attention to what went on at the main altar. I'd heard someone mention a midnight Mass at the Lyon Cathedral on Wednesday, and I'd become intrigued.

I'd had an unproductive day, at work and with the murder investigation. Disgusted with myself, I'd decided to attend the service to see what such a large cathedral looked like at night.

It was dark outside as I entered. The church was dimly lit with hundreds, if not thousands of live candles, and people spoke in hushed tones, creating an atmosphere entirely different from a daylight service. A more reverent man would've had shivers run down his spine and his mind turned to God. I was ... impressed, but not particularly moved.

I arrived well before the Mass began. I ambled slowly up and down the aisles—quite a journey in a church that big—and admired the chapels that were illuminated with large self-standing candles. I lit a small-one for my old self too.

As the service was about to begin, I reached the last chapels before the entrance on the left aisle. Between them was a confessional made of beautifully carved oak or mahogany, meant for one confessor at a time; there were larger ones in one of the chapels, but those weren't in use tonight. The long line had diminished to a couple of old ladies who had more patience than the younger generations to wait for their turn.

I hadn't confessed my sins since my Confirmation, and I wasn't about to do so now. I'd be here until morning in that case. I studied the chapels leisurely, but I kept a side eye on the confessional. People attending these things interested me. Were they true believers or going through the motions?

The second-to-last person in line, a tottery old lady with a full veil in her fetching hat, entered the booth and didn't spend much time in there. Either she didn't consider herself sinful or she'd confessed recently. She exited the booth, but instead of joining the service, she headed straight to the exit.

That was a tough one to figure out. Someone who found confession more important than receiving the Holy Communion? Or maybe it was past her bedtime already and she didn't have the energy to stay.

There was one more person in line. The moment they confessed, a young priest who had waited nearby crossed the aisle and went into the confessional, only to exit instantly and head out of the door at a brisk pace.

I frowned, puzzled. That wasn't terribly devout of him. And even though it was none of my concern, or particularly interesting, I found myself following him. I'd seen the church already anyway.

The old lady with the veil hadn't made it out of the narthex yet, and the priest hurried past her and out of the door, letting it fall closed behind him with an echoing thud. I hastened my steps to exit, holding the door for the old woman while my attention was on the priest.

He was rounding the cathedral already, pulling off the collar with a forceful yank as he went and throwing it into the nearest trashcan.

Now *that* was my kind of interesting.

The moment the old woman was past the door, I hurried after the fake priest. I'm not sure why. Maybe I was bored.

He headed down a narrow, cobbled pedestrian street to the north between the cathedral and small shops and restaurants in the medieval buildings. There weren't many people around at that time of night, and even though my steps had to be echoing off the stone walls no matter how silently I tried to walk, he didn't seem to notice me following.

He passed the back side of Palais de Justice where the criminal and appeals courts sat, and then turned west down another similar medieval street. It was quiet and dark in there, the streets barely lit, and I couldn't see him well. But I wasn't about to give up now.

He turned north again at the next corner. I hurried up, as quietly as I could, but when I reached the street corner, he'd disappeared.

I swore quietly. I had no reason to follow him, but losing him annoyed me nonetheless. I walked a few meters down the street he'd taken—and was yanked into a neck lock by a man who'd been hiding in a door recess. It robbed me of breath, more for the surprise than for the tight hold.

I hadn't expected the ambush. No one would've dared to attack Jonny Moreira and I'd become accustomed to being the apex predator. I hoped I lived to regret that mistake.

Jonny would've extracted himself from the hold in a heartbeat and then proceeded to beat the crap out of his captor. Eliot Reed was a different man.

I relaxed against the hold, and it eased a little, allowing me to breathe better.

"Tell Dobrev that if he wants his files back, he needs to do better than kill Fabre," the man said in French into my ear. Then he pushed me forward so fast that I fell on my face. Only my years of yoga prevented me from hurting myself.

I climbed up and faced the man, but he wasn't there anymore. Baffled, I turned around—and almost collapsed into someone. I was about to launch an attack when I realized it was a woman and not the fake priest.

An old woman.

"I'm so sorry, Madame," I said, sounding a bit breathless to my embarrassment. It had been over a decade since I'd been at the receiving end of an assault.

"Never mind that," said a curiously familiar voice from within the full veil, pushing me aside. "Where did he go?"


I BLINKED, STUNNED. I peered at her face, but it was too dark to see it clearly through the veil. "Ada?"

What the fuck?

She didn't bother answering. She stepped around me and ran down the street, curiously hunched but fast. Ada or not, she most assuredly wasn't an old lady.

Since I couldn't just stand there staring at her retreating form, I ran after her.

She'd already turned the corner toward the river when I caught up with her. My handmade Italian leather shoes weren't made for running, and certainly not on cobblestones. She was wearing sturdy orthopedic shoes, but her skirt and hunched back slowed her a little.

She turned right at the next corner, and then immediately left to the river down another narrow medieval street. It was lined with restaurants on both sides, and the tables and chairs of their terraces had been piled by the walls for the night. Maybe she was able to see the man past them, because she kept running.

We reached the main street by the river. The light was better, and she paused briefly to look around. "There!"

The fake priest was walking unhurriedly toward Palais de Justice, returning to where he'd come, clearly believing he'd given me the slip. We followed, slowing down and keeping our distance.

A car was rolling toward us down the one-way street almost soundlessly, pulling over by the curb to intercept the man. I lengthened my steps to catch the license plate before he escaped in it.

When the fake priest was almost at the car, a window on the driver's side lowered and a hand stretched out. The car's headlights were blinding me, but I glimpsed a weapon pointed at the priest—and us.

I didn't pause to think but threw myself over Ada, tackling her down when the first shot rang, then two more. The car pulled off with tires squealing and was soon gone.

"Get off me!"

Startled, I obeyed the determined hands pushing me. I rose and pulled her up, looking around.

A body was slumped on the sidewalk a few meters from us, blood spreading fast around him.

"Fuck."

Ada spotted him too, and with a startled noise, made to go to him, but I held her back. "I don't think it's a good idea for you to be here when the police arrive."

She shook off my hand. "I can't just leave him there. He needs help."

"He's beyond our help. I'll deal with it. Now go!"

She nodded, reluctantly, and made to turn around when a brief blare of a police siren halted her. A patrol car drove slowly to us from their guard post next to the courthouse, lights flashing on the roof. Two uniformed officers exited, and I found myself staring at the business ends of two Sig Sauer Pros.

For an enforcer like me, it was a familiar sight, but it had usually been a fellow criminal holding the weapon.

"Act feeble," I hissed at Ada, but she was better than me at this.

As I lifted my arms, palms at the cops, she covered her face with her hands and began to wail. "Mon Dieu, I'm going to die…" Even her voice belonged to an old woman now.

She collapsed against me, forcing me to lower an arm to wrap it around her or risk her falling.

"We're unarmed," I said in English, not knowing the equivalent in French. An oversight on my side; I should've known I'd need the phrase sooner than later.

"Who was shooting?" one of the officers demanded in passable English, while the other went to the dead body, concluding like I had that there was nothing we could do for the fake priest.

"It was a drive-by shooting," I said. "I didn't see their face, but it was a black Citroën."

The officer checking the body holstered his weapon and spoke to a radio attached on his shoulder. The other came to us, the weapon still out. The old woman in my arms—it was difficult to think of her as Ada—pressed closer to me. I wrapped another arm around her, patting her on the back and making soothing noises like I would if she were my grandmother.

The officer grimaced and holstered the weapon. "What are you doing here at this hour?"

"We were at the midnight Mass." I nodded toward the cathedral that peeked behind the Palais de Justice. "The lady became dizzy and I offered to escort her home."

"On foot?" he asked, dismayed, and I shrugged as if I found it odd too.

"She said she lived right by the church, but now I'm not sure she quite remembers where she lives."

"Madame, are you all right?" the officer asked in a kinder tone in French. Then he frowned. "Why are her clothes torn?"

"I … had to tackle her when the shooting began," I confessed, hoping that he found saving an old lady's life more important than manhandling her. "The line of fire was from the car toward us."

"How many shots?"

"Three."

"They're all in the victim, then," the other officer said, coming to us. "Do you know who he is?"

"I have no idea," I said truthfully. "He was walking ahead of us when we came to this street."

"Why were you walking toward the church if you came from there?" the officer demanded.

Good question. "She thought her home was over there," I said, pointing behind us. "But when we got there, she said she wasn't sure anymore, and her key didn't fit the door. I thought I'd walk her around a bit in case it would jolt her memory." I glanced at the sobbing woman in my arms. "But I fear this has only made it worse…"

An ambulance and an unmarked police vehicle arrived at the scene, and the officers went to brief them. I glanced around and located a chair on the terrace of a café a few meters down. With a nudge, I led Ada there and she sank onto the chair, to all appearances a feeble old lady.

Remarkable.

The detectives had exited the car and I stiffened when I recognized them. "Bellamy and Gagne," I said in a low tone.

"*Merde*…"

They photographed the body and went over his pockets, finding a phone, keys, wallet, and a small, black gift box. Ada stiffened under my hand that was resting on her shoulder. But I couldn't ask her why, because Gagne was approaching us.

His brows shot up when he recognized me. "Monsieur Reed. I take it this is a coincidence?"

"Or bad luck," I said dryly.

"Would you mind if I searched you anyway?"

I minded very much, on principle, but I stepped away from Ada and spread my arms. "Not at all."

The search was quick and impassive. He didn't find anything, and he didn't even suggest he do the same to Ada, which was good, because I suspected the hump in her back wasn't the only unnatural thing about her, but he insisted on looking into her handbag.

"It's all right," I said in a soothing tone, as if I was her caretaker or something. "He only wants a peek."

It took some coaxing—she was really good—but eventually she agreed to open the bag and Gagne looked in without touching the bag. He was good too. Then he straightened and glared at me.

"Now, if you could tell me what the hell are you doing here?"

# 12

## ELIOT

I GAVE GAGNE THE SAME STORY I'D given the uniformed officers, and he listened like he believed me. A unique experience. "And you don't know this lady at all?"

"No. She was at the cathedral, waiting to take a confession when she started to feel weak. As the service was starting and I was the closest, I helped her out. But then she wanted to go home. I couldn't very well abandon her."

"Of course not. Do you know her name?"

"It hasn't come up."

He crouched in front of Ada and peered through her veil. I could only hope he couldn't see her face clearly. "Madam, do you know your name?"

She pulled straight. "Of course I do."

I bit my lip and Gagne shot me an amused glance. "And do you know where you live?"

"At 11 Place Antonin Gourju," she said promptly, if feebly. "Can I go home?"

"Absolutely," Gagne said, getting up. "It's right across the river," he said to me, pointing at the nearly identical houses on the opposite bank. I had no idea how Ada knew the address, it's not like she'd had a chance to google it, but I doubted it was where she truly lived.

"Ah. No wonder we didn't find the right building. Maybe I should see her there."

"No, she can take a taxi. I need to talk to you." He gestured at a taxi that had idled nearby to come over, the driver busy ogling at the goings-on.

I helped Ada up and we walked slowly to the taxi with her leaning heavily on me. I helped her on the front seat. "Do you have money?"

She gave me a confused look that was so genuine that I sighed and dug into my pocket. I pulled out a couple of twenty-euro notes, all the cash I had with me. I wrapped her hand around them with a stern command to pay the taxi with it. I glared at the driver for further measure, in case he thought to swindle an old lady.

The taxi took off and I returned to Gagne. Bellamy had joined him too. "Now, what happened here?" Bellamy asked.

I told them about the drive-by shooting, as clearly as a person who had been lying on the ground, head covered with hands, could.

"And there was nothing that triggered the shooting?"

"Nothing, no words or warnings. I don't think the victim even noticed before the first shot rang out. But I think the shooter knew the victim would be here. He was driving slowly, clearly looking for him."

"So not random?"

"No."

My conviction was based on the fact that the victim was involved in Fabre's case somehow, but I couldn't tell that to the detectives without blowing holes into my story.

"They didn't even try to eliminate us, even though we witnessed everything."

"Did you see the shooter?" Gagne asked.

"No. It was dark and the headlights were on. I don't even know if there was more than one person in the car."

"Did you see the weapon?"

I gave it a thought. "All I saw was the silhouette. Pistol, large, with a silencer, single-shot or semi."

"Well, it certainly made an impact on the victim…" Bellamy said dryly. "His name was Vincent Brunet." He gave me a questioning look, but I shook my head.

"The name doesn't mean anything to me."

"Would you like to see the face?"

"Yes."

The victim was already on a stretcher, waiting for the coroner to transport him away. There were three large holes in his chest, overkill if anything was, from such close range.

Gagne lit the face with his phone and I studied it carefully, but apart from being the fake priest I'd been following, it wasn't familiar.

"I've never seen him before." The lapel of his suit jacket had fallen open and I saw the designer label. "Expensive clothes though."

Maybe that was why I'd followed him. I'd subconsciously noted that he was too well-dressed for a priest.

"I was hoping this would connect with Fabre's murder somehow," Gagne said.

It did, but since I didn't know how, or had no way to tell it to them that wouldn't implicate me and Ada, I lifted my brows in a polite inquiry. "Bit of a stretch, don't you think?"

Gagne put his phone away. "There aren't that many murders in this city. Usually when those occur back-to-back, they're connected. Are you sure he wasn't at the party?"

I gave it a proper thought. Maybe I'd seen him there and that's why I'd followed him. "He wasn't anyone I talked to, but I was busy the whole night with people pitching at me to notice everyone."

"Maybe he's a random person on his way to a late birthday party." Bellamy opened the small gift box the victim had been carrying. "An external drive?"

I controlled my face, but it took effort. I knew that drive. And now I knew what Ada had been doing in the church—and how the victim was connected with the case.

"Robbery wasn't a motive, then," I said lightly.

Bellamy cursed in French. "It has to be gang related."

"With clothes like his?" Gagne said, looking dubious.

"High-end organized crime," I suggested, and the detectives grimaced.

"Great."

"You know, it could be connected with Fabre anyway," I continued, as if coming up with the notion only now. "Just because he was a successful businessman doesn't mean he couldn't have been involved in organized crime somehow. Innocent people don't get shot in their homes."

"Maybe there's something interesting on this drive," Bellamy said, but he didn't look hopeful. I bit my tongue not to sound too eager.

"Maybe it's why Fabre was shot in the first place?"

"By this victim?" Gagne shook his head. "Why would he be walking around with it days after, then?"

"I … have no idea."

But at least the police now had the piece that was missing from their murder investigation. Maybe I could let the matter be.

The body was taken away, and the detectives dismissed me too. "Can we offer you a ride home?" Gagne asked. It had been a long night, but I shook my head.

"Thank you, but I think I'll walk. It gives me a chance to clear my head after … this."

They didn't press the matter. They drove away and I walked two and a half kilometers home down the riverside that looked beautiful and serene at this time of night. I took my time, needing every minute. I even climbed the stairs up to my apartment instead of using the elevator.

I opened the door to my place and knew instantly that it wasn't empty. My hand went inside my jacket, only to come out empty, as I still wasn't carrying.

As quietly as I could, I walked down the hallway to my living room. Lights were on, but no one was there. Kitchen was empty too. I grabbed a filleting knife from the knife block. It would sink between the ribs of the intruder beautifully.

Feeling better now that I was armed, I searched the study. The door was open and the room was dark. I switched on the lights and went through it, keeping my back against the wall like the good cop that I wasn't. It was empty. That left my bedroom.

The door was slightly ajar and made no noise when I opened it. Lights were on, as were the lights in the bathroom. I could hear water running in the shower.

What the fuck?

I crossed the floor in a few steps, safety forgotten, and yanked the door open just as the water cut. The glass door of the shower opened, and Ada stepped out. Naked.

MY MIND WENT BRIEFLY blank as my blood relocated south with a woosh. If it was a deliberate attempt to throw me off my guard, it worked. Anyone could've attacked me and I wouldn't have cared.

She looked gorgeous, and not just because she was the first naked woman I'd seen since moving here. Water ran down her body, demanding I follow with my gaze. Tilting my head, I let my eyes roam. Her long limbs were muscled and graceful, her hips curving, and her breasts—

A wet washcloth hit me in the face, thrown with incredible accuracy across the bathroom.

"Thanks," I managed to say, backing out of the bathroom. I closed the door and fled to the living room, only there noticing that I'd taken the washcloth with me. I was holding it in one hand and the filleting knife in the other. It was a miracle I hadn't stabbed myself in the face.

I put them hastily on the counter between kitchen and the living room—I wouldn't return to the bathroom in a hurry—and went to my liquor cabinet. I'd fantasized about a cold beer as I was walking home, but that wasn't sufficient for recovering from the sight I'd just witnessed. I poured a measure of whiskey for myself instead and took a large gulp.

Warmth spread through my body, but it didn't help with my arousal. Needing to gain control before Ada returned, I opened the balcony door and stepped out, hoping that the cool night air would do the trick. I stared with unseeing eyes at the dark park below and the river slowly flowing by, taking deep breaths—thanks, yoga—until I was in control of my body again.

I sensed Ada behind me but didn't turn to look. Instead, I studied the balconies of the lower floors, placed at uneven spots on the wall, like large stairs or Minecraft blocks, the lowest close to the ground and each within grasp from one another. A minor challenge for a parkour enthusiast—or a cat burglar.

"Did you come up using the balconies?"

It was only the third floor, but it was still impressive, especially in the granny clothes she'd been wearing.

"You need a better lock on your balcony door," she said, returning inside. I followed.

"Do you want one?" I asked, showing my glass, but she shook her head as she took a seat on the couch.

She'd dressed and was wearing black leggings that instantly brought back the memory of her naked legs, as they perfectly hugged her contours. Her T-shirt was black too, and she wasn't wearing any makeup. She looked even younger than she normally did.

I liked the fresh face. She was beautiful.

I took a seat in an armchair next to her. "Care to tell me what happened tonight?" I asked, taking a sip of my glass. Her brows shot up.

"Me? You're the one who was playing spy. Poorly, I might add."

I made a face. "It was on a whim. Why did you follow him?"

"I was following you," she said dryly. "What did he say to you when you so foolishly let him capture you?"

She'd seen that? Damn. There went my credibility as a former security expert.

I rubbed my face, trying to remember. "Something like 'tell Dobrev that if he wants his files back, he needs to do better than kill Fabre.'"

She straightened. "Fuck, fuck, fuck."

The excessive swearing seemed out of character. "I take it that it means something to you?"

She reached a hand to my glass. "I think I'll take some of that after all."

I gave the glass to her and she downed the expensive whiskey in one gulp and then held her breath to keep it in, her face scrunching tight. When she was able to speak again, she sounded calm.

"Dobrev is a Bulgarian drug lord and human trafficker I've been tracking for months. He's basically untouchable. There was some indication in the ledgers I showed you that all this had something to do with his businesses, and now I'm sure."

The name didn't ring any bells, but I hadn't been at the acquisition end of my boss's drug businesses. "So how did Fabre get involved? Why did he have the external drive?"

"I have absolutely no idea. I was hired to steal it, so I did."

I hid my surprise that she finally admitted to being the burglar. Not that I hadn't been sure before.

"And you dropped it off at the church tonight?"

"Yes. And the man we followed picked it up."

"And got killed for his trouble. By Dobrev's men?"

She pursed his lips. "They would've taken the drive from him in that case. They killed Fabre when he didn't have it."

She was right. "So who shot the fake priest?"

"Fake priest?"

"He was dressed as a priest. He fetched the packet you left and fled. His name was Vincent Brunet."

She shook her head. "Doesn't mean anything to me. But it's French."

"As opposed to…?"

"Bulgarian."

"Fabre's French."

"True." She sighed. "I thought I was on a verge of a breakthrough with my case, but now I understand it even less. I should've left the drive be, but my intel pointed at Fabre, and I wanted to see what was on it."

"Do you often steal evidence for your cases?" I asked, genuinely curious.

She rolled her eyes. "Never. But the intel turned out to be solid and the contents connected with my active case. Which created problems for me…"

"You falsified evidence?" I don't know why I was so dismayed. I was a criminal; she was a criminal. It should've been par for the course with us.

"Only after the ledgers turned out to be important," she said, sounding defensive.

"What's the connection?" She hesitated and I gave her a stern look. "I'm in this too. No use pleading confidentiality now."

She rubbed her face with both hands, looking tired. It was getting late. "Keyword to one of the accounts is *Arctos*. It's a yacht that belongs to Dobrev's right-hand man, Artem Melnyk."

That name didn't mean anything to me either, but I nodded. I rose to refill my glass, thinking over the case, trying to make what we had make sense. *Benevolence* had also been a keyword. That couldn't be a coincidence.

"Could there be a coup brewing inside Dobrev's organization?"

She tensed. "I have no idea. I don't know what kind of person Melnyk is other than that he loves his yacht and spends a lot of time partying in Monaco." Her eyes narrowed as she gave it thought.

"How would it fit our case? Fabre gets his hands on Dobrev's ledgers, Melnyk wants them and hires me to steal them. Dobrev sends someone to kill Fabre to get the ledgers back but is too late, so they stake one of Melnyk's men to see when he gets the ledgers, and instead kill him and leave without the ledgers?"

"That doesn't make any sense…"

She sighed and pushed up. "I'm too tired to think. I'm going home."

I put the glass down. "I'll get you a taxi."

She went to collect her things while I made the call. I didn't own a car, which pained me, as I loved fast cars. But the system of one-way streets in this city was infuriating, my office and everything important was a short walk away, and public transportation was cheap and efficient.

She probably would've refused the lift anyway.

I walked her downstairs and waited with her for the taxi to arrive. "You didn't take the taxi here, did you?"

She gave me a slow look. "Please…" she drawled. "I drove in the original taxi to the exact address I gave to the detectives. The front entrance to that building isn't locked, which is why I chose it. I've used it before. I went in, waited for the taxi to leave, and then got myself another one. Thanks for the cash, by the way. I didn't have any money. I can't carry plastic with my actual name when I'm in disguise."

That was sensible.

"Do you need more?" I put a hand into my pocket to see if there was any cash left, but she shook her head.

"I didn't use it all."

The taxi arrived and I walked her to it. "So ... keep me posted on the case?"

She just smiled and waved as she got in the car. She closed the door before giving the address to the driver, making sure I couldn't hear it, and the car was soon on its way.

As it turned in the corner, I had a brief déjà vu, as if I'd watched her drive away from me on this street before. It was such a strong recollection that it had to be true.

I was back in my apartment when it hit me: *Sandrine*.

A slow smile spread on my face, and I shook my head, impressed. She really was good.

# 13

## ADA

THE SHOOTING HAD RATTLED ME badly. I'd never witnessed someone being shot to death before, for all that I'd been a Met detective. Even the explosion that had supposedly killed my husband had happened where I couldn't witness it.

I hadn't even noticed the weapon or realized that a shooting was about to happen, not even when Eliot threw himself over me and pressed me against the pavement. I'd been stunned and angry for the sudden manhandling, both because I hadn't expected it of him and because I hadn't even had time to react, let alone pull a nifty self-defense move despite having a black belt in jiu-jitsu.

Maybe I should be more understanding of the timid housewives in Laïla's self-defense class from now on.

The dead body had been a rude awakening to a reality with which Eliot was evidently more familiar. I didn't believe he was a secret agent, like Laïla hoped, but he must have been excellent private security.

When it dawned on me that I might have died if it hadn't been for his swift thinking, I hadn't had to pretend to be a feeble old lady. My knees had barely held. I hated to be so helpless, but my body hadn't cared for my opinion.

I lay awake most of the night going over the events, my mind churning for possible explanations. Nothing made sense though. I simply didn't have enough data to work with.

I tried to push the problem aside, but then a new question emerged: why had Eliot been at the church? I hadn't thought to ask, and he hadn't volunteered the information.

Had it been a coincidence that he was following Vincent Brunet? Or did he have information about the case he wasn't sharing with me?

I found it incredible that he would've simply decided to follow him like he claimed. But where would he have gained intel about Brunet? Unless … he was a secret agent after all.

I laughed aloud in the darkness of my bedroom.

I was almost certain that he hadn't been there because of me. At least he hadn't expected me to be the old lady for whom he had held the door open. The stunned look on his face when he collided with me in the dark street made me chuckle.

Remembering how he had looked at me when he surprised me in the shower wiped the laughter away. It had been ages since a man had so openly admired my naked body. The heat in his gaze had been … exhilarating.

I blushed in the dark. Sleep was impossible after that.

There were dark circles under my eyes in the morning, and despite the careful makeup I applied, Laïla noticed the moment she saw me. Her face turned concerned.

"Are you all right?"

"Absolutely," I assured her. "I didn't sleep well, that's all. The case kept churning in my mind, no matter what I did."

"Did you find anything interesting in the laptop?"

It took me a moment to remember what she was talking about. "I didn't have a chance to look yet."

"Do. I think you'll find it useful."

She looked so hopeful that I nodded and promised I would do it the first thing. I didn't want to lie to her, again, and so, after morning emails and other routines, I opened the folder where she had saved the contents of the laptop.

I didn't expect to find anything interesting. Or anything useful for my case. The connection between them was a scam, after all.

But since it could be useful for some future investigation, I went dutifully through every folder, file, and software there had been on the laptop.

Most of it was in Bulgarian. I didn't speak it and it slowed me down, as I had to make quick online translations to see if the file was worth devoting time to. Most of them weren't, but there were enough that I couldn't abandon everything outright.

I found a list of names in one file particularly interesting. None of them were familiar to me, but they might be to someone else's case, now or in the future. That was what Interpol did best: connected evidence from various and even unlikely sources. I had no idea if it was a list of accomplishes or clients, or a hitlist even, but I flagged it as interesting and added appropriate tags so that my colleagues could find it.

My phone rang just as I was about to head to lunch. "This is Detective Gagne," the man at the other end introduced himself. My heart skipped a beat, but when he continued it was clear he didn't suspect I'd been the old lady the previous night. "We met at the residence of Eliot Reed the other day."

"I remember, Detective. How may I help you?" I was proud of how calm I sounded.

"There was a shooting last night and we're having trouble identifying the victim. I was hoping you'd have better resources."

My brows shot up, but fortunately he couldn't see the stunned expression. I thought they had a name. "Absolutely. Do you have anything to go by?"

"We have a name but it's fake. His fingerprints aren't in our system, but you could check more widely."

We had good resources for it, so I said I would do it. "Is it connected with the Fabre case?"

"We're hoping so. You have access already, so you can take a look yourself to see if anything catches your interest. Thank you for that hint about the keywords, by the way. We haven't been able to connect them with anything tangible yet, but we will."

They would, now that they had the ledgers.

"You can get the prints straight from the documentation," Gagne continued. "There are two sets of prints, neither of which we have a match for, so if you could check both."

My entire body went cold. "Two?"

"There were a couple of partial prints on a gift box we found from the victim that we hope will lead to somewhere."

I had trouble breathing. "I'll do my best."

I SAT AT MY DESK AFTER the call ended, trying to ward off a panic attack. I'd never had one, but if anything merited it, this did.

I'd left fingerprints on the gift box! I couldn't fathom how I had been that careless. When had it happened? I'd been wearing gloves when I put the external drive in.

With shaking hands, I logged onto the local police database and the correct case. Then I just stared at the files, unable to see the contents. I squeezed my eyes closed and held my body rigid for a few heartbeats, holding my breath. When I released myself, I was calm again.

I read everything the detectives had on the case. There were numerous new interviews of people who had attended the rooftop party on Saturday, but they hadn't had anything worthwhile to say. None of the faces on photos from social media posts of the party looked familiar, and I'd been there.

At least I hadn't been captured on the background of any of them.

There was a link to the drive-by shooting, marked as a potential connection. They'd added Eliot's eyewitness account, with comments from the detectives that they needed to keep an eye on him. I would've done so too if I'd been the detective on this case. It was an odd coincidence that the same man showed up on two shooting cases.

Again, I wondered if it was a coincidence, but I knew that he hadn't shot Brunet and I had no cause to suspect he'd shot Fabre either. Besides, I'd been on both sites too, and I certainly hadn't killed either man.

They had accessed the external drive and found the ledgers, but they weren't treating them as suspicious yet. They'd forwarded them to an investigator of economic crimes, but that would take time. Police work was slow. Perhaps I could add a helpful note about connecting the keywords with the ledgers.

I pulled out the fingerprints. One set was complete, taken from the victim. The other was a couple of partials.

I uploaded the partial prints to our search program and clicked "search." It could access prints from people who had been arrested and or convicted of crimes all over the world, and since neither had happened to me, I wasn't surprised when the search came out empty. Then I checked the outstanding cases with prints from crime scenes that hadn't been identified yet. That search came out empty too.

At least I hadn't been so careless that I would've left my prints on crime scenes for the police to find.

The third search was more specific: Interpol personnel. It was a smaller database, so the search was quick. And to my amazement, it didn't point at me.

Relief washed through me with such force it almost blinded me. I pressed a hand on my mouth to ward off the nausea, taking shallow breaths.

"Are you all right?" Richard asked, concerned. I barely managed to speak.

"Yes. I slept poorly last night. I think it's time to head for lunch."

"Mind if I join you?"

I would've wanted to be alone with my nausea, but since I didn't have a polite way to refuse, I nodded.

"Let me just add these notes first."

He leaned over my shoulder to look at my monitor. "What are you searching?"

"Fingerprints for the local police. There was a drive-by shooting last night and they need us to identify the victim."

He was appropriately horrified and kept asking questions while I sent a note to the detectives that the partial prints most likely belonged to someone working at the shop where the gift box had been purchased.

Despite my misgivings, a lunch with Richard improved my mood considerably. And then he had to ruin it.

We were having the obligatory shots of espresso after lunch, and he gave me a teasing look over the rim of his cup. "So ... how are things going with Eliot Reed?"

A memory of the shower incident flashed to my mind, and I blushed, horribly. With my complexion, it was basically a whole-body experience. A slow leer spread on his face.

"That well, huh?"

"No!" I denied vehemently, but with the blush it was useless trying to make him believe me.

He teased me all the way back to our desks, where I finally pleaded the needed to work, and he left me alone. But the rest of the day, whenever I happened to catch his eyes, they twinkled at me.

One of us was enjoying this at least.

I don't know why I was so embarrassed by it. I was a grown woman, not a schoolgirl who was surprised by a boy in a locker room.

Then again, no schoolboy had ever looked at me with such heat...

I had been surprised by him. I might have shrieked; I wasn't sure. The filleting knife in his hand hadn't helped.

I'd needed a shower after the night I'd had—and the climb up to his balcony, which had been more straining than I'd given him to believe.

I hadn't thought beyond locating the shower before peeling off all the horrid layers of clothing I'd been wearing. It hadn't occurred to me that he would react with violence when he found an intruder in his home—which should've been self-evident, given what I knew of his background.

At least I'd been exiting the shower already when he found me, otherwise we would've been reenacting the shower scene from *Psycho*...

Before I spiraled down that horror scene, the search for the shooting victim's prints finished, claiming my attention. Our databases of criminals, convicted or otherwise, didn't find a match. Brunet's prints didn't show up in the passport registry either, but I couldn't be sure if it meant he wasn't French or simply didn't have a passport.

I rubbed my face as I tried to come up with other options, but I had to give up. "Are there any official, legal databases that collect fingerprints that we have access to?" I asked Richard and other colleagues within hearing distance.

"The military, but we don't have access," one of them said.

"Law enforcement," another one said, and even though I was certain the victim wasn't a cop, I logged on to that.

"Casinos," Richard said, and we all turned to look at him, surprised.

"Really?"

"They're paranoid about security. Each civilized country maintains a national database of their personnel."

I hadn't known that.

I would need to access each country separately, but since the man had a French alias and had spoken French, that's where I began.

I had an instant hit. "Bingo. He worked at the Casino in Monaco." The official name was Casino de Monte-Carlo, a luxurious entertainment complex from the nineteenth century that contained *Opéra de Monte-Carlo* too, but everyone simply called it the Casino with a capital C.

"Jean-Michel Lepine, thirty-one, worked as security there for a year."

There was a photo too. It showed an average looking man that matched the photo of the victim. Delighted to have been able to help, I sent the info to the detectives.

Something about the name nagged at me, as if I'd come across it recently. Since the only list of names that I'd read today was the one from the laptop, I pulled it out again.

I skimmed the list of maybe twenty names and there it was. My heart skipped a beat. Was my scam case connected with my real one after all?

It wasn't entirely unbelievable. I'd chosen a recent drug bust especially since Dobrev smuggled drugs as well as people. The smugglers' boat had been captured right outside the French maritime border. Linking it to Dobrev without the false evidence would be difficult, but not impossible.

Lepine had mentioned Dobrev, and here was Lepine's name on a list taken from drug smugglers. Now I only had to figure out why the list existed in the first place. What sort of idiotic smuggler carried this much incriminating evidence with them?

Unless it was planted. But by whom? Was there a power struggle within Dobrev's organization after all, like Eliot had suggested? But between whom? Dobrev and Melnyk? Or was there a third, unknown party at play?

I had a sudden need to talk about the case with Eliot, but since he wasn't here—and it would get me fired for sure—I turned to Richard again.

"If a drug bust comes up with evidence that's too good to be true, would you suspect an internal struggle or an outside coup?"

He shook his head, bemused. "You have really odd questions today."

"The name of the shooting victim is among the drug bust evidence, and I want to know why."

He scooted his chair to my desk to study the monitor himself. "Run this by me."

"Frontex raided a boat a couple of months ago, hoping to find illegal immigrants from Africa. They found drugs instead and two Bulgarian nationals. There was also a laptop, which had a list of names, one of which was the victim's." I pointed at the screen.

"And you simply happened to come by it?"

There was nothing simple about it, but I shrugged. "I'm grasping at straws with my human trafficking investigation. Since Dobrev runs drugs too, I'm going over everything we have about drug smuggling."

"Huh. So how does a guy who works security at the Monte Carlo Casino in Monaco end up on the list on Bulgarian drug smugglers' laptop?"

"That's what I'm asking you. Is it genuine or planted?"

"By whom?"

I threw my arms up, perplexed. "Melnyk, Dobrev's right hand man, spends a lot of time in Monaco. Lepine could be his man. And now he's dead."

"So Melnyk gives a tip to Frontex about a suspicious boat, which gets taken down, and his boss retaliates?" He looked dubious, and I didn't believe it either.

"There would be names of Dobrev's men on the planted evidence, then."

"Presuming that Lepine isn't Dobrev's man. And presuming it was planted. Some people really are so stupid they carry incriminating evidence with them."

I knew Lepine hadn't worked for Dobrev, but I couldn't tell him that.

"So where does that leave me, vis a vis the power struggle?"

He grinned. "Fucked if I know. Maybe there isn't one. Or maybe a third party is trying to take over and is starting with bit players to rattle Dobrev and Melnyk both."

Great. Just great.

"I'd best send this list to the detectives. Let them deal with it."

Richard patted my back and scooted back to his desk. "Let me know if I can be of more assistance."

"I will," I promised. "But first, I have the movements of two boats to track."

It wasn't as straightforward as I'd hoped. While I could pull the data of all maritime traffic from the past year on Mediterranean, input the boats' registration numbers to a software and let it do the job for me, it tended to give hundreds of false hits.

After removing the latter for a better part of an hour, I gave up and called Laïla. "Is there software that compares the routes of two boats more efficiently than the current one we have? Or better yet, tracks all the boats that have been in the same place with one of them?"

"Hmm… It's not exactly a challenge, only time consuming. Give me the registration numbers and I'll see what I can do. But don't expect results until next week."

"Thanks, you're the best."

I sent the information I needed to Laïla and then concentrated on *Arctos*. It had been in Nice for several days now. The Cannes Film Festival was in full swing, and all the jetsetters gathered there. Melnyk had money and power, and he liked to show off both, and there was nowhere better for it than an event that gathered glitz and glamour in one place.

Only, the yacht wasn't there anymore. Baffled, I leaned closer to the monitor. The tracking data was almost real time, and according to it, *Arctos* was on its way to Monaco and would arrive there tonight.

Melnyk spent most of his time there, so it wasn't an unexpected move. But with a third sign pointing at Monaco today, it was clear what I needed to do.

I would travel to Monaco.

# 14

## ELIOT

My week had been so odd and unsettling, with its thefts, deaths, and brushes with law enforcement, that I decided I deserved a relaxing weekend. Long, relaxing weekend, starting on Friday and lasting maybe until Monday.

Unplanned vacations weren't exactly new for me, though in the past I'd used them as a pretext to visit the locations where I needed to stash IDs and money. Not that I hadn't fully enjoyed those places once I got there.

I didn't have to do that anymore, so no need to head to Kuala Lumpur or wherever. Moreover, I didn't want to fly. My Italian passport and new looks were good, but why tempt fate with airport security.

I was spoiled for destinations regardless. There were dozens of places in France alone that I wanted to see, and my Italian passport ensured that I could travel through the entire EU without problems at borders. The excellent train network would make it possible without setting foot on a plane.

I spent most of Thursday listing the places I wanted to see and visit without taking a whole week off. Not that I couldn't take a week off—or not work at all, for that matter—but I did have business related meetings scheduled for the next week, so a long weekend it was.

How had my life turned into business meetings?

Paris was only a two-hour train journey away, and it was my number one option, but there were places like Venice and Rome only an overnight's train ride away too. I could've rented a car just as easily—the mountain roads around here were spectacular—but I'd set my heart on a luxury train. I would arrive rested and relaxed instead of with cramped muscles after a ten-hour drive.

Or I could go to the Riviera…

The blue Mediterranean sea and white beaches instantly began to call me. A long weekend soaking in the sun was just what the doctor ordered. Nice—or Nizza, as they called it here—was only four hours by train.

But it wasn't to be, to my disappointment. The Cannes Film Festival was on and Nice was fully booked down to the last lousy Airbnb. And even though I didn't know anyone in the film industry, I didn't want to spend my weekend swarmed by American tourists. I'd had enough of my vacationing countrymen when I ran the hotel. And the chances of someone I knew being there was too big.

But it wasn't far from Monaco, and the sea and sands of the Riviera continued there. The glitz and glamour of the European jet set would fill the famous Casino and I would fit right in.

I began instantly to search for hotels. I didn't dare to stay by the Casino, no matter how badly I itched to see how luxury hotels there were run. Many of the whales who frequently gambled at the Casino had visited my hotel too, and I couldn't risk being recognized. Besides, they were fully booked.

The Jewel of Monaco, a five-star hotel a couple of miles to east, looked perfect, but the film festival had filled the hotels in Monaco as well. They only had a two-bedroom luxury suite left and I booked it before it was snatched too. Then I booked a first-class train ticket on a TGV—the highspeed train—which would depart at six this evening, and a table in the first-class dining car. The train would arrive at the Monte Carlo station at midnight.

My arrangements made, I hurried home to pack everything I thought I might need on my journey, from swimming trunks to a tuxedo. It was only three—or maybe four—days, but it was my first proper vacation in ages. I was almost giddy with excitement—or as giddy as a former mafia enforcer ever came to be. I had no idea what I would do in Monaco, but I would be properly dressed for it.

A taxi took me to Lyon-Part-Dieu train station at the appointed time and a porter showed up to carry my luggage. I had a sleeping cabin to myself, which in first class came with a proper bed instead of a narrow ledge folded down from the wall. I didn't plan to sleep there, but I appreciated it.

As the train pulled off from the station, I had a sudden notion that I should've asked Ada to come with me. I would've enjoyed her company—and it wasn't even the bed that gave me the idea.

But I cast the impulse aside. She couldn't just abandon her work like I could, and a long weekend together would be too much like an opening gambit in a relationship. One that would break rules number three and eight simultaneously.

Dating an Interpol analyst would be just about the stupidest thing I could do.

Pushing the fanciful thought aside, I checked my appearance—Armani suit with a crisp shirt and no tie, which I hoped wouldn't be required—and headed to the restaurant car.

I won't lie to you: it was everything I hoped for. A veritable James Bond experience complete with an excellent three-course meal and a femme fatale in a form-hugging silk gown that left nothing to imagination.

She sashayed through the restaurant car, saw me checking her out, and asked if she could join me. She was a step or two removed from a professional, a woman who coasted through high society with no money, relying on men like me for keeping her up in style. But her appreciative smile as she checked me out in return, and her luxurious black locks that fell across lush breasts, were enough for me to deem her worth paying her dinner for.

It was exhilarating to have a woman check me out without fear being her first reaction, like used to happen when I was still the size and shape of Jonny Moreira.

She was my age, cultured and intelligent, and we had a wonderful, leisurely dinner together. And if I took her to my cabin for a leisurely and immensely satisfying test of the double bed, that's no one's business but ours.

She disembarked in Nice, to join her friends there. I wasn't sad to see her go; I'd got exactly what I needed from her.

Only after she left did it occur to me that I didn't even know her name.

FRIDAY AFTERNOON FOUND me on the terrace of the brasserie of Casino Café de Paris, a smaller gambling establishment outside the more famous Casino. It was chock-full of tourists, but I had an excellent table at the side of the terrace with a view of the Casino over a verdant piece of greenery full of colorful flowers and palm trees, and the luxury cars parked outside the Casino.

My hotel was a leisurely half an hour walk from the Casino. I slept late, enjoyed breakfast on the balcony of my suite that overlooked the Mediterranean, and swam several laps in the excellent pool of the Roman style outdoors spa of the hotel. My new body was perfect for swimming—and swimming trunks. I'd discovered I loved the exercise when I was trying to reach my current size and shape.

I'd dressed in tan linen trousers and a white shirt with sleeves rolled up to the elbows, suede loafers, and a stylish, white Panama hat with a wide brim to shield my face from the relentless sun that was heating up the day.

My sunglasses were *Dolce & Gabbana*, my sunscreen was SPF 50, and my attitude was full-on enjoying life.

Judging by the lingering looks the young women at reception gave me, I'd chosen well. I couldn't have pulled off the look in New York without getting a lot of raised eyebrows, but here I fit right in. I smiled in return, and they perked. I wouldn't need to look far for company tonight…

My leisurely walk along the seashore took me past crowded beaches, but if—when—I wanted to soak up the sun, I would return to the hotel. The hotel itself was on a low cliff on the side of the mountain by the sea, but the beach and marina below were gated and reserved for hotel guests.

There were several cafés and restaurants along the promenade, but by the time I'd climbed what had to be hundreds of steps onto the hill where the Monte Carlo Casino was, the midday heat pressing on me, I didn't feel like returning to any of them. I'd beelined to the first restaurant I saw instead.

I couldn't see the sea from here, as the Casino and all the high-rises that lined the seashore blocked my view, but there was plenty to look at, like a fashion shoot on the greenery in front of me. There were a lot of people strolling past me on their way to and from the luxury shops lining the square. I even spotted a couple of celebrities who had opted to stay in Monaco instead of Cannes or Nice for the duration of the film festival.

They were followed by a flock of paparazzi, and I was glad I'd kept the hat on, even though a shade over the table shielded me from the sun. I hoped it shielded me from the eager photogs too. My former boss didn't read gossip magazines, but my mother did. She would recognize me instantly, no matter how good my new looks were.

It was a good reminder that I couldn't let my guard down for even a moment.

I was, therefore, mentally prepared to be recognized when I spotted familiar faces exiting the Casino, heading determinately toward the brasserie terrace, as if they'd noticed me there. Gagne and Bellamy. They'd discarded their suits and wore summer chinos and white, short-sleeved shirts, with linen blazers folded over the arm, but I didn't doubt for a moment they weren't here on an official business.

My gut tightened. Had they followed me here?

The smart thing to do would've been to pull the brim of my hat down and pretend I hadn't seen them. But evidently I wasn't as smart as I'd believed, because I straightened and waved at the men as they came near.

"Detectives! Care to join me?" I asked in French.

The surprise and dismay on their faces indicated that they hadn't expected to find me here. Their eyes narrowed, and I could almost hear them making calculations.

This had been an epic mistake...

Then Bellamy smiled, pleased, and they made their way to my table past the flower arrangements that separated the terrace from the street. "Monsieur Reed. This is a surprise."

"Eliot, please," I said with affability I didn't feel but could fake well, gesturing at the free chairs at my table. "I feel like we know each other well enough for that already."

"Alan," Gagne said, offering his hand, and I shook it. Bellamy did the same.

"René."

They took seats and I gestured at the waiter to bring two more glasses. I'd been nursing a bottle of chilled rosé for the past hour, but there was plenty of it left—though it wasn't cold anymore.

"May I offer you lunch, Detectives?"

"Only if you're having," Alan—Detective Gagne—said.

"I already had mine, but I could use the company," I said. "And some help with this bottle, or I won't be able to walk back to my hotel."

He lifted a quizzing brow. "You're not staying up here?"

"No, the Jewel of Monaco at the Monte Carlo end of this place."

The waiter took their orders, which I told him to put into my tab, poured the rosé in our glasses and left. Bellamy gave me an assessing look.

"Not a gambling man, are you?"

I shrugged. "I do my gambling on stock markets." Then I reconsidered. "But I will obviously visit the Casino."

"So, what brings you here, if not gambling?" Gagne asked.

"Sun, mostly," I said lightly. "I would've gone to Nizza, but it was full. I take it you're here on official business?"

"Mademoiselle Reed didn't tell you?"

I tensed. "No. But we're not that familiar with each other. And if it's related to an active investigation, she's not likely to share."

Apparently.

Bellamy took a sip of his glass and made an approving face, before giving me a curious look. "How did you two meet, if I may ask?"

"At a self-defense class," I said easily—the truth, even if it wasn't the first place where I'd met her.

"She's studying self-defense?"

I gave him an admonishing look. "She's teaching it."

"Ah, that's the chauvinistic Frenchman told," he said with a smile. "You are more enlightened in the States?"

"Hardly. And I'm partly Italian, so…"

I wiggled my flat hand in 'it could go either way' gesture, and they laughed, like I'd hoped. I wanted them to see me as a harmless playboy, not a potential threat.

Their food arrived and they dug in. I waited until they'd satiated the worst of their hunger before probing: "So what is it that you hoped Ada had told me?"

Gagne put down his utensils and wiped his mouth into a napkin. "The shooting victim, Vincent Brunet, turned out to be Jean-Michel Lepine. He worked as security here at the Casino. We're interviewing his colleagues."

No wonder they'd been dismayed to find me here. It was as if I'd gone out of my way to implicate myself.

"Did his colleagues know what he was doing in Lyon?"

"No one had a clue," Bellamy said, not as opposed to sharing as Ada apparently was. "But he was well liked, and the news of his death has upset many people. The shift changes around two, and we'll go interview the rest then."

"Are you staying the night?"

Gagne snorted. "We wish. Even if our supervisor would accept the expense, which he won't, there aren't any rooms available."

I don't know what came over me. It had to be the heat and the alcohol. But I found myself opening my mouth. "I have a spare room in my suite, if you don't mind sharing. It has two beds."

Was I suicidal or something?

Bellamy studied me. "I would've thought that a man like you would like to bring a woman over."

I smiled. Then I remembered the woman on the train, and it deepened. "I had plans, but they were met already on the train here…"

The detectives laughed again, understanding.

"I didn't take you as the kind to take a train," Gagne said.

"You don't get to have a three-course meal and a sexy woman when driving a car," I said wryly, making them grin. Then, because I really seemed to have a death wish, I leaned closer.

"I could use the company. I've been in Lyon since March, and I haven't had time to make friends yet."

"Are we friends?" Bellamy asked with a quizzical brow. I barely suppressed a shudder.

"You are company at least."

The men exchanged glances. They clearly knew each other well enough that no words were needed.

"We'd be happy to take your offer," Bellamy said.

"Great!"

Just great…

# 15

## ELIOT

WE HAD A VERY LONG, VERY FRENCH lunch, with a lot of small talk. The detectives were good at interviewing while making it sound like a casual conversation. I had to appreciate their skills, even if I was the target.

"What made you move to Lyon?" Bellamy asked.

"A woman I dated while I lived in Frankfurt recommended it for me," I told them, casually enough. Conversations like this was why I'd dated Elizabeth in the first place.

"Was she why you moved to Europe?" Gagne looked mildly curious, but something told me they'd checked me up and were only confirming what they knew.

"No, that was … someone else."

I hoped I looked awkward enough that they wouldn't enquire more, but I had a name and dates ready. They referred to a real person, but not anyone I'd even met; she was a colleague of Elizabeth's whose move to Europe and back to the States matched my story.

"I'm sorry it didn't work out."

I shrugged. "I was too, but the truth is, it wouldn't have worked no matter where we lived, and it gave me a chance to move here. I never would've done it otherwise, and I would've missed out on a lot."

The detectives didn't share much in return, but I did learn that they were both Lyonnais, though Gagne, despite his French name, was of Algerian origin like I'd thought. Algeria had been a French colony until 1962, and millions of people with Algerian origins lived in France.

"My self-defense teacher is Algerian," I said conversationally.

"Ada?" Gagne asked, baffled, and I smiled.

"No, her name is Laïla Diab. She works at Interpol too."

He pursed his lips, thinking. "There's Samí Diab in my daughter's class, but it's a common enough name."

I hadn't thought of him having a family, but of course a man his age would have. "Do you have many children?"

He smiled. "Three. My daughter, the eldest, is eighteen and the boys are fourteen."

I congratulated him and looked at Bellamy, who shuddered. "No children for me."

Gagne immediately began to tease him about it, like the old friends they were. I listened with a smile. It was nice to see people who were friends. I hadn't had good, close friends since my youth. Some of them had died, some were in prison, and the rest had either distanced themselves from me for my criminal life or turned into rivals. It was difficult to make new friends when I hadn't been able to fully trust anyone.

I still couldn't. I'd best not to forget that.

Eventually the lunch came to an end. I paid the check and we vacated the table, which was instantly claimed by a loud American family.

I hadn't realized we were loud as people until I moved to Europe.

"Would it be possible to come with you to the interviews?" I asked as we crossed Casino Square to the Casino. Bellamy gave me a sharp look.

"Why?"

"Apart from being curious? I used to work in security. We handled the security of a casino and I'm not above industrial espionage, even though I've left that world behind."

He tilted his head. "It's a bit irregular, but since we don't have jurisdiction here either and are only offered a courtesy by the casino security, you might as well hang around."

I'd been waiting to enter the Casino the entire time I'd sat staring at the ornamental sandstone façade of the huge nineteenth century building. The entrance lobby was cool after the relentless heat and as grand as I'd hoped: black and white marble floor and golden marble walls with heavy columns of the same material supporting a balcony that lined the space on all four sides, creating an atrium that was covered by a stained-glass window three stories above.

I'd seen pictures, of course—the lobby of our hotel in Red Hook had taken inspiration from this place—but the real deal was still impressive.

The casino itself was towards the left. Through open double doors, I spotted a large room with white and gold walls that wouldn't have looked out of place in an imperial palace. It was full of slot machines though, and people were busy feeding coins in them like in any casino, ignoring the surroundings.

Beauty was wasted on some people...

The entrance to the *Opéra de Monte-Carlo*, the opera that took half of the building, was straight across the lobby. The doors there were open too, so I ambled closer past the milling tourists. It was a larger space than I'd imagined, with walls that were floor-to-ceiling heavily ornamented gold. The boxes in two rows and the stage were closed with deep red velvet drapes.

If a Vegas casino had tried to pull this off, people would've called it garish and ridiculous. Here though…

Okay, it was still so ostentatious it made my eyes bleed, but somehow, they could pull it off. It was full of history.

We waited in the lobby for the head of security to come and fetch us. I studied the security arrangements with genuine curiosity born of professional interest.

"Is there a reason you sold your private security business?" Bellamy asked, noticing my interest.

They'd definitely checked me out. At least he wasn't questioning the story I'd woven.

He managed to take me by surprise though. I had a rote answer, but genuine interest in his eyes made me reconsider. What could I say that sounded believable?

"The business was changing fast," I settled with, remembering the conversations I'd had with the security at my hotel. "It's become more about protecting data than people, and relying on algorithms. It wasn't fun anymore. I got an excellent offer for my firm and didn't hesitate."

"What sort of algorithms?" Gagne asked. This I could answer.

"Take a place like this," I said, gesturing around. "Not many actual guards around, but dozens of cameras. There's a room full of monitors somewhere in this building where people sit studying every gambling table and slot machine for signs of abnormal behavior. It's the algorithms that determine when people are acting out of norm, cheating or trying to hack the system. They study body temperature, gestures, pupils dilating, how much one bets and how often. Everything."

As a manager of a casino hotel, I'd loved the system, but the turnover of security had been constant, as they got bored pretty fast.

"And you're more an old school kind of security?"

"Yes."

Was I ever.

The casino's head of security arrived, a man in his mid-forties with a neat haircut and large mustache. He gave me a sharp look. "You weren't here this morning."

"I'm an outside consultant," I told him with a polite smile and introduced myself. The detectives didn't contradict my claim, and the man took us through the staff area to a small conference room.

Not a speck of gold or ornaments of any kind there.

"The shift has changed, so you can talk to the rest of the staff," he told us and exited the room to fetch the first person.

"What's the plan, then?" I asked, taking a seat with the detectives.

"Basic interview. We ask about Lepine, who his friends were and such," Gagne said. Bellamy reached a sheet of paper over the table to me.

"We also have a list of names Mademoiselle Reed provided us. It was taken during a drug bust right outside our sea frontier. Lepine is on it, and chances are some of these names belong to his friends."

I worried the inside of my lower lip as I read the names, none of which rang any bells. I tried to come up with an angle that would justify my presence here.

"Lepine was well-dressed. The security here isn't wearing designer suits and aren't paid well-enough to afford them."

I knew what I'd paid for my people, and Monaco was easily as expensive to live in as New York.

"You're saying he was high up in the drug business?" Bellamy asked sharply. "Because no one we've talked with so far indicated anything like it."

I spread my arms. "The money had to come somewhere, and mere drug runners don't make all that much."

Middlemen, maybe, but the money flowed up and you had to be at the top to make a good payday in the drug trade. Not that I could tell that to the detectives—or disclose how I knew.

"But could be he was providing escort services to rich ladies or something. There's probably a good market for that here."

I didn't believe it myself. Lepine had mentioned Dobrev, so he was involved in that business, either drugs or human trafficking. Pity I couldn't tell it to the detectives either.

Interviewing people was the same whether it was about crimes, people, or for a job. Boring and repetitive. And a lot less violent than interrogating them for your mafia boss.

I'd been great at those kinds of interviews once.

One by one, Lepine's colleagues came in, most of them with red-rimmed eyes and only good things to say about him. The detectives probed about the money, but no one admitted knowing where it could've come from.

The head of security returned after the last interviewee was gone, giving us a questioning look. "Was this helpful?"

Gagne shook his head. "Not for our investigation."

We got up and made to leave, when something occurred to me. "What kind of turnover do you have in this place?"

"Are you planning to interview all the past employees too?" he asked, amused. I shrugged.

"I'm merely interested in whether they leave town or move to a different place here."

He nodded. "There's some movement between casinos and hotels. Good security is sought after, even poached. The rest are hired for a season or a longer time."

"And which one was Lepine?"

"The latter. If I recall correctly, he worked at the Jewel of Monaco hotel before."

"Have you lost anyone to them recently?"

He gave it a thought. "There was one, at the end of last season. Bruno Travert."

I kept my brows from shooting up, but only just. That name was on the list Ada had provided.


"I TAKE IT WE'LL HEAD to interview Bruno Travert next?" I asked the detectives once we were outside the casino. Gagne nodded.

"I think we'd best. But we must inform the local authorities before we continue, especially if we need to take him into custody. We're not in France anymore."

I kept forgetting that Monaco was an independent principality, forty-thousand people living in an area less than a square mile—a little over half the size of Central Park on Manhattan—and about third of them millionaires enjoying the tax haven status.

"And you likely won't be able to sit in on that one," Bellamy added.

"Fair enough," I said easily. I'd been more curious about the Casino security than the murder case anyway.

We headed to Bellamy's car that was parked outside the casino, a sleek Audi R8 sportscar that fit perfectly among the expensive cars and revealed that not only did he not have children, he didn't have a wife either.

It was also a more expensive car than a detective could buy with his salary, so he had to come from money.

A red convertible BMW pulled over into a free spot near the front steps of the Casino, drawing my attention. I used to own an X6 and I had a soft spot for BMWs.

A well-formed leg in a stiletto-heeled sandal emerged from the open door, and I instantly found that more interesting than the car. I glided my gaze up as the woman exited, taking in a tall and slim body clad in a red halter-neck silk dress with a deep neckline that showed just the right amount of nicely curving breasts and hugged a perfect bottom.

Her black hair was in a short bob and covered elegantly by a red silk scarf she'd wrapped loosely around her throat, like a walking advertisement for convertibles. Large sunglasses obscured her features, but the lush red lips and high cheekbones were perfect.

She sashayed into the Casino, and I found my head tilting as I watched her go. Then I froze.

I knew that bottom and that walk…

I turned to the detectives, who had been following the woman go too. "Perhaps we could meet at the hotel in an hour so you can check in?"

"Or maybe two?" Bellamy suggested with a wry grin.

That was fine by me. I barely waved the men goodbye before returning to the Casino.

The woman wasn't in the lobby anymore, but there was only one direction she could've gone. I would find her. Provided she didn't change her looks again...

I had to walk through the entire huge building before I found her in the last room, Salle Blanche, or White Salon. It wasn't entirely white; the floor was azure blue and the inescapable gold trimmings were everywhere, but compared to other rooms it was airy and bright, with sunlight streaming in from large windows that opened to a balcony facing the Mediterranean.

The salon was dedicated to roulette, with about a dozen tables filling the large room, a couple of which were occupied at that time of afternoon. Having been in the gambling business for a long time, I knew the odds in winning at roulette were just about nonexistent, but it was the most popular game of chance everywhere.

A curving bar desk decorated with tiny azure and gold tiles stood between the doors to the balcony, and the woman had taken a seat on a tall stool in front of it, one long leg resting on the floor, the well-formed calf looking perfect. She'd wrapped the scarf around her shoulders and lifted the sunglasses on her head, but even so I had to look twice to make sure I'd identified her correctly.

I propped my hip against the bar next to her and leaned closer. "May I buy you a drink?"

Her startled gaze shot to my face, but she didn't drop character. Her upper lip curled in amusement, and she

161

nodded at the bartender. "In that case, I'll take champagne." Her voice was low and held a hint of Slavic note.

I smiled, slowly and utterly delighted. I couldn't help it. "Make it a bottle," I said to the bartender without moving my gaze from her face. I'd likely be served a six-thousand-euro bottle for failing to specify, but it would be worth it.

Her transformation was incredible. Her eyes were deep blue and heavily lined to slant up, with false lashes adding to the effect. Her cheekbones seemed sharper and her mouth bigger. The tips of her black bob reached her chin, somehow changing the shape of the face.

"Let's go to the balcony," I said, helping her off the stool. Keeping her arm lightly wrapped around mine, I walked her out. I chose a table for two outside the glazing that protected the roulette tables from the Mediterranean wind, and held a chair for her.

She sat down, crossing her long legs and stretching them along the side of the small table. I stretched mine on the other side and leaned back in my chair. The waiter brought the bottle in a cooler and poured our glasses, and I waited until he'd left.

I raked my gaze down her body and back up, shaking my head in disbelief. Or I believed—I'd seen her transform before—but still…

"I'm Eliot Reed," I said, my tone husky. I was painfully aroused.

She smiled, the look holding a promise of pleasures to come. "You can call me … Natasha."

# 16

## ADA

"NATASHA," HE PURRED, THE SOUND destined to make a woman's knees weak. I know mine were a bit wobbly. "Lovely name."

I couldn't believe Eliot was here. He looked like he belonged too, his pose relaxed, his clothes clearly expensive despite only being a white shirt and tan trousers. The sleeves were rolled up and the collar was open just so, revealing lightly tanned olive skin and corded muscles. He'd removed the hat and run fingers through his hair, leaving it in a careless disarray. His seafoam green eyes were shielded as he studied me.

He looked ... good.

That he knew who I was and was pretending not to made this like a delicious roleplay, a rich playboy picking up a beautiful and poor immigrant who hoped to find her true love—or someone rich—at the Casino.

He took a sip of his champagne, and I followed suit. His eyes instantly dipped to my mouth, and he swallowed, heavily.

Okay, this was getting too much...

His lips quirked, but his tone remained low and seductive. "So ... where are you staying?"

I bet even Natasha in her need to find a rich man would be appalled by such a fast approach. "I … don't have a room. I was hoping to find someone … friendly."

It was mostly true too. The entire town was fully booked, but I hadn't planned on seducing some man for a room.

Not that I was seducing him!

He grimaced, pained. "Couldn't you have arrived two hours earlier? I gave my spare room to Bellamy and Gagne."

I blinked. I blinked again. "What the bloody hell did you do that for?" I was too stunned to keep character anymore.

"You're the one who sent them here in the first place. And I didn't know you would be an option." He tilted his head, taking me in once again. The effect on my body didn't lessen.

"What are you doing here anyway, and looking like this? Planning a … job?"

I blushed, more annoyed than embarrassed. I didn't like that he knew what I was, and I liked even less that he thought it was some sort of lark.

"I'm following a lead in my case."

He cocked a brow. "And you couldn't come as yourself?"

"I'm not a detective anymore. I have to be subtle, and Natasha fits this place. I can't afford to be caught doing investigative work when I'm not mandated to."

"I'm not a detective either, yet I was able to sit through the interviews Gagne and Bellamy did."

I frowned. "Is that why you're here?" And why hadn't he told me?

"Hardly," he snorted. "I wanted a nice, relaxing weekend on the Riviera. It's not my fault you lot followed me here."

"Aww, poor Eliot."

He grinned, his cheeks creasing.

"And what did you learn in the interviews?" I asked to distract myself from the effect. I hadn't been this aware of him in Lyon. It had to be the character I was playing affecting me.

He made a face and took a sip before answering. "Nothing. Lepine was well liked and no one admitted knowing where he could've got enough money for a designer suit."

"It has to be related to drugs," I mused.

"Yes, but how? His job kept him here and wouldn't allow him to do the actual smuggling, and while this is a perfect place for customer retail, he would've been caught by now."

He was right. "He had to be someone his drug boss trusted to send him to fetch the hard drive, so he could hardly be a seller. A bodyguard?"

His eyes narrowed as he gave it thought. "Maybe for someone who doesn't live in Monaco permanently, because he still had a full-time job here. His other boss could've paid for the suit in that case, so that he would look good next to him."

"Melnyk is in town regularly, but doesn't live here permanently…"

It was impossible to get permission to move here, even if you could find accommodations, which you couldn't—hence all the yachts filling the many large marinas. Most people who worked here, cleaners, waiters, shopkeepers and such, lived on the French side of the border, but even most of those who could afford to live here weren't able to.

He tapped the stem of his glass absentmindedly as he thought. "Whoever sent Lepine to fetch the hard drive most likely didn't anticipate problems." His gaze sharpened as he focused on me. "How was the drop-off arranged?"

I glanced around, but there was no one near and the glass separated us from the players on one of the roulette tables filling the balcony.

"Through the same anonymous system that they used for hiring me in the first place. Coordinates and the exact drop-off time."

"And it was days after the theft and in the same town. Is that usual?"

"It depends…" The topic was making me amazingly uncomfortable. I don't even know why. My father had been a safecracker and I'd been married to one too. We'd had conversations like this daily.

"If the item is hot, it needs to move far away from the original location as fast as possible. With the external drive though, I could take it more slowly. But I expected the drop-off to happen elsewhere, maybe over this weekend."

I'd asked to have the Friday off already when I accepted the job, anticipating I needed to travel for it. I had random vacation days saved especially for my other job.

He picked the bottle and filled our glasses again. I hadn't even noticed I'd emptied mine. I had to be careful or I wouldn't be able to drive. "The shooter knew to expect Lepine at that exact place and time. So who blabbed?"

Good question.

"Except, he wasn't shot outside the church. He rounded three blocks first, yet the shooter found him as if they'd agreed on a location before."

His glass halted midway to his mouth and his eyes shot to mine. "The shooter was his ride?"

"That's the only explanation that makes sense. But why such a public execution when the driver could've taken him anywhere quiet? And why didn't the shooter take the hard drive?"

His lips tightened as he gave it a thought. Then he inhaled, sharply. "The hard drive doesn't matter."

MY MOUTH DROPPED OPEN. "What do you mean it doesn't matter? I was paid well to steal it."

He leaned forward, excited. "It's a distraction, or a trigger. Or a means to an end."

"What end?"

"I don't know, the coup? Or ... Fabre's death!"

I studied him, bemused. "You mean, the goal of the theft was to get someone to kill Fabre?" I blinked, trying to wrap my mind around the idea. "Wouldn't it have been easier to just shoot him?"

"Maybe your client doesn't like to get their hands dirty." I nodded as it made sense and he continued. "If there were only two players against each other, Melnyk challenging Dobrev, one of them might have shot him outright. But if there's an outsider pushing them against each other..."

I straightened when I understood what he was getting at. "Make one party believe the other is behind it, so they take each other out and you can move in unchallenged."

"Exactly. For whatever reason, Fabre had been trusted with the cooked books. Their theft made him look either incompetent or untrustworthy, both of which are death sentences in a crime organization. Lepine seemed to think Dobrev had Fabre killed, which is likely."

"But if Lepine worked for Melnyk, why would he be fetching the hard drive if a third party was actually behind commissioning me?"

He spread his arms. "I'm only starting with this theory. But maybe Lepine only thought he was doing it for Melnyk."

I took a sip from my glass, testing his theory. "No, he only wanted you to think he's working for Melnyk. He clearly assumed you were Dobrev's man when he gave you that warning. You would've returned to your boss with the message and Dobrev would've gone after Melnyk for the theft."

"Only I wasn't, and Lepine is dead. So who killed him?"

I stared out over the glistening sea, not really seeing it. "Maybe Lepine used to be Melnyk's man, but he switched to the third player. Maybe he was the inside man for the third party. Melnyk found out and had him killed. Publicly, as a message."

He nodded, impressed. It made me absurdly pleased, which was really embarrassing. "That works. Lepine asks Melnyk's man to come with him to Lyon, not telling him what the errand's for, maybe to recruit the guy for the third party, only the guy goes to Melnyk instead and gets the execution order."

"So now the next question is, why did my client need me to drop-off the hard drive if it's not important."

He shrugged. "To make sure you didn't become suspicious? Or maybe he does want the ledgers. If not for a leverage, then to learn about Dobrev's operation."

I worried the inside of my lip. "What happens when he doesn't get them?"

"It's hardly your concern. He'll learn about Lepine's death soon enough, if he already hasn't, and that the police have the external drive. He also gets the message Melnyk sent him with the shooting. It's not you he'll come after."

That was a relief to hear.

"Now we only have to find out who the shooter was. We have no leads into Melnyk's operation."

He perked. "That's not true. There's a name on the list that you provided to the detectives. A security guard who used to work here and now works at the Jewel of Monaco. Gagne and Bellamy will interview him later today."

My heart skipped a beat in excitement. *Arctos* was docked in the hotel marina. This would be my chance to get close to Melnyk. "I need to be in on that!"

He tilted his head. "Not like this you will…"

I'd forgotten the disguise. "I need to change. Where are you staying?"

"At the Jewel of Monaco. It was the only one with a vacancy."

Perfect. "I'll meet you there in an hour."

I didn't wait for his answer but got up and sashayed out of the balcony, remembering my character at the last moment. I could practically feel his gaze following me out, but I didn't turn to look.

It was only three in the afternoon, but the gambling rooms were filling with tourists. No one paid any attention to me as I made my way out and to my car. I fetched a tote from the boot and returned inside.

The opera auditorium was open for visitors, and I slipped in with a bunch of tourists. I'd been here before—a really exciting job—and I knew that a hidden door in the front wall led behind the stage. It was never locked, and it was a moment's work to slip in unnoticed as everyone's attention was on the ostentatious decoration, unable to peel their eyes away.

The hallway behind the door was as utilitarian as the auditorium was extravagant. Dim lights showed me a way up the narrow concrete stairs, and I took them all the way to the attic, where the dressing rooms of the choir were. The place was empty at this time of day, but it would soon change. They would be performing Puccini's *Madame Butterfly* this evening and the singers would start arriving for their makeup.

Good thing I was an expert in fast changes.

With liberal use of the makeup removal lotion on one dressing table, I removed all the traces of Natasha and changed into practical but boring off-white linen trousers and a light green, sleeveless chiffon top suitable for work. The high-heeled sandals gave way to my usual ballerinas, and the large designer sunglasses to less flashy ones. My own hair only required some fluffing with my fingers, and instead of full makeup I put on some mascara and lip gloss.

Natasha went into the tote, and I was ready to go. I exited through the opera staff entrance at the side of the building and rounded it to my car. I'd rented it in Nice, having taken an early train there, amazed that they had any cars available. I loved it and was sad to give it up so soon, but Ada Reed simply couldn't drive a car this flashy.

I drove the car a few blocks north, right to the Monaco-France border to a branch of the car rental chain that had rented it to me. I took my luggage out of the trunk, returned the key, and hailed a taxi. Half an hour later, the afternoon traffic being heavy, I entered the lobby of the Jewel of Monaco Hotel as my own self.

Bellamy and Gagne were there.

# 17

## ADA

I HALTED, THE SURPRISE NOT FEIGNED, as I hadn't thought I'd run into them this fast. "Detectives! What brings you here?"

Bellamy hurried to take my luggage, even though it had wheels and I obviously didn't need help. "Mademoiselle Reed. A pleasure to see you again. We're here to interview people who knew the shooting victim. Thank you for your help with that."

"My pleasure." I headed toward the reception desk at the side of the lobby, with the detectives following. After the Casino, the off-white marble and wood interior seemed wonderfully calm—and incredibly boring.

"Are you here to meet Monsieur Reed?" Gagne asked. I halted and whirled to him, my eyes large with—feigned—surprise.

"He's here?"

He cocked an amused brow. "Come now, Mademoiselle, we're all adults and you're not doing anything wrong."

I shot him a withering glance. "I do not have weekend assignations with men I've only just met."

With that overly prim comment—I was probably pushing this role too far—I turned to the receptionist with a polite smile. "I have a reservation with the name Reed."

I didn't, but I had to throw the detectives off the scent.

The woman behind the desk clicked her computer and, to my utter amazement, smiled. "Ah, yes. Monsieur Eliot Reed has already checked in."

I pulled straight. "Not Eliot. Ada."

I ignored the chuckles behind me.

The receptionist looked more worried now. "I'm sorry, but there is no reservation for Ada Reed."

Of course there wasn't as I hadn't made one, but I didn't let that stop a good show. "What do you mean? I reserved the room ages ago."

"I do not understand what has happened. Maybe two reservations with the same name messed with the system. It probably assumed a double booking by a married couple and cancelled the extra," the woman said apologetically.

Their system couldn't be that lousy, but I wouldn't say that to her. "And naturally it's the woman's reservation that is deleted." I was getting into the spirit of things, my anger sounding natural. I brushed with my hand. "Never mind, just book me into another room and there's no harm done."

"I'm truly sorry, but we're fully booked. There are no rooms."

I inhaled, incensed, ready to give the woman a piece of my mind, when Eliot spoke behind me.

"Is there a problem?"

I swirled to him and unleashed the ire on him. "You! You've ruined my holiday!"

He lifted his hands and stepped back. "I only got here. How did I manage that?"

"They've given my room to you!"

For a moment he looked like he would argue and reveal I hadn't even booked a room—or point out that it wasn't possible. But then he turned to the receptionist and flashed her a warm smile so effective I could practically see her melt.

"I'm sure there's a special room kept free for occasions like this. Book Miss Reed there."

The woman looked even more apologetic. "That's gone too." She leaned closer over the desk and lowered her voice. "A special celebrity guest. I'm can't tell who, but they're opening in Cannes tonight."

Eliot rubbed the bridge of his nose, thinking. "That's unfortunate. I have a spare room with twin beds, but that's for the detectives." He gestured at the men who had remained mercifully quiet through my act. Then he gave me a sideways glance.

"But I have a large double bed..." I glared at him. "...there are large couches in the sitting room."

"I will not sleep on a couch!"

He flashed me a smile. "Fine, I'll take the couch. But I'll need to use your bathroom." He addressed the receptionist. "Would that be possible?"

"Of course," she said, relieved that the matter was solved so easily. She checked us in and gave us our keys. "And here are complimentary drink coupons and tokens to the hotel casino, with our apologies."

We took the offerings with the keys and headed to the lift that would take us to the top floor. "That went well."

I was rewarded with laughter.

"WE HAVE A PROBLEM," Detective Gagne said after we'd settled into our rooms—Alan, as he'd introduced himself now that we were sharing a suite.

The entire suite was excellent if a tad dated and oddly appointed, with faux-wood and red walls, stone floors and an occasional Barcelona chair by Le Corbusier. The greatest attraction, however, was the Mediterranean view that opened from the windows in all rooms and a *loggia* type of balcony in the sitting room, deep and covered to protect the occupants from the glaring sun. The sitting room wasn't large, but it had room for a dining table for four, and the red leather sofas were roomy enough for even Eliot to sleep on.

Not that he looked happy about it when a hotel maid came to make a bed on one of them.

"This is not how I imagined my vacation…"

For our part, the detectives and I were happy with our accommodations. My room had a huge bed where Eliot and I could've spent a perfectly chaste night, but I didn't want the detectives to get the wrong idea.

Besides, the mere notion of spending the night with Eliot, no matter how innocent, was just too much. I hadn't spent a night with a man since Danny, and I wasn't in the right space of mind to start now. It was bad enough that the room smelled of him and that his clothes filled the closet already.

How much clothes could a man need for a short holiday anyway?

"What sort of problem?" Eliot asked Gagne.

Eliot was looking a bit rumpled, having walked back to the hotel. Not that the detectives believed he had, judging by their knowing smiles. They clearly thought that he'd been having a good time with Natasha and had taken a taxi like a sensible person, but they didn't want to say it aloud, in case I'd be upset.

It was impossible to make them believe we weren't here together.

"The local authorities weren't happy that we'd operate on their turf in a case this big. We tried to say that it's only an interview, but since it's related to two murders and a drug bust, it needs to go through proper channels."

Eliot dipped his chin. "What's that, then?"

"Me," I told him with a smile. "That's why Interpol exists in the first place."

He smiled. "Good thing you're here, then."

"Not what *I* thought I'd be doing on my holiday…"

It was exactly what I'd hoped to do, but the detectives didn't need to know that.

I picked up my phone and made a call to the local Interpol office. Nobody answered. It was a small office, and it was close to five p.m. on Friday, but I would've thought someone would be manning the place over the weekend.

Unfazed, I called my boss instead. That man never left the office before six. "You want to work on your day off?" he asked, amazed—and approving. "Naturally I'll authorize it, but why would you want to?"

"It's related to a case I've been investigating," I told him. "It would be helpful."

"Very well. I'll mark today as a workday for you, and you can take the Monday off instead. But since you're already there, you can't deduct the travel expenses."

I'd be back at my desk by Monday, and I definitely wouldn't deduct the expenses even if I could—the rental of a luxury sportscar wasn't exactly easy to explain, especially since I hadn't done it with my own name—but I thanked him and placed a call to the local police.

It took a surprising amount of diplomacy and sweettalking to arrange the very simple matter of interviewing a person who wasn't even a Monaco citizen. I groaned when I was put on hold for a second time.

"Maybe we should wait until he's home so we could do this on the French side of the border," I suggested to the detectives.

"He's on duty tonight. I'd rather not postpone it," Bellamy said. "You're doing fine. He'll cave."

Bellamy was right. We got the permission to operate in Monaco, provided that I was present at all times—yay—and that we'd call them the moment we needed to make an arrest. They would come and handle it for us.

Gagne rubbed his hands together, looking pleased. "Now that that's sorted out, let's talk about what you know about the case that we should be aware of before we go in."

I didn't glance at Eliot, but it took an effort. "It's mostly circumstantial," I hedged. While I had more facts about the case than they did, the speculation Eliot and I had done didn't stand on very solid ground, especially since I'd falsified some of the evidence. But the link between the drug bust, Lepine, and Travert was real.

"It's still more than we have."

I tried to set my words so that I didn't accidentally reveal my role in acquiring the external drive. I'd never had to balance between my two roles like this before and I had no tools for it.

"I've been tracking the movements of a Bulgarian drug and human trafficking organization in the Mediterranean. For that, I've studied the evidence of all the drug busts done within the past year—which isn't all that many. The list I gave you is from one such bust."

Gagne nodded. "And how does it link to the shooting of Fabre?"

"I'm not sure it does. However, Fabre might be linked with one of the main operators of the organization, one Artem Melnyk."

"How?" Bellamy asked.

"Among his phone contacts was *Arctos*. That's the name of Melnyk's yacht." I paused and they looked suitably intrigued.

"And where is the yacht currently?"

I smiled. "Here at the hotel marina."

The detectives pulled back simultaneously. "You're not here on a holiday, are you?" Gagne said with an admonishing smile. I shrugged.

"I was supposed to be. Him being here is a wonderful coincidence. Of course, having tracked his movements for months, I could be reasonably certain he'd show up here this weekend."

"But nothing links Lepine to Melnyk or Fabre," Gagne pointed out, and I nodded.

"Not that we know of." Or could reveal, at any case. "But based on Lepine's clothes, he had a wealthy sponsor of some kind. He wasn't working for them full-time, because he had a job at the casino, but he clearly had extra income and a need to wear a designer suit."

"Maybe a part-time bodyguard?" Eliot made the same suggestion as earlier. I smiled at him for nudging the conversation for the right direction.

"Yes. Melnyk usually docks at this hotel when he visits Monaco. A good chance for Lepine to make some extra cash between his own shifts."

Bellamy pursed his lips. "Lepine used to work here, but that was a year ago."

"The arrangement could still have continued. Or he could've had a similar arrangement with a client at the Casino."

"That may be so, but it doesn't explain why Lepine was in Lyon getting shot," Gagne said.

I spread my arms. "No idea. Was there anything interesting in the external drive he was carrying?"

"Cooked books," Bellamy told us what we already knew. At least they'd figured out that much. "Though we have no idea whose or how to interpret them."

This would be so much easier if we could tell them where the drive originated. I glanced at Eliot, who shook his head minutely. He wouldn't want to be outed as an expert on money laundering then.

We could let the contents be for now. "That it was masked as a gift suggests a need for secrecy. Maybe Lepine was transporting the drive, to or from Lyon. Maybe to Melnyk, or whoever he worked for on the side. Or maybe he'd stolen it and was shot for it."

Gagne perked, but Bellamy shook his head, clearly figuring out the essentials. "The shooter would've taken the drive in that case."

Eliot rubbed the bridge of his nose. He did that a lot, as if marveling at the shape. "Maybe Lepine didn't steal it. Maybe he was supposed to deliver it somewhere days ago, only he didn't and was shot for the delay, the shooter unaware that he had the hard drive all along."

That was a good way to direct the focus to what we suspected was behind the shooting. But Bellamy was still skeptical.

"Then how did the shooter know where to find Lepine? Lyon is a long way from Monaco. Both had to be there on purpose."

"Did his colleagues tell you why he was in Lyon in the first place?" I asked. Eliot hadn't mentioned it. But Gagne shook his head.

"They hadn't even known he'd gone there, so they likely hadn't alerted the shooter."

"Maybe the client lives in Lyon," Eliot suggested. "Lepine might've been there on a job for them. Perhaps the client asked him to deliver the external drive back to Monaco. Maybe the shooter travelled with Lepine or had agreed to meet him there."

The detectives looked baffled. "How does that work?"

Eliot shrugged. "It's the most logical explanation. Drive-by shootings usually take place outside the victim's home or workplace. Somewhere regular and fixed. Lepine was on a random errand in a random place, in the middle of the night. The shooter had to be Lepine's ride, or the person he was there to meet, and they'd agreed to meet outside the Palace of Justice, or maybe the client lived near there, but Lepine was double-crossed and shot."

"And the shooter can't be the person Lepine was delivering the external drive to, because then the shooter would've taken it," I added.

Bellamy rubbed his eyes. "None of Lepine's colleagues make a promising suspect. I'm putting my money on Travert."

"As the shooter?" I asked, and he shrugged.

"At least someone who might have more information about Lepine's side business. They were both on that list, after all."

I nodded. "Let's go talk to him, then."

Gagne shot Eliot an apologetic look. "I'm sorry, but you can't sit in on this one."

"That's all right," he said with an easy smile. "I've been waiting for a chance to hit the beach the whole day."

He disappeared into the bedroom to change, and I decided it would be best we left before he emerged. The way he'd affected me this afternoon, I don't think I could've handled seeing him in nothing but swimming trunks.

"Are you really here for *Arctos*?" Bellamy asked when we entered the lift, one brow cocked and looking a tad hesitant. "Because if there's nothing going on between you and Eliot, I could ask you out."

He managed to take me by surprise, and I struggled to come up with an answer. The proper one would've been "I'd like that," because he was a good-looking man with a steady job and I hadn't really been out since my husband's so-called death.

"No?" he quizzed before I managed to speak, and I blushed lightly.

"Maybe once we're back home?" I suggested. "I don't want holiday flings to follow me home."

I couldn't afford anything to follow me home.

# 18

## ADA

SECURITY WAS LOCATED IN THE hotel's basement. They had a large surveillance room monitoring the slot machines at the hotel casino and other high-risk points, a couple of offices, break and dressing rooms separate from the rest of the hotel staff also located at the basement, and their own gym.

Wes Morris, the head of security, had an office in the middle of a long hallway, with small, arched windows close to the ceiling for some daylight, most of which was blocked by shrubbery and flowerbeds that lined the hotel on all sides.

He was a British man in his late forties with a heavy Yorkshire accent even in his French—of which he mercifully opted out when he realized I was English too. I hoped the detectives could understand his accent, which he made no attempt to soften. I had to struggle a little with it too, but it also made me nostalgic for home. Not that I'd ever lived in Yorkshire, but one seldom heard the accent abroad.

But not even our shared nationality made him willing to let us interview one of his employees. "What would the guests say if they saw the police after one of the people trusted to keep them safe?"

"They'd likely be much happier than if it turned out he was involved in something and you didn't do anything," I pointed out.

He studied me from under his bushy brows. He was seated behind his desk, and we'd taken the guest chairs. "What's he's supposed to have done?"

"Nothing as far as we know," I assured him.

"But you think he could shed light on your case?" he asked the detectives. Gagne nodded, indicating he'd followed the conversation just fine.

"His name came up in a drug bust a while back."

"Bugger." Morris rubbed his face with both hands, then gave us a weary look. "We've had some trouble with drugs here, as you can imagine. We've even had to let some people go when it became obvious that they were involved in the business on a larger scale."

"Do you have any names?" Bellamy asked.

"He wasn't convicted of anything, so it wouldn't be proper to implicate him."

"Was it Jean-Michel Lepine by any chance?"

Morris' brows shot up. "Well, in that case, I guess I can confirm that much. Was he caught?"

"He's dead," Bellamy said.

Morris pulled back, stunned. "What happened?"

"He was shot in Lyon on Wednesday."

"Shot? In Lyon?" Morris exclaimed. I wasn't sure which stunned him more. "By whom?"

Gagne shook his head. "We don't have suspects at the moment. What can you tell us about him?"

Morris ran fingers through his thinning hair. "Nothing much. He did his job well enough, but he was always more interested in making connections among the wealthy clients. We discourage it, but it happens all the time."

"Any guest in particular?" Gagne asked before I had a chance. This was not my interview. I was only liaising.

"Well, there's this young Bulgarian guy, fast money, no manners, even less taste. Dresses horribly, surrounds himself with idiots like himself, and women who are probably prostitutes and whom he treats like shit. Makes a lot of noise about his security. Definitely in drug trade. Lepine was his bodyguard here."

We'd guessed that right.

"Could I have a name?" Bellamy asked, though I already had a pretty good inkling before Morris spoke.

"Artem Melnyk. Owns a yacht he stays in while here. *Arctos*."

The detectives were decidedly not looking at me.

"And what about Travert?"

Morris nodded. "Nothing so brazenly overt, but I think he's Melnyk's new guy here."

"You mentioned there were other guests Lepine was maybe working for too?" I asked. "Anyone in particular?"

He had to think. "There was this French guy, though I don't know what his deal was other than money. What was his name...?" He was quiet for a moment as he searched his memory and then straightened.

"Fabre ... Dominic Fabre."

You could've knocked me over with a feather. If Fabre and Lepine were connected, was Fabre linked with the unknown player too? Or with Dobrev?

I was getting a headache from all this speculation.

"Can you confirm the connection in any way?" Bellamy asked, and Morris shot him a sharp look.

"Why?"

"Because Fabre is dead too."

Morris startled. "By the same shooter?"

"That's what we're trying to find out," Bellamy said calmly. "Did Fabre visit here often?"

"Once a month, maybe. He likes—liked—to gamble at the Casino. Baccarat."

"Did he win or lose?" I asked and he gave me a sardonic smile.

"When do they ever win…?"

Fabre had had the deeds to his house, so he probably hadn't gambled so recklessly he'd been in debt. But I couldn't say that aloud. If I'd known cracking a safe would lead to this, I would've found a way to return everything I didn't need.

"Did Fabre spend time with anyone in particular while here?" Gagne asked. Morris shook his head.

"He always picked up a woman at the Casino, but it was seldom the same one more than two, three times in a row. Then he would give them a bauble as a thank you and send them on their way."

That explained the odd jewelry in the safe.

"Did he know Melnyk?" I asked.

"I never saw them together, but who knows what happens on those yachts. But Fabre wasn't the type to hang out with trash. I think he fancied himself James Bond or something, always wearing a dinner jacket, always with pretty ladies and gambling."

Laïla's notion that Eliot was a secret agent returned to me and I almost snickered. Eliot could pull off the look. Fabre … not so much.

"Did he gamble with the same people?" Gagne asked.

"I don't know. It's not like I have a direct line to the Casino, and if you think they're going to tell you, you have another think coming."

Gagne nodded, calmly. "Anyone else you could think of that he spent time with, other than Lepine and the women?"

"No one springs to mind. I'll have to ask from the staff. Is there anything else or should I fetch Travert?"

I gave it a thought. "Did Fabre pay for his stay himself or did someone pick up the tab?"

Three pairs of baffled eyes turned to me. "He was filthy rich," Bellamy said. "Surely he could afford to stay here."

"It's not about affording, it's about being paid for services without it showing."

Gagne nodded, understanding. "Can you check that?"

Morris's brows shot up. "I have no idea how we'd do that."

"Just go through the records for the past couple of months," I told him. "If Fabre's name comes up, he paid for his own stay. If it doesn't, someone else did. Then we'll just have to figure out who."

He promised to do that after he fetched Travert and left the room. Gagne furrowed his brows.

"It appears Fabre had a secret side no one knew of."

"His gambling habit didn't come up with the interviews?" I asked, and he shook his head.

"His housekeeper knew he left town regularly, but she had no idea where."

"We'll have to check his financial records now," Bellamy said with a sigh. "It'll take forever."

"So where does this leave your investigation?" I asked, trying to fit the new information with the theory Eliot and I had.

Bellamy spread his arms. "Maybe Fabre was shot for gambling debts?"

Casinos preferred people paid with credit cards instead of cash or debit cards to prevent money laundering. But who paid the credit card bills?

"Could Melnyk be bankrolling?" I asked, then discarded the notion. "Nah, there's no indication that he's in a loans business. And Fabre was rich."

Could it be the unknown third party? It would blow the theory Eliot and I had completely.

Not that it was on firm ground as it was.

BRUNO TRAVERT WAS a few years younger than me, in his late twenties maybe, medium tall, and a bit too muscled for the black-on-black uniform of the hotel's security, his biceps bulging out of the T-shirt with the hotel logo on it.

"Boss says you wanted to talk to me," he said, taking the seat Gagne indicated. His French had an Occitan accent, so he could be local, as it was one of the official languages in Monaco. Then again, Occitan was spoken from Catalonia in Spain through the south of France to northwestern Italy, so it didn't mean much.

"We wanted to ask about Jean-Michel Lepine," Gagne said in a conversational tone that indicated we were here having a chat, not interrogating him.

"I'm not familiar with the name," Travert stated. Gagne lifted a brow.

"Oh? Our records indicate that you worked at the Casino until recently when you changed here. Surely you know him?" He gave Travert the Casino ID photo of Lepine, and the young man gave it a brief look.

"Oh, him. Yeah. He worked on the Casino floor and I was mostly in the surveillance room. Didn't speak to him much. Didn't know his name."

"So he didn't recommend that you relocate here?"

Bellamy asked. Travert snorted.

"No. I wanted here because I could get out of monitor duty. Here I can interact with the guests."

"And that's important?" I asked, and he shot me a contemptuous look.

"Of course it is. The tips are insane if you get to do favors for the rich."

"And what kinds of favors is it that you do?" Gagne's tone was still affable, but Travert tensed.

"You know … favors. Private. I can't disclose them."

Gagne nodded, as if it was a perfectly reasonable explanation, but you'd have to be stupid not to realize it meant getting them drugs.

"Have you ever acted as private security for any of these rich people?"

Travert perked. "Yes. That pays best of all."

"Anyone in particular?"

"I'd rather not say," he hedged. Gagne's eyes sharpened.

"I'd rather you would."

"Why?"

"Because this is a murder investigation."

Travert pulled back. "Whose?"

"Lepine's."

Travert tensed. Then he shot up and bolted out of the door.

We shared brief baffled glances. Then Bellamy rushed after him, with me at his heels. The hallway led to two directions and there was no sign of Travert anymore.

"Which way?" he asked, then headed right without waiting for my answer, so I went left.

My ballerinas weren't made for running and they slid off as I rounded the corner, so I paused, picked them up, and continued with bare feet. It wasn't comfortable, but I had better traction on the concrete floor.

The hallway ended at a metal security door with a push bar handle. It was firmly shut, so if Travert had come this way, he was well ahead of me, but I pushed the door open anyway.

I burst onto a small landing at the side of the cliff on which the hotel was built, startling a couple of women in hotel maid uniforms having a smoke. Sturdy steps led up to the guest level, and down toward the beach. I chose down, mostly because I really didn't want to run up.

The surface of the steps was rough against my bare feet, but I ignored the sensation and headed down as fast as I dared. There was another landing at the bottom, with paths leading to the beach and the marina. The entire area was fenced in by chicken wire, so if Travert had come here, he was trapped.

There was no sign of him though. If he'd sought refuge in one of the yachts, I had no way of getting to him, as I didn't have jurisdiction here—or anywhere, actually. But I wasn't ready to climb back up—or rather, take the scenic lift along the side of the cliff that carted people from the hotel to the beach.

I chose the only direction available and ran down the beach terrace. A tiki hut type of bar with reed walls made a good place for him to hide. Without slowing down, I rounded the bar to take a look—and collided with a firm chest.

A *bare*, firm chest.

# 19

## ELIOT

I WAS EMBARRASSINGLY CURIOUS about the interview I hadn't been allowed to participate in. I was a mafia goon, for crying out loud, a career criminal since I was strong enough to beat people up. I should not be interested in a criminal investigation that wasn't about me.

But I was and this wasn't even my first time being involved in investigating a crime instead of perpetrating one. Back at home, I'd accidentally befriended a private investigator in the making, a woman more enthusiastic than adept, yet she always caught the bad guy in the end. She'd staged my fake death too. She and her PI boyfriend were the only people I'd found myself able to trust.

However, my involvement in her investigations had usually been about providing inside information on the various criminal organizations in New York and New Jersey. But this time I was in the middle of the investigation, and I didn't like being left out.

The hotel beach had all but cleared, as everyone had headed to their rooms to prepare for dinner, and the sun wasn't as scorching as earlier. It was quiet and glorious—and I couldn't relax. The drive-by shooting kept churning in my mind.

Giving up, I pulled the backrest of my sunchair to a sitting position, opened the sunshade, and gestured for the bartender to bring me another mocktail of some tangy fruit juice. I'd had enough alcohol for the day, even if we hadn't finished the champagne bottle with Ada. I mean *Natasha.*

Incidentally, it'd only cost me two hundred euros. The bartender was more sensible than I gave him credit for.

Lounging in the chair, enjoying the small breeze I caught in this position, I pretended to read a book I'd purchased from the hotel gift shop. It was a techno thriller by an author I'd never read but whose books had been bestsellers at the gift shop of my hotel too.

Whatever its appeal, it couldn't hold my attention more than a paragraph at a time. I let my attention wander, watched the sea and the people on the beach, and the luxurious yachts at the marina.

The latter made my gut tighten and roil uneasily, and it didn't take a licensed therapist to figure out why. I'd died on a yacht. On my boss's yacht, to be precise, though it hadn't been nearly as grand and luxurious as the ones filling the marina here.

Destroying it had been satisfying, nonetheless.

The PI's boyfriend had rigged it to explode by remote in the most spectacular fashion, allegedly while I was inside. There had been plenty of witnesses on the wharf outside my hotel by the East River—essential to the plan—and even though it had been a day earlier than we'd agreed with my coconspirators, I'd had everything ready for my grand escape and I hadn't thought twice about going through with it when the opportunity presented itself.

And then some idiot had boarded the yacht at the last minute to escape the police. I'd already moved the yacht away from the wharf so that people there wouldn't be hurt in the explosion. Being forced to turn back when I'd been primed for a different action had made my blood boil.

I'd considered driving away with him on board, but knowing he was the prime suspect in the case my PI friend had been investigating had halted me.

The idiot had attacked me, forcing me to fight for my life for the first time in ages. He'd been bigger than me, looking much like I had before I began my transformation, and as a firefighter his muscles weren't for show. He could've—would've—overpowered me, but I'd been armed.

In the scuffle, the gun went off. It didn't hit the guy though. It hit the gas tank where we'd attached the bomb.

I reacted with instinct rather than reason. I jumped off the boat and dove as fast and far as possible in the murky and cold East River. If the small oxygen tank I needed for my escape hadn't already been attached to a holster on my shoulder, I wouldn't have had time to grab it. Without it, I wouldn't have made it back to the shore.

I barely made it with it.

It felt like the bomb went off right as I reached the water. I was deep enough not to feel the heat, but the shockwave pushed me with a force I had no chance to resist. It stunned and disoriented me, and it took ages to get back on the surface. I struggled to stay afloat long enough to cast off my clothes I'd worn over a wetsuit and attach the mouthpiece of the oxygen tank, before starting to swim.

I spared no thought for the other guy, but I doubt he survived the explosion.

I'd taken my time swimming ashore, diving just under the surface for much of it. No one was looking for me as far as I could determine, but I didn't want my movements to catch anyone's attention in the darkness. The people who had been on the wharf were shouting and screaming, but I was too far away to hear individual words. I hoped my boss had had the nasty surprise of a lifetime when his yacht went up.

There were ladder rungs attached to the concrete at the end of the quay, close enough to the hotel to make it practical for my purposes but hidden enough in the darkness that no one would see me climb them.

Before taking them, I removed the wetsuit—not easy to do while clinging to the ladder—and let it sink to the bottom with the oxygen tank. Wearing only swimming trunks—a man had to have some standards even in a staged death—I climbed up, the task amazingly exhausting after the swim in the cold water.

I'd hidden a small bag behind a bollard by the ladder, which contained a hotel bathrobe, towel, and slippers. I put them on, hanging the towel over my head so that it covered my face, and hurried to the closest entrance of the hotel. If anyone saw me, they would think I was just a hotel guest checking out the commotion outside.

The private wing of the hotel had minimum security to protect the privacy of the exclusive guests. Basically, only the elevator was monitored, so I took the stairs all the way to the roof and the bathroom of the helipad lobby there.

I'd hidden another bag in a cleaning cupboard, this one containing a change of clothes: black cargo pants and a turtleneck, and a black blazer with the emblem of the royal Saudi family on the chest, a member of which had arrived at the hotel in a helicopter an hour earlier.

The helicopter was waiting for me. I'd arranged it with the prince, who insisted he owed me a favor after my PI friends had got his stolen diamonds back. He might've expected Jonny Moreira to board the chopper, but the pilot had no idea who his passenger would be.

I'd shaved my hair completely off the previous day and worn a wig that looked like my regular hair. The wet rug went into my bag and was replaced with a messy dark blonde one—not a good look on me, but if anyone asked questions later, they would describe a blond guy. I wore a cap too, just in case. With my trimmer body, the cap shading my face, I looked different enough to fool the camera that was monitoring the exit to the helipad.

I took the duffel bag that was holding the old disguise, the first of my fake IDs, and enough cash to see me through months, and boarded the chopper that was already warming up its blades.

"We have to wait a moment before we can take off," the pilot told me, barely checking me out to see who I was. "Coast Guard's orders. There was an explosion of some kind."

"Yeah, no problem," I said, even though I was ready to highjack the chopper to get away. I'd made it this far and with every second of delay I risked being caught.

We were given permission to leave before I burst a vein. But instead of heading to our destination, the pilot went to check the explosion site, where rescue boats had gathered. He hovered the chopper in place for at least ten minutes, lighting the water with its powerful headlights so that the divers could see better.

I sat still, squeezing the edge of my seat so hard that my knuckles were white, hoping that no one would look up and recognize me.

Finally, we moved on and flew north. The chopper was large enough to fly long distances—we landed once to refill in Albany—and flying under diplomatic privileges. We crossed the border into Canada without any delays.

A limousine was waiting for me at the heliport outside Montreal—no one expected a fugitive to be in a limo—and the border security didn't give me any trouble after taking one look at the emblem on my jacket. They just gestured the driver to move on.

Before the night was over, I was a free man.

I ABANDONED THE BOOK disgusted when the main character, a supposed military veteran, didn't know the first thing about handling firearms. If the state of the US armed forces were as bad as that guy indicated, we'd never win any wars.

Not that I cared much. I'd never been drawn to the military, and now that I lived in Europe, the defense politics of my home country were even less interesting.

But I did miss being able to carry.

I emptied the juice glass and decided it was time to return to my room. I needed to cool off, but the thought of plunging into the sea made me tense. Another trauma I'd be carrying for my fake death.

Maybe I'd be able to take a shower before Ada returned.

Maybe she'd return while I was in the shower…

More eager now, I got up and began to pull on the hotel bathrobe, when I saw someone run down the main dock of the marina. A person running is always interesting, as it usually indicates they're fleeing from something. But this guy wore the uniform of hotel security, which made his actions even more intriguing.

Was he headed toward trouble? Should I rush in to investigate?

Was it more interesting than the possibility of Ada surprising me in the shower…?

The dilemma was solved when I saw Ada run down the steps toward the beach. Was she pursuing the security guy or heading to investigate with him?

Since she was running in the wrong direction, I rushed up the steps to meet her. I rounded the bar—and soundly collided with her.

I wrapped arms around her to stop her from falling, and she dropped whatever she'd been holding to clutch the lapels of my bathrobe.

"Steady now…"

The collision had robbed her of breath, or maybe it was her mad dash. She took a moment to catch her bearings and, realizing it was me, relaxed. "Did you see a guy run down here?"

"Yeah, down the dock," I indicated with my head, and she frowned.

"Shit." She pulled back and I released her, but she still held on to my robe, as if not even realizing it. "If he gets on a yacht, we'll never have a chance to catch him."

My brows shot up. "Who is he and why are you pursuing him?"

What had I missed while lounging on the beach?

"Travert, and because he was fleeing."

"Good, solid cop reasoning. If they're running, they're guilty of something." My teasing smile made her roll her eyes.

"I used to be a cop. And he definitely has something to hide. Come."

She pulled me from the lapel she was holding, and I had no choice but to follow or lose the robe. "You can let go now," I said, amused. She gave me a confused look, noticed what she was doing, and released me, a faint blush rising to her cheeks.

"Sorry."

She leaned down to pick up her shoes she'd dropped, put them back on and hurried up to the marina. I followed, tying my bathrobe closed as I went.

"So, what happened?"

She made to turn down the first fork in the docks, but I pushed her on, as Travert had run past it. She gave me an annoyed look, but it was more for the situation than my hand between her shoulder blades.

"I don't know. One minute he was pretending he'd never heard of Lepine, the next he was bolting."

Her phone rang and she pulled it out of her pocket. "Bellamy," she said to me before answering. "I'm at the marina. Eliot says he ran this way." She listened to the other end. "I know we can't. We'll just look from the dock. Hopefully he's hiding on one of the unoccupied yachts so we can get on board on the pretext of him trespassing." She listened again. "Fine, we'll let the local police do the actual searches…"

She didn't look happy about it.

The docks were shaped like an elongated E, with four prongs jutting toward sea to have room for all the huge yachts to moor and operate. Even skipping the first one, we had three of them to check, each holding five or six yachts on both sides. Most of them looked to be empty, or manned by a skeleton crew, so we had to stop by each, and try to determine if Travert was hiding on board.

Bellamy found us before we'd finished checking the first prong. "Alan is waiting for the local cops. Anything interesting here?" He gave an amused look at my bathrobe that had opened again.

Ada made a face. "There are too many of these damn things and some are sailing under flags of countries we don't have good relations with."

"We'd best split up," Bellamy suggested. "You two take the last one, it's longest, and I'll take the next."

We hurried to the last dock. Just as we reached it, a Jet Ski pulled away from one of the yachts at the far end and headed to the open sea. Not waiting for Ada, I rushed to the end of the dock, knowing I was late already. But there was no question: the guy in the hotel security uniform had to be Travert.

"Two guesses where that blasted thing came from," Ada growled, pointing at the closest yacht. I read the name and nodded.

*Arctos.*

# 20

## ELIOT

I'D RESERVED A TABLE FOR US at the hotel restaurant before I went to the beach. After showering and changing, the four of us headed for a well-deserved dinner.

Not that we were in a mood for it.

The local police hadn't been hopeful that they'd catch Travert. "He won't get far on that thing, but he won't have to before he's on your side of the border—or in Italy."

The border to Italy was only sixteen kilometers away, well within the range of a Jet Ski.

Gagne had asked the French police to head to Travert's home in one of the villages outside Monaco that formed its commuting area, and we hoped he was stupid enough to be there. Ada contacted the Maritime Gendarmerie, but they weren't any more optimistic than the local police.

"He won't head to the open sea, and we don't have jurisdiction on land."

There was nothing we could do about *Arctos* either. There hadn't even been anyone on board when the local police went to interview them, so the disappearance of the Jet Ski would come as a surprise to them.

But the fact that Travert had known how to take it out from a hidden compartment at the side of the yacht told us that he was familiar with the vessel. It had taken the police ten minutes to find the lever on the bow deck that opened a hatch there.

"Dinner is on me," I stated before the rest of our party had opened the menus. Gagne's brows shot up.

"This is starting to feel like you're trying to influence our investigation," he said, only half in jest. I bit the inside of my cheek to keep my first reaction in.

"I'm rich. You live on cops' salaries. This isn't a cop salary kind of establishment, and I want a relaxing dinner without monetary worries." I'd checked the prices on the menu from the hotel network while I waited for my turn to shower, and they'd made me lift my brows a couple of times.

"Besides, I like to treat people."

That was true too, although the number of people I'd treated at my hotel's restaurants could be counted on the fingers of one hand. Basically my mom, her sister, and my PI friends, though the latter probably thought it was on the hotel.

"In that case, thank you," Ada said. She could afford to eat here—her side job had to be lucrative—but she couldn't do so with the detectives present. Judging by his car, Bellamy probably could afford the place too, but I didn't want to presume.

When the waiter had left with our orders, Gagne leaned forward. "Monsieur Morris called. Fabre didn't pay for his stays here."

The other two looked pleased, but I had no idea what he was talking about. "Fabre?"

How did he factor into this?

Ada was seated next to me and turned to me to explain. "We learned that he stayed here at least once a month and gambled at the Casino."

"Money laundering," I stated before I considered the wisdom of it. The detectives didn't suspect Fabre was involved in that. Even if they figured out that the books on the external drive were cooked, they had no idea it connected with him.

"What makes you think that?" Bellamy inquired, but not like he suspected me of anything. I picked my words carefully.

"Gambling is the easiest way to move large amounts of cash between two people. Turn cash into chips, play against a fixed opponent, bet excessively, and lose everything. The winner cashes the chips. Clean money. If Fabre didn't pay for his stay, he probably didn't play with his own money either."

Gagne's eyes narrowed as he considered my explanation. "Wouldn't the casino become suspicious?"

"They might, unless they're in on it." Like at my boss's establishments, though it was mostly his money that was being laundered.

"Fabre liked baccarat," Ada said. "House usually gets everything."

I pursed my lips. "That doesn't work quite as well, unless it's *chemin de fer*, which is player against player. Poker would be better."

Gagne nodded. "We're checking Fabre's finances to see if there are irregularities. Meanwhile, we have nothing to work on."

"I could go to the Casino and sniff around," I suggested lightly.

"Not alone you won't," Gagne stated, but I shook my head.

"You two look like cops no matter what you're wearing."

"Then you'll take Mademoiselle Reed with you."

Ada startled, but then she nodded. "I can do it. But I won't be some silly arm candy."

"Pity," I drawled, making her roll her eyes.

"What should we do?" Bellamy asked Gagne. "Our interview was a bust, but I'm not ready to give in."

I considered him. "Did you bring any party clothes?"

"No, but I can find some. Why?"

"Someone ought to keep an eye on Melnyk, in case he emerges. You could hang out on the rooftop bar. I hear that's where the party gang spends their nights."

He grimaced. "I'm getting a bit too old for that scene, but I guess I could have a drink or two. What about you, Alan?"

"I'll go to bed early. This is the first time in weeks that I'm going to have a nice, quiet night without three children demanding my constant attention."

"Another reason not to have any children…"

Our starters arrived before that could escalate, and we moved on to other issues. The food was excellent, though not worth the price. I enjoyed every bite, luxuriating in the dinner.

This was the first proper social engagement I'd had since my death. Business lunches didn't count, my dating with Elizabeth hadn't included her friends, and Fabre's party had turned out to be work too.

I hadn't realized how much I'd missed the company of people who seemed to like me, even if they didn't know the real me—or because of it. I found myself relaxing for the first time in months.

That was dangerous. I couldn't afford to forget it.

"You know our family situations. What about you, Ada? How come you've not been snatched up by some handsome fellow?" Bellamy asked at some point. She made a small shrug.

"I'm a widow."

That silenced the detectives. "I'm sorry. How did that happen?"

"He was a cop who responded to a bank robbery that went wrong. A bomb exploded. He died."

Gagne patted her hand that rested on the table. "I'm sorry. It's this job. That's why I prefer being a detective. Fewer chances of dying in the line of duty."

She nodded, not contributing more. We kept the conversation light after that.

When we finished dinner, we returned to the suite to change clothes for the night.

"Do you have anything suitable?" I asked Ada. I was fantasizing about the red dress she'd worn that afternoon, but obviously she couldn't dress in that.

She gave me a slow look. "Of course." She closed the door to the room before I had a chance to remind her my clothes were in there too.

Never mind. I could wait.

A STEADY STREAM of people was climbing the steps to the Casino when the taxi left us outside it. Some were heading to the opera, but there was a long line to the Casino too. At this time of night, you had to pay to enter.

"You're looking lovely," I told Ada, taking in the dove-gray silk sheath dress that hugged her front and hung loosely from the shoulders in a U-shape to reveal a lot of skin at the back. She wore the same high-heeled sandals as Natasha, but I doubt the detectives had noticed. They'd been too busy ogling when she emerged from her room.

I'd ogled too, but I wasn't going to admit that.

I was dressed in the tux that I hadn't had a chance to wear since purchasing it, the shirt crisp and the cufflinks understated platinum. I felt good—and looked good too, if the interested flash in Ada's eyes was anything to go by when she saw me.

A delighted smile had spread on her face. "So you are a secret agent…"

Hardly.

"Where did you get that notion?" I asked, amused, and she grinned.

"Laïla. She said your backstory is too good for an ordinary person, and apparently secret agent is the best explanation for it."

My gut tightened. "You've talked about me?"

A slight blush rose to her cheeks. "She was curious."

"Right…" I drawled, making her blush deepen. Inside, I was shivering. I'd made a mistake somewhere when creating Eliot Reed. If Laïla was suspicious, others would be too.

The countdown to my exit had started faster than I could have imagined. I'd only had a couple of good months as Eliot Reed and now I would have to change. But I had identities ready. I only had to choose which one and where.

But the twinge in my heart seemed to indicate that at some point during this last week I'd forgotten rule number three as well as eight.

The exchange had unsettled me so thoroughly that I hadn't paid attention to her jewelry. "Where did these come from?" I asked, as we lined up, pointing at the ruby and diamond earrings and bracelet.

She flashed me a smile, and leaned closer, lowering her tone. "Fabre's safe."

I stared at her, stunned. "Isn't that risky?"

"He had several exactly similar sets there. I wondered about it at the time, but it turns out he gave them to his mistresses when he ended a relationship."

I tried to take the information in. "And he had several sets?"

"As if he'd had a bulk discount of them. They're not great quality though, so they can't have been that expensive."

I was stunned by the notion that he automatically assumed there would be a next woman to whom to give the trinkets, but of course there would be. A place like this lured in hopeful women in search of moneymen. There had been those at both of my boss's casino hotels too.

"And you decided to keep them?"

She shrugged minutely. "It's not like I can get a good price for them. But tonight I'm wearing them for a purpose."

"And that would be?"

"Pretending to be one of Fabre's women. Maybe whoever he played cards with will recognize them."

It was a longshot, but we didn't really have anything else to go by. "You should've worn Natasha's wig too. I think she would be exactly the kind of woman who attracted Fabre."

"Well ahead of you," she said with a smug smile, opening the small evening bag she was carrying. It didn't look large enough to hold anything but a phone, but she'd managed to stuff the wig inside too.

"The moment we're in, I'll disappear into the ladies' to fix myself up."

All the rooms had been opened for the night and they were full of people. It was far from the elegant affair you saw in movies, and most of the people were here only to ogle and maybe have an expensive drink or two.

Nobody paid attention to Ada as she slipped into the nearest toilet, only to emerge as a completely different person. Even her eyes had changed to the blue of Natasha's, and the makeup had become stronger.

"You fit all this in there?" I asked, amazed, pointing at the clutch.

She smiled. "I've learned to pack efficiently." Even her voice and accent were Natasha's now.

She was amazing.

There were more security personnel present than during the day, and I marked their locations as we made a leisurely round through the rooms like the tourists we were. It was an automatic habit from the time it had been my job to make sure a casino was well secured.

"We'd best get something to drink," I said when we reached a bar that didn't have a wall of people in front of it. "Champagne?"

"What, not dry martinis?"

Grinning, I headed to fetch our drinks, but my insides had turned cold. It was only a matter of time before she realized the discrepancies in my backstory weren't because I was a government operative but a criminal in hiding.

"It's Bollinger," I told her when I handed her a glass of champagne. "I hope that's Bond enough for you."

"Since I don't plan to drink it, lesser stuff would've sufficed."

I wasn't planning to drink it either, but appearances mattered when one was undercover. "The bartender would've noticed if I'd ordered cheaper stuff. If security starts asking questions about us, he'll say I have money but not much taste."

She tilted her head, taking me in. "I don't know … nothing distasteful about your looks."

Her gaze warmed the cold inside me, but I stifled the sensation. I'd be gone soon and didn't need to leave people that mattered behind. "That's because the tux is by a French tailor."

That made her laugh.

"Should we head to the baccarat tables?" I asked.

"Yes, but I don't think Fabre played on this floor. The big money games are in private rooms upstairs."

"We'd best get ourselves invited to the big boys table, then."

I wasn't as eager to do that as I sounded. The risk of being noticed by one or two of the high rollers that had frequently visited my casino was too high. But it would be a chance to test my disguise too, so I located the floor manager and led Ada there.

"Where can I play in a more private setting?" I asked. He gave us a dispassionate once-over and, deeming us wealthy enough, nodded.

"It's a minimum deposit of ten thousand euros to enter. What would you like to play?"

"Baccarat. For fifty."

I gave him my credit card and the man made a quick transaction, giving me a pile of chips in a wooden tray, and a passkey to the private rooms.

"Take that door. Next floor up, at the back."

The security guard at the door was one of those we had interviewed that afternoon with Gagne and Bellamy, but if he remembered me, he didn't indicate it in any way as he checked the passkey and opened the door marked "Private" for us.

Ada shot a worried glance at me as the door closed behind us. "Do you know how to play? That's a lot of money to lose."

It was, but I had plenty and I wasn't emotionally attached to it. "I know the rules, but baccarat is a guessing game where you're likely to lose anyway. I'm ready to part with this money in order to get more information."

There was a staircase right behind the door and we took it to the next floor. Rooms there didn't fill the entire building, only one wing, and they were smaller, but like downstairs the passage to the last room was through the others.

It gave us a good chance to look at the people at the card tables. The first two rooms had four tables each for pro poker, then there were blackjack and roulette, which I couldn't imagine anyone playing with high stakes, but which I'd seen happen often enough. The smallest room at the back was for baccarat and other special games.

The interior was polished wood, red-carpeted floors, and no gold trimmings. There weren't as many people filling the rooms as the common area, but still more than I would've thought. Most of them were onlookers; some of them were paid to be there. Everyone looked wealthy enough to belong.

I recognized two men at the poker tables from my casino, but their eyes were tightly on their cards; they paid no attention to what was happening around them. Still, their presence reminded me to keep my guard up.

We strolled to the last room and took a casual look around. Ada tensed. "Melnyk's here."

She couldn't point, so I let my gaze sweep the room again. At the back corner, facing us, was a man in his early thirties with short-cropped black hair and a rather square-shaped face with a large nose and heavy brows. He was wearing a silver silk shirt that hugged a powerful torso under a tight white-on-white suit. He'd left the top buttons open and heavy golden chains hung towards a hairy chest. A huge gold watch was on prominent display on his wrist. Judging by the sullen look on his face, he was losing.

"What is he doing here?" Ada wondered in a low voice as we turned to round the room.

"Losing at baccarat."

"Do you think it's deliberate?"

I shrugged. "If it is, he's hiding it well."

"Do you think it was Melnyk's money that Fabre was playing with?"

I had no idea. "I think I've lost the plot of this play completely. But I think it's best to assume that Dobrev and Melnyk still work together, at least outwardly. Melnyk won't openly challenge Dobrev until he's ready."

And he would take his life in his own hands when he did. I'd never been tempted to take over my boss's operations, but even if I had, the consequences would likely have kept me from doing it.

"So Fabre played with Dobrev's money that Melnyk coordinated?" Ada asked.

"That would be the easiest explanation. Now that Fabre's dead, Melnyk has to do the losing himself."

"Then who is he losing to? I thought the point was to circulate the money through the Casino? Fabre plays with Dobrev's money and loses it to Melnyk."

"If the dealer isn't in on it, the casino will become suspicious if two men played month after month and one always loses to another."

She nodded, her gaze taking in the people in the room. "So a handful of people, one of which was Fabre, playing with other peoples' money, winning and losing to each other, and then handing the money back."

"That would be the sensible option. Of course, there's no guarantee that these people are sensible."

A small smile tugged her mouth. "Let's take a look at Melnyk's table, then, to see who he's playing with."

"And then I should try to get invited in."

"Why you?"

I cocked a brow. "Do you play baccarat?"

"No, but if the point is getting into that table, does it matter?"

I tilted my head, giving it a thought. "No, but there are no women at that table and I'm guessing they're the kind of men who don't value women."

"Melnyk is, anyway, if Morris is to be believed." She sighed. "I guess I'll be the arm candy, then…"

# 21

## ADA

I TRIED TO GET INTO MY ROLE as Natasha as we made our way slowly around the room to Melnyk's table. I held on to Eliot's arm, all but wrapped around him while looking at other men like I was keeping my options open. I was so far from my comfort zone I needed a passport, but Natasha would be here solely for that. She didn't have to like it, but a girl does what she must to survive.

For all that I always wore disguises, I'd never had to spend any time interacting with people when in them. Their sole purpose was to distract the possible onlookers. The old lady had been difficult enough to pull off, and everyone had kind of dismissed her. But Natasha wanted attention on her.

"You can circle the room or stay standing behind me," Eliot said in a low tone. "But don't get into my line of sight. I find you too distracting."

Before I had a chance to comprehend his meaning, he paused at Melnyk's table and flashed the men the polite but charming smile of a used car salesman.

"Gentlemen, there seems to be a free spot at your table. May I join you?" He opted for English, as the average tourist here wouldn't speak French.

The oval table had room for seven players, with the dealer on one side and the players on the other, but only three seats were occupied. Melnyk was sitting at the right edge of the table, leaning an elbow on the table as he fidgeted with his whisky glass, looking sullen.

Coming face to face with him for the first time after spending months tracking him was exciting and unnerving—and disappointing. He didn't strike me as a man who could be the second most important person in a large crime organization. He seemed like a little boy, even though he was about my age. Shouldn't he exude authority, or at the very least, violence?

At the other end, the last seat was taken by a handsome and debonair man in his late thirties, with elegantly overgrown black hair combed back, a hooked Roman nose, and an olive complexion that said "Italian" even more clearly than Eliot's did. His tuxedo was tailored and the accessories, like his watch, were understated luxury.

I wouldn't have turned my nose up if I'd found that watch in a safe I broke into.

There was quiet authority about him. He would make a much better leader than Melnyk, though maybe not of a crime organization. A CEO of a large company maybe. And he didn't seem like a person who would spend his time at card tables playing with other people's money either.

He wasn't wearing a wedding ring, but he had a signet ring in his left pinky finger. Natasha would've gone after him and been disappointed. He wasn't the kind to waste time on cheap women.

The chair next to him was empty, but the next after that was taken by an older businessman in a white dinner jacket. He was staring at the cards the dealer set on the table with a tight focus that indicated he was taking this far too seriously for his own good.

Here's the thing about baccarat: it's purely a game of chance. The players don't touch the cards and they can't make decisions about them to improve their odds. Two sets of cards are dealt, for the bank and the player, and the participants make bets on which of the hands wins or if it's a tie. The odds favor the bank over the player, but a tie gives the best results. Even if you were able to count cards, a practice that places like this detect pretty fast, you'd still improve your odds only marginally.

I couldn't imagine how money could be directed from one person to another in this game, unless the entire table was in on it, including the dealer—and even he couldn't direct the results unless the cards were prearranged into the shoe. None of the men at the table tonight looked like they were here for anything but winning. The dealer looked perfectly professional.

Maybe Eliot was wrong in his assumption about money laundering. Maybe Fabre had simply loved the game.

But Melnyk was here and that couldn't be a coincidence.

The businessman didn't pay attention to Eliot's question. Melnyk just glowered. The handsome man smiled politely and nodded.

"The more the merrier."

"More people for you to fleece, you mean," Melnyk spat. Apparently the handsome man was winning.

Since no one opposed, Eliot took the middle one of the three empty seats, sitting between Melnyk and the desperate businessman. He placed the chip tray on the table and the dealer nodded.

"Thousand euro minimum, ten thousand max per bet."

I knew Eliot had money—he hadn't batted an eye before purchasing the chips. I could've afforded to lose fifty grand too, but the mere notion sat uneasy with me. I took my risks in front of safes, not at gambling tables. If I absolutely had to gamble, I would try my hand at poker, where skill played at least some part in the outcome. This game was as much in the players' control as roulette or craps.

I stood behind Eliot and placed a hand on his shoulder like the good arm candy that I was. The handsome man gave me a polite, welcoming smile and a quick sweep down my body that wasn't intrusive. His smile turned appreciative.

Pity I wasn't here as Ada. If I judged his character right, he would've been more interested in the real me.

But I couldn't get involved with random men. Danny had been perfect for me, as he'd been a crook too. I hadn't had to hide what I was.

I didn't have to hide what I was with Eliot either, because he already knew, but I couldn't entirely relax with him. He only had to say a word to the detectives and I'd find myself behind bars.

The businessman didn't react to my presence in any way. If I'd been the dealer, I would've suggested he leave the table while he still had money left, but this one let him play. He'd probably seen too many desperate acts to be moved by them anymore.

Melnyk leaned back in his chair and let his eyes wander around my body in an insolent manner that made my skin crawl. His upper lip curled. "If you're looking for Dominique, he's dead."

I inhaled sharply, and it wasn't entirely pretense. I wouldn't have thought he'd bring it up. But I found it interesting that he immediately recognized the jewels.

I felt Eliot tense under my hand. "Who's Dominique?"

"No one," I assured him with Natasha's purr, though it didn't sound as natural as earlier.

"For women like her, they're always no ones," Melnyk said with a sneer. Eliot glowered in return.

"I'm Salvatore Bosco," the handsome man introduced himself, claiming Eliot's attention. Despite the Italian name and looks, there was only a hint of accent in his cultured British English.

"Eliot Reed." The businessman and Melnyk didn't bother with introductions.

"First time in Monaco?" Bosco asked.

"Yes. But hopefully not the last."

"Are we jabbering or are we playing?" Melnyk demanded. Bosco gave him a cool smile, but nodded at the dealer.

"By all means, let's play."

Everyone placed their bets. Eliot put a thousand on the bank, as did Bosco. Melnyk put five thousand on the player and the businessman two thousand on a tie, all that he had left.

I tensed as the last cards were revealed, but Eliot remained calm under my hand. Bank won. The businessman pushed up abruptly and marched out of the room without even a nod at the dealer. Unfazed, the dealer removed the losing chips and gave Eliot and Bosco their winnings.

"Place your bets, gentlemen."

"So where do you hail from, Mister Reed?" Bosco asked as he placed the same bet as before. For a big money game, he was a conservative better.

"Originally? New York. But I currently live in Lyon."

I had my attention on Melnyk and I saw him startle. "Did you know Dominique?"

"I'm not sure…?"

"Fabre. Dominique Fabre."

It was Eliot's time to inhale, all pretense, of course. "I knew him briefly, yes. He's dead, you said?"

"Yes. How did you know him?"

The dealer dealt the cards and the conversation halted. This time it was a tie, probably for the first time in the game.

Bosco sighed. "Pity the gentleman didn't have money left for this round…"

Dealer collected the lost chips and Eliot glanced at Melnyk. "Fabre and I were talking about investing in a tech startup together. How did you know him?"

The men placed another round of bets. Eliot switched to player, though it didn't make a difference in his chances to win. If Melnyk was here to lose deliberately, he was doing a great job. And if Bosco was part of the money laundering scheme, he was doing well too. But I didn't get the notion that that was happening here.

"Why?" Melnyk's question was accompanied with a hostile glare.

"Since he's dead, I'm open for new investors," Eliot said.

"I'm not here to talk business. I'm here to play."

Eliot gave him an easy smile and turned to Bosco. "What about you?"

"I'm more in an import-export business than investing in tech startups," he said apologetically. "Odds for breaking even aren't good in startups."

Eliot won the round. "Just about as good as in this."

He and Bosco laughed. Melnyk pushed his lost chips at the dealer before he could collect them, took his remaining chips—not all that many—and stormed out without a glance back.

MY HAND MUST'VE tightened on Eliot's shoulder, because he patted it. "Would you get me a drink." He glanced at Bosco. "Anything for you?"

"Thank you, I'm set."

Eliot gave me a chip for a hundred euros, and I gave him a smile that I hoped suited Natasha—admiring and ready to please—and left the room.

One didn't really need to fetch their own drinks in the private rooms; there were several waiters in each room for that. But I wasn't really looking for a bar. I was after Melnyk.

Melnyk didn't have that much of a head start, but by the time I reached the next room he wasn't there anymore. I wanted to run after him, but that would've attracted too much attention. So I held my head high as I sashayed through the rooms as fast as I dared, meeting the gazes of men admiring me straight on, like Natasha would, stifling the uneasy shivers some of them caused.

I counted my lucky stars I didn't have to make my living on these men for real.

I kept an eye on Melnyk, but it seemed he hadn't felt like trying his hand at other games because there was no sign of him. Heading down the stairs to the public part of the casino, I hoped he hadn't taken a hidden staircase or lift meant for the rich and powerful who didn't want to go through the riffraff of the main floors. I'd never find him in that case.

I glanced around as I emerged to the main floor, and to my relief spotted him at the bar in the adjoining room. He got a shot of vodka, emptied it in one and instantly gestured for another, treating it the same way.

The bartender didn't bat an eye. People drowning their losses in spirits had to happen several times a night here. One really shouldn't be playing if one couldn't afford to lose.

Melnyk should be able to afford to lose though. But maybe he just really hated it.

I made my way to the bar, leaned against the desk next to him, and gestured at the bartender as if I didn't notice him there.

"Did he send you away so that grownups can talk about business," Melnyk drawled in my ear. I stifled a shiver of disgust as I turned to him, feigning surprise.

"It happens." My shrug was full of acceptance of my fate.

He sneered. "If I were to speak Russian to you, would you understand?"

I would, oddly enough, but I couldn't speak it like the native I was supposed to be. But I couldn't be the only woman here who pretended to be something she wasn't in order to attract wealthy patrons.

"Some men like exotic," I said easily, still keeping the accent.

"Did Dominique?"

I touched the bracelet, as if absentmindedly. "For a while. Is he really dead?"

"What does it matter? He never entertained the same woman again once she'd received his parting gift. So how come I never saw you with him here?"

I hadn't expected that question. "You often played with him?"

I got the whisky I'd ordered for Eliot as a ruse and paid with the chip. I was given cash in return. I put the coins in the tip jar and slipped the notes inside my bra. Melnyk sneered.

"You are Russian after all," he said, switching to that language, though he didn't seem to speak it any better than I did. I shrugged.

"Maybe." I could say that much in Russian without sounding like a fraud.

I turned to leave and he grabbed my arm, holding a bit too tightly. "You could come with me to my yacht. We could talk about Dominique there."

Part of me wanted to, to keep him talking and to have a good snoop around his yacht, but I wasn't that stupid. I gave him a cool look.

"Why would I want to? He's dead and I have someone new."

"You're better off without Dominique anyway," he said, releasing my arm. "You have no idea what he was involved in."

I lifted a carefully painted brow. "Oh?"

Would he reveal to me that he was a drug smuggler and human trafficker?

No such luck. "I hope you have better luck with the new guy."

With that, he pushed through the people lining the bar and headed out of the room. I wanted to follow but I knew where he was going. His yacht. I had a drink to deliver to Eliot to keep up the ruse, so I headed back to the private rooms.

I hadn't learned anything useful from Melnyk, other than that he'd definitely known Fabre. But had they been working together, or against each other? And how did the gambling factor in?

Maybe Fabre's death wasn't linked to money laundering. Maybe it was about gambling debts after all. But who was indebted to whom? Melnyk to Fabre, or vice versa?

Then why did Fabre have the external drive? As collateral? Maybe it was Melnyk who hired me to steal it to get out of the debt. But who killed Fabre, then? Was there a third man in play after all?

Eliot was right. We'd really lost the plot of this case and we didn't have enough players to make it work.

There seemed to be more people in the private area than earlier, and it took me a while to get to the last room. I glanced at the table at the back where I'd left Eliot—and halted.

The table was empty. Eliot wasn't there anymore.

# 22

## ADA

I WAITED FOR A WHILE IN CASE Eliot emerged from the nearest bathroom or something, but he didn't. He wasn't downstairs either. There was no point in hanging at the casino alone, so I took a taxi back to the hotel. I kept checking my phone, hoping he had left a message for me, but there was nothing.

He didn't owe me a message, but if he had wanted to talk business with Bosco more privately, it would've been nice to let me know.

The suite was dark and quiet when I entered. Only slight snoring from the other bedroom indicated anyone was there. I thought about going to bed, but it was barely midnight and I wasn't tired.

I removed all signs of Natasha, sighing in relief when I kicked off the shoes. I dressed in black leggings and a black tunic that could double as a party dress if I removed the leggings, wrapped a black scarf around my neck in carefree fashion, and put on black sneakers. I kept Natasha's blue eyes, but changed the black bob to a long blond wig in a ponytail.

I switched the clutch to a black evening bag with a long enough strap that I could wear it over the shoulder.

In it, among the necessaries like the room key, some money, and my phone, I put vinyl gloves and a set of lockpicks.

You never knew when those would come in handy.

I slipped quietly out of the room and headed back to the lobby and through it to a low side wing, on top of which the roof bar was located. I could hear loud Euro techno as I approached the place, and pitied the guests who had rooms on that side of the hotel.

The bar wasn't large or particularly unique looking, but the view toward the sea was spectacular at that time of night, even with the moon only three quarters full. The railing surrounding the roof was lined with lush seating groups that were lit by soft yellow garden lights hanging from pergolas. All were taken up by loud parties of young, wealthy people who looked beautiful and carefree. One corner was closed off with a velvet rope, and I studied the people there hoping Melnyk would be among them. No such luck.

But as I circled the roof to the bar, he arrived with two bodyguards in tow, neither of which was Travert. The party in the VIP area greeted him loudly and eagerly, and like a king he sat in the middle of the largest sofa and spread his arms on the backrest. Two beautiful women instantly sat on his sides, and he kissed them both. A waiter brought in shots and he emptied one of them.

Either he always drank a lot, or he was still aggravated about the losses at the gambling table.

I contemplated my options. I could try to get invited to his party. I wasn't dressed sexy enough though, and I'd pretty much got what I could from Melnyk already. Besides, I didn't care to spend any more time around him.

But I was dressed for stealth work and Melnyk's yacht was currently empty...

I didn't spare a glance at him as I made my way to the stairs that led down to the marina, the same I'd already taken earlier that day when I chased Travert, only this time all the way from the top.

Since they ran along the cliffside, one would have to hang over the railing of the rooftop bar to spot people taking them, but to make sure I remained invisible I wrapped the scarf around my head so that it obscured my face.

A blond wig wasn't exactly best for going unnoticed in the dark, but it was the only other wig I had with me besides Natasha's.

The beach was lit by garden lights too, not so bright that they would ruin the atmosphere, but light enough for people partying there not to hurt themselves. I spotted Bellamy eagerly dancing to a summery tune with a hot girl half his age dressed in a bikini top and micro shorts.

He was supposed to keep an eye on Melnyk, but I couldn't blame him for giving up and switching to partying when Melnyk hadn't been there. I would've chosen the beach over the rooftop too, and not solely because the music was better. If he wasn't too distracted by the woman, he had a good spot for keeping an eye on Melnyk arriving at his yacht.

Many of the yachts were brightly lit and there were parties on them too. Music and laughter filled the marina, and no one paid any attention to me as I made my way to the last yacht at the last dock.

*Arctos* was quiet and only dimly lit. But it wasn't empty. I could see two men in white short-sleeved steward's uniforms in the large salon on the upper deck. Melnyk could be back with his guests at any time, so I'd best be fast.

Looking around carefully to make sure that I wasn't seen, I slipped on board.

THIS WASN'T THE FIRST time I was on a luxury yacht, not even the first time I was on one uninvited. But it was the first time that I wasn't commissioned by a client, and the first time the yacht was occupied while I was there uninvited.

Yachts this large all looked basically the same. Bridge at the top front. Below it, on one or more decks, depending on the size of the yacht, were the common areas both in and out: lounges, dining areas and the galley, maybe an office squeezed in somewhere. Below decks was the master suite and, depending on the size of the yacht, several cabins and baths. Everything was always teak, brass, white leather, and navy blue.

If there was a safe, it was either in the office or the master suite. The office was a good place to start while the yacht was still empty.

The lower deck was mostly a large lounge area, with the galley at the bow. I could hear noises from there. The room didn't look promising, so I took the spiral staircase to the upper deck, giving it a careful peek from the stairs in case the two men were still there.

It was a small dining area, but whatever the stewards had been doing there, it wasn't setting the table. The place was clean and empty. Maybe Melnyk had had a late dinner before heading to the rooftop and the stewards had been clearing the table.

I hurried through the dining area to the door at the other end. It opened onto a cramped space with a door to a toilet on one side and a door to an office on the other. The latter took the rest of the front, with a nice view over the bow deck below and the hot tub there.

I put on my vinyl gloves and began to go through the few drawers there were. They were mostly empty and nothing was incriminating. Melnyk didn't use the office for his businesses, then, despite spending most of his time on this yacht. I powered up the laptop too, but the prompts were in Bulgarian and I didn't understand them to try to crack in.

Where was Laïla when I needed her…?

I considered taking the laptop with me, but I wouldn't be able to use its contents as evidence, and it was too large to fit into my bag anyway. With a sigh, I shut it down and left it where it was.

I found the safe behind a cabinet door under the narrow wall-to-wall desk. It was fairly large, reaching from floor to the desktop, but to my relief not very modern. I could crack the digital dials of modern safes just as easily if needed, but not without proper tools.

This one only required a good ear and a steady hand on the tumbler.

There's something about cracking safes that speaks to me. It exhilarates and excites me, even when I'm not committing a crime. The simplest explanation would be that it was an interest I'd been able to share with my often-absent father who taught me the trade. But I'd kept at it long after he died, taking pride in honing my skills, learning about all the new safe models out there.

It was something I was good at. That it came with nail-biting tension and a huge adrenaline rush didn't hurt either.

I had the safe open in under two minutes, which wasn't my record with this type, but I'd been slowed down by the noise coming from the nearby yachts.

I opened the door carefully in case of alarms and peeked in. My brows shot up.

About a hundred, tightly wrapped, brick-sized packets of cocaine filled the bottom half. I knew Melnyk smuggled drugs, but I hadn't expected them to be in the safe of his yacht where anyone could find them. Well, anyone who could crack it.

There were also a few smaller, consumer-sized portions in tiny plastic bags, which I had expected.

The rest of the safe was filled with cash in neat, bank-issued piles of hundred euro notes and dollars. Easily a couple of million in what looked like clean money. I wasn't an expert on the drug smuggling business, but I couldn't fathom why there would be so much cash when there was so much cocaine. Didn't one usually get traded for the other?

If I'd been here as a thief, I would've taken as much of the cash as I could carry. But I was here for information, and while the contents of the safe were interesting, they didn't really reveal anything new about Melnyk's businesses. I closed the safe door but not all the way, in case I needed the authorities to have easy access, and considered my options.

If Melnyk didn't have any interesting and incriminating papers in his office, they had to be in his cabin. Would it be worth the risk to go check it?

Maybe I should create a pretext instead for the local police to come and raid the yacht, find the cocaine and arrest Melnyk. The world would be a marginally better place for a while, but it wouldn't shut down Dobrev's business. I might even be playing into Dobrev's hands by removing Melnyk.

Since I was here, I might as well check Melnyk's suite. As silently as possible, I headed below decks and to the cabin at the bow. It was large and most of it was taken by a bed with black satin sheets. There were mirrors on the ceiling and on the doors of the closets that were fitted in the walls, and handcuffs in short chains attached to the headboard.

Someone liked kinky…

I went through the room fast and meticulously. The bedside drawers held a sex shop's worth of condoms, lubes, and toys. I didn't want to touch any of it even with gloves on, but where better to hide things that you didn't want to be found than underneath them?

I only got mild nausea for my bravery.

The closets were filled with clothes in drug lord chic. And at the back, I found a cache of weapons that could take down a small army. Huh.

I considered borrowing a pistol for my safety, but I'd never been comfortable with firearms. I was an expert in weaponless self-defense, which wasn't worth much against bullets, but I'd take my chances.

I found nothing that would help me to crack the case. I couldn't understand it. I'd been tracking Melnyk for months and my intel pointed clearly to his importance in Dobrev's organization. I didn't expect there to be dungeons where smuggled people were held, but I also hadn't expected a party boat.

Was Melnyk a decoy? While I and other investigators kept an eye on him, Dobrev could smuggle people and drugs right under our noses.

I didn't like the idea of having been duped, but everything I'd learned about Melnyk today indicated I'd been wrong.

The yacht was still silent, so I decided to check the other cabins too. There were a couple of smaller ones in the midship, both empty, and another large suite at the back. It had a regular double bed and no excess of mirrors. Maybe this was Melnyk's real bedroom.

I went through the bedside drawers first, but they were empty, as were the closets at the side of the cabin. This wasn't in regular use.

There was one more large closet by the door. I didn't put much hope on it, until I tried to pull the door open and found it locked. A shiver of anticipation coursed through me as I slipped a hand into my bag and took out the lockpicks. I selected the correct ones and made to insert them, when the door suddenly rattled from the inside, making me jump. I might have shrieked.

Another shove from inside the closet, more forceful this time, made the door buckle. It would make a loud noise when the lock broke. Someone might hear and come to check.

"*Tais-toi!*" I hissed in French, trying to insert the pick into the lock that was jumping under my hand.

The door stopped rattling and silence fell. Then:

"Ada?"

# 23

## ELIOT

SENDING ADA AFTER MELNYK WITHOUT backup made me uneasy, but we'd come here for information. The Casino was full of people, and she was a cop. She would be fine.

I followed her progress with my gaze, admiring as ever the easy sway of her hips as she crossed the floor. I should really remember to ask her if she'd been a gymnast or a dancer at some point in her life.

Bosco cleared his throat. "Women like her aren't for keeps, you know."

I bristled, and then remembered the role Ada was playing. "But they sure are nice to look at…"

He smiled and gestured to the table. "Do you want to continue?"

Since the reason I'd chosen the table had left, I didn't need to stay, but I couldn't let him know that. "Maybe a couple of rounds more?"

We both bet on the bank. I'd chosen my bets more or less random, and the results were equally random.

"So, what were you saying about that business opportunity?" Bosco asked. I spared him a quizzical look as the dealer revealed the last cards. We both won.

"I thought you weren't interested."

He shrugged. "As you pointed out, the chances of breaking even in investing to startups are about as good as in this game."

He had a substantial pile of chips in front of him, so I'd say he was doing just fine at the cards table. I'd worked on casino floors since my late teens, and I knew that people usually left with fewer chips than they'd arrived with.

"Seems like you've broken even here too," I said with a smile.

Bosco made a very Italian so-so gesture that made me suddenly miss my nonna, a first-generation immigrant who had spoken with her hands as much as with her mouth. She died when I was ten, and I hadn't thought about her much, but now it came back.

Maybe I should locate to Italy next.

"Do you want to try another game?" he asked. "Poker, maybe. I could make it worth your while."

I laughed. "I've heard that line before…"

He grinned too. "In that case, how about drinks on my yacht? We can talk about that startup there."

I didn't really care about the startup; Fabre and I hadn't had any deals together. But I could always use a drink, and I was curious to see one of the yachts.

"Where is it docked?"

"At the marina of the Jewel of Monaco hotel."

I nodded. "I'm staying there too."

We handed our credit cards to the dealer to cash our chips. Modern technology had made gambling an efficient operation. No need to line to the cashier when each dealer had a device for handling the transactions and taxes. We tipped the dealer and left the table.

"I have a car waiting. We can take the private stairs."

I followed Bosco across the floor to where a door marked "Private" almost disappeared into the wall. A security guy masking as a doorman opened it for us and we emerged into a narrow hallway with a staircase up and down. We headed down.

We'd left so abruptly that Ada hadn't returned, but I couldn't wait for her. She might spend the entire night following Melnyk. I wanted to send her a message, but Bosco would find it odd. She was supposed to be a casino fancy who would pick another man when the first one left.

She would figure out I'd returned to the hotel when she couldn't find me.

At the bottom of the stairs was another narrow hallway and a locked door that opened to the street at the side of the casino, with its own doorman slash security to keep the unwanted people out. The night air felt cool after the hot rooms inside, and I relished the sensation. Tux jackets were warm.

A Bentley glided to the door, and I gave Bosco an impressed look. "Nice…"

His shrug was elegant. "It's not Italian, but it'll do."

I'll say…

A bodyguard in a black suit rounded the car and opened the back door for us. The driver was similarly suited and looked like a bodyguard too. Bosco was clearly a more important person than I'd thought. Maybe I should've made a quick online search before getting into his car. I might be out of my league here, and I didn't even have a real investment to offer for him.

I'd make something up.

The car glided almost soundlessly down the hill, and I leaned back in the soft seat. I'd had a long day, with a lot of walking in the sun, and the darkness and comfort hit me hard, making it suddenly difficult to keep my eyes open.

"Have you been investing in startups for long?" Bosco asked, and I forced myself to pay attention.

"Less than a year. Since I sold my company."

I'd best stick to my usual story.

"What did your company do?"

"Private security."

The men at the front perked. They didn't say anything, but I saw the bodyguard assessing me through the rearview mirror. There was something familiar about him, and I hoped he wasn't anyone who had visited my hotel with the VIP guests. I knew I hadn't met Bosco before, but that didn't mean the bodyguard hadn't been there for someone else's security.

The drive to the hotel was fast at that time of night, but instead of pulling over outside the entrance, the car continued about half a kilometer before turning down a road that wound down the side of the cliff straight to the marina.

There was a manned security gate at the bottom, but no one came to check us as the driver opened the gate with a keycard and drove through. He pulled over at the parking lot inside, next to high performance sportscars and other luxury vehicles.

"Do you guys rent these cars at every marina, or are these always here?" I asked curiously as I exited the car. Bosco smiled.

"My yacht stays here all year round, so I own my car. Many of these people are the same. It's impossible to find housing around here."

"Got to get that tax exemption somehow…"

His mouth tightened. "One is not eligible for a citizenship when one lives on one's yacht. Besides, citizens aren't allowed to gamble here, and I like it too much to apply for it."

Good to know.

The car park was at the opposite end of the marina from the hotel beach, but I could hear distant music drifting over the water from there. There were parties on many of the yachts too.

Bosco's yacht was at the car park end, opposite to Melnyk's *Arctos*. They hadn't indicated they knew each other well at the card table, but I'd arrived late to the party.

"This is my *Serenata*." He looked proud, and for a reason. The Bentley hadn't adequately prepared me for this. Yacht seemed an insufficient word. It was a small ship.

"Wow."

"It's a hundred and seventy-feet superyacht, three decks above, two below. Five crew. Has everything a man could want from a home on water."

My boss's yacht, the one I'd blown up, had been under sixty feet, and the only person who ever drove it was me, as my boss hadn't bothered to learn.

"Probably everything a man could want from a home on land too…"

We got on board and climbed to a comfortable lounge on the middle deck. I would've loved a tour, but Bosco gestured for me to take a seat. He went to a bar cart at the side of the room.

"Whiskey? I prefer red wine, but I know how Americans love whiskey on the rocks. Or is it bourbon?"

"I don't mind what you call it, but hold the ice."

He offered me a generous glass of eighteen-year-old Scottish single malt and I savored the smoky scent before taking a sip. Excellent stuff.

He sat across me with his red wine and leaned comfortably against the backrest, crossing his legs. He gave me a calm, assessing look and I prepared for a barrage of insightful questions about a bogus startup. Good thing I had answers ready.

"Tell me," he asked, "where is the external drive from Fabre's safe?"

THE WHISKEY GLASS halted on my lips as my entire body tensed. I couldn't stifle the startled look I shot over the rim, but I could pretend.

"What external drive?"

Two Sigs were suddenly pointing at me, one on each side. I hadn't even noticed that the bodyguards had remained in the room. If I had, I would probably have been better prepared for this turn of events.

Who was I kidding? I hadn't had an inkling this was coming.

Bosco tilted his head, studying me. "If you want to pass as a businessman, you shouldn't go about interviewing people about dead men."

So that's why the bodyguard looked so familiar. He worked as casino security.

"Lepine?" No point in pretending I didn't know what he was talking about, but could I pretend to be a cop? "What do you know about his death? Was he working for you?"

"I commissioned a theft of the external drive from Fabre's safe. Lepine was supposed to bring it to me, so where is it?"

I gave him a calm look. "If you mean the external drive that Lepine was carrying when he was shot, it's in the police evidence locker. How did Fabre come to be involved?"

He shrugged. "He had a gambling problem. Dobrev got him in his snares. Fabre turned out to be good at cooking books, so he started to do that for him. Dobrev gave him gambling money as a reward and kept the winnings if there were anything. Clean money and dirty books, and the taxman none the wiser about either of them."

We'd sort of got it right, then.

"And what do you want with it?"

His gaze hardened. "That's hardly your business."

"This is a murder investigation," I countered calmly. "Two murders, in fact. If you had Fabre killed, I need to know."

"Fabre's death was a natural consequence of him losing the external drive. Dobrev isn't one to suffer such mistakes."

I leaned forward. "Was that your intention? Getting rid of Fabre by having him take the fall for the theft?"

He shrugged. "It was an inconsequential side effect. Fabre was inconsequential."

"Then who shot Lepine?" I glanced at the men pointing guns at me, but neither of them looked like they'd been commissioned to do it.

"Melnyk, of course."

I pulled back. "Then why didn't he take the external drive?"

"He didn't know about it. Dobrev doesn't share everything with him anymore. Only thing Melnyk cared about was punishing a former employee who had entered my employment. When Lepine went to Lyon, Melnyk saw it as an opportunity to do it without the blame falling on him."

"Did he shoot Lepine himself or send someone?"

He cocked a brow. "Does it matter?"

"Yes."

"Weren't you chasing a bodyguard of his today? One that Melnyk helped escape?"

It wouldn't stand in court, but I took that to mean Travert had shot Lepine like we assumed. It had been only a coincidence that it linked with the other investigation. But his words also meant that he had known from the start who I was. He'd had a ringside seat to our search on Melnyk's yacht that afternoon from here.

Bosco took a sip of his glass. "Now, how will you get me the external drive?"

"I won't. That's not my problem."

He leaned forward and placed his glass on the low table between us. "Come now, *Mister Reed.*" I could practically hear the quotation marks when he said my name. "I had you thoroughly vetted and what my people found makes me certain that it's an assumed identity."

My stomach tightened painfully, but I regarded him calmly as I took as sip of my glass. The whiskey burned down my throat and didn't really help with the tension the way it should.

He continued: "I don't know how you got involved in the investigation, but I'm sure the detectives would be interested in learning about your past—or the lack of it."

I tilted my head. "Are you trying to blackmail me?"

I sounded calm but I was making calculations. I wasn't armed and I could only take one of the bodyguards before the other shot me. Not worth the trouble.

"There aren't many reasons for why a person would have a new identity. You could be in a witness protection program, but you'd keep a low profile in that case."

I thought I had, but I didn't say it aloud.

"You're Dobrev's man, masking as a businessman to keep an eye on Fabre. Why else would he have died only months after you moved to Lyon? You shot him."

The absurdity of the claim made me snort. "That's Melnyk."

"Please, that idiot?" He all but rolled his eyes. "He's a flashy fool that provides Dobrev girls to smuggle."

I took another sip as I tried to wrap my mind around his version of reality, but the alcohol seemed only to muddle my brain. I hadn't had that much to drink today, had I? I couldn't tell anymore.

I pinched the bridge of my nose, trying to make my brain work. "We presumed there are three players trying to move each other out of the way and take the entire Mediterranean operation to themself, Dobrev, Melnyk, and someone unknown, which … is you? Only, you say Melnyk isn't in the play?"

Bosco shrugged. "Not much longer, anyway."

"What do you mean?"

"I mean that I've planted a hundred kilos of cocaine and two million euros of his boss's money on his yacht. Dobrev received an anonymous tip of his treachery and is on his way with a small army to deal with it. What would've made it even better is the external drive. That would really have pissed Dobrev off."

That was one way to handle it.

"Well, this has been fun." It was difficult to form words and I had to force them out. "Thank you for clearing our case for us, but I must be going now."

I made to push up, and the bodyguards stepped closer.

"You're not going anywhere," Bosco drawled. "If you're not Dobrev's man, you're a cop and you know too much."

His face was blurry. I blinked to get it to focus, but it didn't. I couldn't understand it at first and then I did, and my heart almost stopped. I had been roofied.

How fucking ... *stupid* ... was ... I...?

# 24

## ELIOT

I WOKE UP IN A TIGHT SPACE. I was standing up, my back propped against one corner, my legs against another with so little room between them that I couldn't fall or fold my knees. It was dark. I tried to straighten up and instantly banged my head, adding to the headache that was throbbing behind my eyes.

My legs didn't feel like I'd been standing here for long, but I'd incapacitated people with drugs often enough when I was still a full-time enforcer to know that it took time to recover from them. It could be morning already.

Whatever I'd been given had cleared already though, and my mind was working well enough. I wasn't dead yet, so I had time to escape.

I listened to the sounds around me, but it was so quiet my ears were probably deceiving me. Was there someone in the room with me?

I felt around in the darkness and located what I judged to be the door. I pushed it. Locked, naturally, but it gave a bit under my hand. I was most likely in a closet or a wardrobe, which meant the door would probably give with a little pressure.

I rattled it but nothing happened. I rammed my shoulder against it but there wasn't enough space to really put force behind it. I pulled back, ready to try again, when someone hissed on the other side.

"*Tais-toi!*"

The words, in French, meant "Be quiet," but that wasn't what halted me. It was the voice.

"Ada?"

Silence on the other side. Then metal clicked against metal and the door opened. I almost fell out—straight onto the woman behind it, who caught me by wrapping her arms around me.

"Ouch. You're heavy."

I pushed to my feet, and they held. I stared at Ada, amazed and happy, and a little touched too. "How did you find me?"

We barely knew each other and she'd come to my rescue. She was dressed all in black, wearing vinyl gloves and a blond wig with the blue contacts, and held lockpicks in one hand. A true stealth operation.

She stared back at me, utterly amazed. "I wasn't looking for you. What are you doing here?"

Huh?

"Apart from the obvious?" I glanced around to get my bearings and to get over the disappointment. We seemed to be in a cabin of a yacht, but best make sure. "Is this Bosco's yacht?"

She pulled back. "Bosco's? No, this is *Arctos*."

I blinked. My mind had to be addled by the drug still. "How the hell did I get here?" And why hadn't Bosco killed me where I'd been? Unless he found it more amusing to have Melnyk do it. "I need to sit down."

"You can't do that. We have to get out of here. You might be injured."

I dropped heavily on the bed, ignoring her protests. "I was drugged, but I feel fine. How long was I gone?"

"I don't know. Half an hour, hour?"

"What?" That wiped away what drug residue there was.

She studied her wristwatch with narrowed eyes, tapping the watch face as she calculated. "I spent ten minutes locating and speaking with Melnyk, by which time you'd left, ten waiting for you, twenty getting back to the hotel, twenty changing clothes, ten getting to *Arctos* via the rooftop bar, and about half an hour searching it. That makes an hour and forty minutes since I left you at the casino."

"That's … pretty precise."

She shrugged. "Timing is everything in my line of work."

I didn't need to ask which work she was referring to.

I couldn't manage the same, but I hadn't spent all that much time speaking with Bosco on his yacht. "I must've been brought here right before you came, then."

She gestured impatiently, making the lockpicks tingle. "But why were you brought here? And by whom?"

A smug smile spread on my face as I recalled what I'd learned. "I've cracked the case." Her brows shot up, eyes large, and I amended. "Well, it was revealed to me, but I think it's a pretty accurate version."

She groaned. "I'm dying to hear it, but we have to go. I think this yacht is about to leave."

Now that she mentioned it, the buzzing under my feet was the engines warming up and not some residue of the drug.

"That's not the worst of it," I said, getting up. "Dobrev's about to attack here."

She stiffened. "What?"

"Safety first, explanations later." My hand went inside my tux jacket, only to come out empty. And I wasn't looking for my phone, which was still there. Ada tilted her head.

"If you're looking for a weapon, Melnyk's got you covered."

She led me out of the cabin to the other end of the yacht. The sounds of the engine were growing stronger, and if I wasn't mistaken, people were climbing on board. It was only a matter of time before someone came down here.

That didn't prevent me from stopping on the threshold of the cabin to take in the large bed with black satin sheets, the mirrors, and…

"Are those pink handcuffs attached on the headrest?"

She shot me an amused glance. "If that shocks you, don't look into the bedside drawers."

I looked into the bedside drawers.

"I've never understood the purpose of sex toys," I mused, wishing I'd heeded her. That was way too much information about Melnyk. "What can you do with them that you couldn't do with ten fingers and a tongue?"

"Umm…" Her cheeks had turned red. I grinned.

"Either you know the answer to that question or you're dying to find out what I can do without toys."

She pulled a closet door open. "I'm more curious about finding out what you can do with these."

I whistled as I saw the contents. "What couldn't I do…"

"You can't take them all," she said sternly, like a mother to a child in a toy store. Which was pretty much how I felt.

There was everything from tiny pistols to assault rifles, complete with ammos and other accessories like silencers and night vision goggles. Everything seemed to be in factory condition.

"Is he arming a revolution somewhere?"

She startled. "That didn't occur to me, but maybe? Maybe he wants to branch into arms dealing, and Dobrev doesn't?"

"Well, he won't have much time for that, because Dobrev's coming for him, and he wants blood."

"What is going on? How did you find out that?" She stood with her hands akimbo, looking like she would stand there until I gave her answers, the need to flee forgotten. I faced her, leaving the guns for a moment.

"Bosco's been playing Dobrev against Melnyk. He planted Dobrev's drugs and money here, and then tipped him off."

"Bosco? Is he a cop?"

I sneered. "Hardly. He's the third man."

Her mouth dropped open. "I did not see that coming."

"That makes two of us…"

I ran a hand down my face, not happy to recall the events of the night. I'd gone too native with my not-a-criminal scam and had stopped automatically presuming that everyone around me was a crook. It had almost cost me my life.

"He invited me to his yacht to talk about the business proposal, and like a fool I went. And then he demanded to know where the external drive is. He was your client, by the way."

Her hands dropped from her hips and her shoulders slumped. "I can't believe that. He was such a … gentleman."

Her wistful face indicated gentleman wasn't the first word that came to her mind.

"Judging by his Bentley and the yacht, he's the biggest player around here, and now he wants Dobrev and Melnyk out of the way, so he played them against each other. And it worked, because Dobrev is coming."

I selected a pistol that felt best in my hand, a Glock 26 semiautomatic. It only took nine rounds, and the range wasn't much, but in close confines like a yacht, it would work fine. Besides, it fit into the pocket of my pants.

I checked the chamber and the magazine, and made sure the safety was on before slipping it into my pocket. "Okay, I'm good. You want one? The small ones would fit into your bag."

She grimaced. "I'm not much into firearms."

"In that case, I'll go first."

We exited the cabin and climbed the closest stairs up. I took a peek at the top and halted. "Shit. The party's moved here."

The stairs opened to the bow deck and at least twenty people were busily climbing into a hot tub, more or less naked. They were probably too drunk or high to pay any attention to us, but I gestured Ada to go back down.

We hurried to the stern and the stairs there, but the lounge and back deck were full of revelers too. The music was loud and everyone was in a full party mood already—or still. "Shall we try through here?"

"We'd best. I doubt anyone will notice us."

A weapon cocked behind us. "That's what you think."

MUSCLES TENSE, I turned slowly around, lifting my hands up. Ada was doing the same a couple of steps below me. She looked calm. I'm not entirely sure I was.

Melnyk was standing at the bottom of the stairs aiming a Makarov semiautomatic at us. It's a Russian pistol and you didn't often see them in the US, but they were popular in Bulgaria. If Melnyk's arms cache had held one, I would've taken it as a keepsake.

"What are you doing here?"

The question was for me. I shrugged. "I came with the party."

"And brought her?" He gestured with the pistol, making my gut tighten. "You seem to have traded ... down."

Didn't he recognize her? That would work for us.

I was about to give some bullshit explanation, when she spoke.

"I do not know this man," she said, her English barely understandable, as her French accent was so heavy. "I came to find my boyfriend. He said to meet me here. But there are only these ... women, and not my boyfriend."

"Boyfriend?" Melnyk said with great contempt. "Who?"

"Bruno. Bruno Travert. He works for you, no?"

A slow sneer spread on his face and the gun fixed at her. "Firstly, your boyfriend is dead."

Ada inhaled in shock. "No..."

"That happens when you lead the police to search my yacht. Secondly..." His eyes turned cold. "...if you're going to invent a boyfriend, make sure he isn't gay."

*Oops.*

I slipped a hand into my pocked to pull out the pistol. Melnyk's attention was on Ada, and he wouldn't have time to react if I was fast enough. But before I had a chance, she straightened, incensed, and took a step down, pressing at him.

"My Bruno is not gay!"

Her anger made Melnyk's attention waver. That was all she needed.

She swirled sideways and kicked him in the gut, making him double over and lower the weapon. She took a firm hold of his hand and with a deft move much like the one she'd taught us on Monday, disarmed him, and with another sinuous move clocked him on the temple with the butt. He dropped down, unconscious.

She removed the magazine of the pistol and remembered to empty the chamber too. I could barely tear my eyes away from her.

"Damn, you're hot…"

Breathing heavily, she flashed me a smile. Then she tilted her head and cocked a brow. "That bulge in your trousers had better be a gun and not a reaction to my hotness, because we have to run."

"Oh, it's definitely a reaction…"

But she had a point. I turned to head back up, stumbling only a little as blood returned to my brain. I emerged onto the deck—and came to such a grinding halt that Ada rammed into me. She peered around me to see what had stopped me and inhaled.

"Shit."

We were several meters away from the dock already, moving away fast. I glanced at her over my shoulder.

"Can you swim?"

Her eyes were large. "Yes, but the current is strong around here. We might not make it."

The mere notion of facing the merciless sea made my bones shrink.

"We might not make it if we stay on board."

She worried her lower lip as she gave it a quick thought. "First things first, let's secure our backs and put Melnyk where he can't come after us."

We returned to the lower deck. Melnyk showed signs of waking up already, so I took a firm hold under his arms and began to drag him to his cabin. Ada took his legs, and we soon had him on his bed.

"Isn't this the first place they'll look?" she asked as I attached Melnyk's arms to the handcuffs. They were real cuffs, despite the pink fluff, and needed a key to open.

I had a notion that he wasn't nice to the women in his bed and wished Ada had hit him harder.

"I bet the crew knows not to enter uninvited." I glanced around. "Look for something to gag him with."

She flashed an impish grin, opened the bedside drawer, and pulled out a black silicone ball gag that fastened with a strap behind the head. I laughed.

"That'll do."

Melnyk came to when we had him fastened, his legs bound with a strap he had in the drawers too. His eyes grew large and he began to thrash and make incomprehensible sounds.

"Hush, or you'll choke," I said calmly. "Now, did you know that Dobrev is on his way here with a small army?"

He went completely still. I nodded.

"That's what I thought. I don't know what you did to piss him off, but it didn't help that Bosco fanned the flames by planting his money and coke on your yacht. For your sake, I hope he isn't arriving today, because … awkward."

"Do you think he might not come tonight?" Ada asked, as we turned to leave.

I spread my arms. "Who knows."

"We should find out. Because if he isn't, we can stay on board until we dock again. Melnyk's not going anywhere until that."

"We don't exactly have a direct line to Dobrev to ask."

"There are other ways…" She pulled out her phone and began to click it. She frowned and lowered the phone. "The tracking software doesn't work on this…"

I headed to the door. "We'd best leave and fast, then." Every second put more sea between us and the shore, and the mere notion of plunging into the cold water gave me unpleasant flashbacks.

She halted me, her eyes large with worry. "There's at least fifty innocent people on board. It'll be a massacre if Dobrev arrives now. We have to get them out."

My insides went cold. "There's no way to get everyone on lifeboats. Besides, they're so drunk they'd probably fall off and die anyway." I pulled out my gun. "Let's turn this yacht back to the marina."

"I have a better idea. I'll call Laïla and have her track us."

"What good will that do?"

"She can tell us if we're being approached. If not, we all take a nice cruise in the moonlight and return home none the wiser."

"And if there are?"

She glanced at the arms cache. "Then we'll prepare."

# 25

## ADA

IT WAS PAST ONE IN THE MORNING, but I knew Laïla would be awake. Her sleeping habits were appalling. If she wasn't at work, which was likely—she claimed she got her best work done when no one was around to bother her—she would be playing *Counter-Strike* with her team.

My hands were so dry the touch screen of my phone didn't react at first when I tried to place the call. I chose video, remembering only at the last moment that I was in disguise and pulling off the wig. I could only hope she didn't spot the blue eyes.

She answered almost immediately, so she was at work. I almost cried when her familiar face appeared on the screen. "What's up, girl? How's the holiday?"

"It's ... interesting. I need your help."

She sighed. "You didn't gamble away all your money, did you?"

"I wish. This is more a life and death situation. Emphasis on death."

"What is going on?" Her face tightened with concern. I took a deep breath, not wanting to confess, but there was no getting around it.

"I ... went to snoop where I shouldn't and now I'm

stuck on a yacht somewhere on the Mediterranean with fifty very drunk and high people, and a drug lord is maybe on his way to attack us."

She was silent for a beat. "I'll call the coast guard."

"I can do that myself, but before I do, I need to know if the threat is imminent or if we have time to flee."

"Right. What should I do?"

"I'm on a yacht called *Arctos*, somewhere outside Monaco, heading…"

"West," Eliot said, looking out of the window, where the lights of the coast were still visible in the distance. How were we so far already?

"West," I repeated, even though she could hear him.

"Is that Mr. Reed with you?" she asked, excited. I turned the phone so she could see him in his tux, and she inhaled. "He *is* a secret agent!"

Eliot looked amused, but I shook my head. "Yes, he's here, no he's not an agent. Now, focus. There's tracking software for all the maritime traffic that should tell you where we are and who's near us."

"I know that one," she said, waving her hand dismissively. "It's not good for your situation as there's at least a twenty-minute lag in the data."

A lot could happen in twenty minutes.

I swallowed hard. "Then what should we do?"

"I'll just log on to the satellite surveillance. That's real-time."

"We don't have access to that."

She made a pish sound. "I can access anything."

"Laïla! You can't hack into government surveillance," I said, scandalized.

"I can if I don't get caught." She put the phone on her desk, so all I could see was the ceiling above her. She clicked her keyboard for a few minutes.

"Ok, I'm in. Man, this has a great camera. I can see clearly even in this darkness. I'll just have to realign the satellite a little to your position and zoom in…"

"They'll notice," I said, my gut tightening, but she just snorted.

"They're not conducting any surveillance operations right now. Let's see…"

I waited in tense silence—or as much silence as a yacht full of partying people could be, with a techno beat making the cabin echo. In the corridor, people looking for empty beds to have sex in were laughing, screeching, and banging the doors. Eliot locked the door to the cabin we were in.

"Bad news," Laïla said, her face tight as she peeked into the phone. "You're not heading west anymore. You're heading south and fast, to international waters."

"And that's bad because?" Eliot asked.

"International laws apply. I can't just send our coast guard to rescue you. It would have to be the navy and that'll take time to arrange. There isn't even any of their fleet near enough."

"Fuck." He pinched his nose. "Okay, what's in the south? Where are we heading?"

Clicking sounds. "Corsica, though you'd have to turn east a bit to meet it. Otherwise, it's just empty sea until Algeria."

He looked at me. "I don't think this thing's got enough fuel to make it that far."

I nodded, thinking it over. "But we're not on a cruise at this speed either. We must be meeting someone, maybe a smuggler's boat or something."

He tensed. Then he leaned closer the phone. "Laïla, is

there a ship called *Benevolence* nearby?"

She clicked her keyboard. "Yes! It's not far, maybe twenty minutes away? I can't really give accurate times with this thing."

Eliot had gone pale. "Fuck."

"What is it?"

"We're not rendezvousing with a smuggler boat. We're heading toward the ship used for moving drugs and people to America. And we have both of those on board."

I stared at him, stunned. "Are you saying that Melnyk picks up a boat full of partiers and then ships them off?" I gestured at the prone figure on the bed. He flipped me a middle finger. I didn't need the answer so desperately I would've freed his mouth.

"Maybe not the entire boatful," Eliot mused. "That would be noticed. One or two, maybe. Everyone's so drunk they won't pay attention to who's on board and who doesn't return with the yacht."

I felt sick.

"We need to turn around, now."

"Agreed," Eliot said, pulling out his gun.

"Make it quick," Laïla said in a small voice. "Two large RIBs full of armed men just left *Benevolence* and they're heading your way."

"WHAT'S A RIB?" I asked Eliot after I hung up. He looked concerned.

"Rigid Inflatable Boat. RIB. Those black, fast things that military uses for stealth operations. Each can take from six to twenty people, depending on size."

I looked at him in horror. "Are you saying forty armed men could be heading at our way?"

"The question is, are they Dobrev's men or Melnyk's."

"Does it matter? They won't be happy with what we've done to him."

We wouldn't stand a chance against such force, even with Melnyk's armory. We needed to flee.

"Can we outrun them?"

He gave me a grim look and shook his head. "We don't have to. We just need to return to France's side of the maritime border."

"Provided they respect that…"

He unlocked the cabin door and peeked out. The hallway was currently empty, though there were a lot of noises coming from the cabins. We slipped out and he locked the door. Melnyk tried to shout something after us, but we didn't heed him. He was the least of our problems right now.

We ran up the bow stairs to the upper deck, then took time to locate the stairs that would take us to the bridge. All around us, the party was in full swing, and no one paid any attention to us, apart from a couple of women who tried to wrap themselves around Eliot. There were empty glasses and bottles everywhere and people dancing and having sex where everyone could see.

At least they'd die happy…

The door to the bridge was locked, unsurprisingly. The crew couldn't risk some drunken idiot invading the place and sinking the boat. Eliot gave the door an officious rap. The lock was turned and the door opened a crack.

Eliot pushed in, forcing the man on the other side to fall back. I followed, closing and locking the door again.

"Turn the boat around!" Eliot ordered, training his weapon at the man at the helm, probably the captain. I still had Melnyk's pistol, and I pointed it at the other man, even though it didn't have a magazine in. He lifted his hands up, so he didn't notice the absence.

"I have my orders to meet *Benevolence*, and I'm more afraid of Artem than you," the captain said.

"We're not going to make it to *Benevolence*," Eliot said. "There's a small army heading our way, fast. Dobrev sent them. They're pissed off and they're not going to let anyone live. Turn. The. Boat. Around."

The men exchanged worried glances. "I can't turn at this speed."

"You can turn it in any fucking speed you want, just make sure we're back in French waters before we're boarded."

The captain slowed down and began to turn the yacht back the way we came. As we turned, I spied lights in the darkness, still far away but approaching fast.

"They're here." My voice broke a little and I had trouble breathing.

The captain accelerated again, but a yacht this size didn't change speed that fast. "We're not going to outrun them," Eliot said, his face grim. "Keep the speed, but prepare to be boarded."

"We're unarmed," the other man said, his face pale.

"Then lock and barricade the door after we leave."

We exited the bridge. "What are we going to do now?" I asked, studying his worried face. There wasn't a safe place on the yacht, but the bridge was hard to reach. We might have survived there.

"We prepare to defend ourselves."

I followed him back down. "We're the only sober people here. We can't go arming this lot."

"God forbid," he said, stepping aside with a shudder when a guy almost puked on his legs. "Do you think they'd listen if we told them they're about to die?"

I grimaced. "Maybe if you cut the music?"

He dipped his chin, considering it. Then he stepped over the puke and marched to the lounge, where the DJ was busy keeping the party up. He didn't ask permission; he just switched the entire table off.

"Hey!" the guy protested, taking off his earphones. Eliot pointed his weapon at him, and he stepped back, his hands up.

"I need to make an announcement," Eliot said, studying the table. The man pointed timidly at a switch, and Eliot turned it. The loudspeakers squealed painfully, but no one reacted. He leaned down to speak to the microphone.

"Attention, everyone! *Attention, s'il vous plaît!* We're about to be boarded by pirates. Please, remain calm."

I rolled my eyes. "Like that's going to work."

The shouts and jeers from the decks indicated people found it a good joke.

He leaned to the microphone again. "Everyone is going to die. Either we're shot by the pirates, or we drown trying to escape. Personally, I'd choose the bullet, but it's up to you."

The front deck cheered and laughed, but from the back came a few tentative screams as they spotted the lights of the fast-approaching boats. A rattle of bullets hit the yacht, audible even to where we were. The engine coughed, and the yacht began to lose speed.

Eliot went pale. "Fuck. They're going to blow us up."

Stomach acid pushed to my mouth, but I shook my head. "They wouldn't have come with such force if that was the objective."

His nostrils flared, as if he was about to lose it. Then

he closed his eyes and breathed deep. "You're right. But I'm not staying to witness it."

"We can't leave these people to die!"

He faced me, unyielding. "They are not worth dying for."

I knew that, on a general level. "They're people…"

People who were busy screaming, running in opposite directions, and pushing each other out of the way in their need to save themselves. The stairs below decks were jammed as everyone was looking for a place to hide. I hoped the lock on Melnyk's door would hold, because I didn't want to witness what would happen when this lot got their hands on his weapons cache.

"The choice is between dying and surviving. I almost died in a boat explosion once. I'm not doing that again."

I looked him in the eyes and believed him.

"Let's find a lifeboat."

He shook his head. "We're a hundred miles out to sea. That won't do much good."

"Better odds on it."

His jaw flexed, but he nodded and we headed to the stern. But the RIBs were already there, a moment away from boarding us.

My insides went cold. I counted ten men in all black, wearing balaclavas and carrying assault rifles, before Eliot turned me around from the shoulders and pushed me forward. "The bow it is."

We rushed through the lounge to the front of the boat. The hot tub had emptied of people, but the most drunken partiers were still sprawled on the seats lining the railing. And among them…

"That's René!"

# 26

## ELIOT

"WHAT THE FUCK IS HE DOING HERE?" I rushed to him just as thuds from the stern indicated the RIBs had reached the yacht. If they were half as efficient as they looked, it wouldn't take them long to board.

"He was partying on the beach. He must've followed the party here."

"Fuck." I reached to pat his cheeks, but he was completely out of it.

"He wasn't this drunk when I saw him earlier," Ada said, worried.

"His glass is almost full. I don't think he's drunk," I said grimly. "He's been drugged."

"We can't leave him here."

"The lifeboat is at the stern. We can't get to it. We have to swim. We can't take him with us."

Her eyes grew large with shock. "We can't swim ashore."

She was right.

I looked around, desperate to come up with a solution, and spotted a lever behind Bellamy's seat. I reached to switch it and a hatch popped open on the floor. I pulled it open and peeked in. It was dark, but there were ladders.

"Down," I ordered Ada, who didn't question the order. I grabbed Bellamy by his shirt, and pulled him on the floor with a thud. My heart beating in my throat, I dragged him to the hatch, then spent an agonizing moment turning him so that his legs went down the hatch first. Stepping onto the ladder myself, I pulled him through, dropping him down the meter or so.

"I got him," Ada hissed from the darkness. I pulled the hatch closed just as I spied the first attackers approaching the bow behind the hot tub that shielded us, assault rifles ready.

It was a dark, cramped space, with barely room to stand up doubled over. I pulled out my phone and opened the flashlight. Ada was sprawled on the floor, Bellamy spread on her, still unconscious.

"A little help?" she hissed, and I crouched to roll him off her.

"No Jet Skis," I said, disappointed. I hadn't come down here when the police searched the yacht earlier. I'd hoped one would still be here.

Ada's bros shot up. "That's what this is for? Can we hide here?"

"Maybe. But I'd rather not test their knowledge of the yacht."

Heavy steps and loud commands sounded over us, but there was no shooting yet. We waited in tense silence, but no one discovered the lever that opened the hatch. For now.

"Okay, they've moving to the cabins. We have to go."

I located the switch on the wall and turned it. A hatch lowered almost soundlessly to form a platform over the water. "We'll swim to the nearest RIB and take it over, then we'll come back for René."

Ada's face tightened. "I don't think we'll have a chance to come back. The moment we leave with the boat, the shooting starts. We have to take him with us." She glanced around and spotted something on the dark wall. "We'll use this."

I went to help her and together we pulled a small raft off the wall. It was basically a foot thick rectangle of floating material, barely wide enough for Bellamy and just about as long as he was tall. It wouldn't float three, but there were ropes on its sides where we could hold while we swam.

We rolled Bellamy onto his back on it, which seemed to take forever. I listened to the sounds coming through the wall, the harsh words, curses, and screams, but no shots yet. That would change when they found Melnyk, and his cabin was right behind our hidey-hole.

"We need to fasten him with something," I said. Ada pulled a scarf from around her throat. It wasn't much, but it reached over Bellamy's chest so that we could tie both ends to the ropes. When he was secure-ish, I took out my phone and pistol and put them into his pockets. Ada did the same.

"We have to strip." It would be too difficult to swim wearing a tux.

"Great."

But she was already pulling off the tunic and leggings, leaving only her underwear. I did the same. Then she took our clothes, wrapped them inside my tux jacket, and fastened it into the scarf from the sleeves on Bellamy's stomach.

"Let's hope it'll hold."

I wasn't feeling hopeful for our chances, but if things went sideways, we could always push Bellamy toward the shore and hope he made it.

We pushed the raft onto the platform, and I glanced up. No one was looking down, and no one seemed to be patrolling on the deck. There was some light coming through the cabin windows, but they were narrow and if we kept to the hull of the yacht, no one would spot us.

"Let's go," I said in a low voice.

We pushed the raft into the water and held our breath until we were sure it floated. The waves were fairly high, pushing water onto the raft, but the raft seemed secure.

I swallowed hard, then dropped into the water. The cold robbed me of my breath. Memories of the last time I'd taken a plunge like this flooded to my mind, briefly incapacitating me. I struggled to gain control, but it wasn't until Ada took hold of the raft and began to swim that I shot back to action.

It was both easier to swim with the raft and much harder. The waves kept pushing us away from the hull, and we had to constantly fight and swim sideways as well as forward. But the distance wasn't long, and we made progress, slow and steady.

I was out of breath when we reached the nearest RIB. It was empty, and there was no one on the other one either. No one kept watch on the deck or the swimming platform at the back. They didn't think anyone would be stupid enough to try to flee on them.

I guess we were.

Ada took a hold of the RIB at the stern, which was lying closest to the water, the two powerful outboard engines pulling it down now that the boat was empty. She built momentum by lifting herself up and down with the waves, and with an upward surf, dove in.

"Lay low," I said, as if that needed saying. I began to untie the scarf that had kept Bellamy on the raft amazingly well, but the knot was soaked and wouldn't open. "Do you have a knife in that bag of yours?"

She nodded, so I handed it to her, and she dug the knife out. Her hands were stiff with cold, and it took her a moment to get the pocketknife open. I turned the raft sideways so that she could reach the scarf more easily. She cut it and lifted our possessions onto the boat.

It took ages to push and pull Bellamy on board. He would have some interesting bruises tomorrow—if he was still alive. When it was done, I rested on the raft, breathing heavily. But we weren't done yet.

"Detach the boat and push it away from the yacht. I'll be right back."

She didn't waste time asking where I was going and went to do as I asked. Clinging to the side of the boat to keep myself from drifting away with the waves, I swam to the other RIB. I untied it, but that didn't seem like enough, so I pushed it away from the yacht as hard as I could with what little strength I had left.

I could hear the men climbing back on the deck. I was out of time. I swam back to the other boat and began to push it away from the stern.

It wouldn't move at first, it was too heavy to push against the waves, but little by little we began to drift away. Hanging on to the ropes, I pulled myself on board. Or tried to. I was exhausted.

Ada took a hold under my arms, and with grunts and curses pulled me on. She dropped on her back, breathing heavily. I was lying on my stomach, doing the same.

"Do you think we can start the engine now?"

My arms were like rubber, but I pushed up with my elbows to peek over the side of the RIB. We were farther away from the yacht than I'd hoped, but the attackers had already spotted the loss of their escape vessels. They couldn't spot us in the darkness; no weapons rose to point at us, and instead they began to search the deck for whoever had released the boats. Two men began to remove their gear, preparing to swim to the nearer boat.

We couldn't allow that.

"You start the boat, I'll handle the other one," I said to Ada. I took out my weapon from Bellamy's pocket, but instantly realized it wouldn't have the range. Rummaging through Ada's bag, I took out Melnyk's pistol, put the magazine back on, and took aim leaning against the round side of the RIB.

Our engine roared to life, claiming the attention of the men on the yacht. They instantly pointed their assault rifles at us and let rip. Bullets were ricocheting off the water, and it was a miracle nothing hit us.

"Go!" I shouted at Ada, who punched the gas. I aimed at the engine of the other RIB and pulled the trigger.

The RIB exploded.

BELLAMY CAME TO midway back, groggy and utterly bewildered. And freezing too, as the water had soaked his backside and we didn't have dry clothes for him.

Ada and I had put on our clothes, but they weren't much help against cold either, as we'd had to pull them on our wet bodies. I checked the equipment box and found one space blanket, which I gave to Bellamy, who wrapped inside it, looking miserable.

"What the hell is going on?" he demanded to know when he'd recovered enough to speak, shouting over the noise the engines made.

"I'll tell you when we've landed," I shouted back, keeping an eye on where we'd come from to see if we were being pursued.

Guided by the compass app on her phone, Ada brought us to the nearest shore, which was somewhere outside Nice. "There's enough juice in this thing to make it back to Monaco," she said. Since that was where we needed to be, I nodded and she turned the boat up the coast, keeping close to the shore.

We reached the hotel marina before we froze to death. Everything was as we left there. We hadn't even been gone that long—two hours maybe, even with the detour. The party on the beach had wound down, but there were a few sleeping figures sprawled on the sunchairs. They didn't stir when Ada revved the engine and pushed us up on the sand.

We were wet, tired, and wobbly as we climbed the terraced deck onto the elevator that would take us to the hotel. Bellamy was able to walk by himself, but we propped him up on both sides anyway.

"Wait here," I told them as we reached the elevator, giving Bellamy's full weight to Ada. As fast as I was able to, my cold muscles protesting every step, I ran to the other end of the docks.

*Serenata* was gone.

Gagne woke up when we entered the suite. He took in our wet, disheveled appearance and his brows shot up. "What's happened?"

"Explanations can wait," I said. "We need hot showers. Can you keep an eye on René? He's been drugged and he might fall asleep in the shower."

I don't know if it was because he was a father or just a good cop, but Gagne immediately took charge of his colleague.

I made to enter the other bedroom, but Ada halted me. "I'll go first."

The mere thought of waiting for a warm shower made me shudder in agony. "There are two shower heads there. We can both go. I have to get rid of these wet clothes."

She hesitated and nodded. "Fine. I'm too tired to argue with you."

"And I'm too tired and cold to get excited about your naked body." I gave it a thought. "Just keep in mind that cold does things to a male body and I'm not at my best."

With a tired grin, she headed to the bathroom, disrobing as she went. I followed with more energy than I'd had a moment ago.


THE COAST GUARD had reached *Arctos* soon after we left, guided by the explosion and Laïla, who had alerted them. She'd followed the events from the satellite until she'd had to give it up when her presence on the system had been detected.

"The attackers were gone by the time the rescuers arrived," she'd told Ada. "They took the lifeboats. There were some injuries among the passengers, most of them self-inflicted when they tried to flee, but the attackers had roughened up a few of them too. Melnyk is dead. He was shot."

The detectives, Ada, and I gathered on the couches of our suite, wrapped up in bathrobes, each holding a large glass of whiskey for warmth.

It was five in the morning and we were exhausted, but this couldn't wait. I kept an eye on Bellamy, but he was recovered from the drug and didn't look like he needed to go to the hospital.

We explained briefly how we had become separated at the Casino. Then Ada grimaced.

"I wanted to check out *Arctos*, so I went to snoop."

Gagne shook his head. "What was the point of that? The police already searched the place, and you won't be able to use anything you found there."

"I didn't even find anything, if you don't count drugs, insane amount of cash, and weapons to equip a small army."

He turned to me. "And what's your excuse?"

"I was drugged."

"At least I'm not the only one," Bellamy groaned. "I wasn't even drinking alcohol. There had to be something in the water the girl drank. I emptied most of her glass."

"But who drugged you?" Gagne asked me.

I told them how I'd ended up on Bosco's yacht and what had been in the whiskey.

"And I know who killed Fabre and Lepine. Well, I know who had them killed, and Bosco was fairly sure Travert shot Lepine, but it could've been any of Melnyk's bodyguards."

"And Melnyk had Travert killed for getting the police involved, so you can stop looking for him at least," Ada added.

I explained everything as clearly as I could without bringing Ada's other job into it.

"It wouldn't have occurred to me that the external drive came from Fabre," Gagne said, frowning when I finished. "Why did Bosco think you'd stolen it?"

I spread my arms, hoping the detective wouldn't fixate on that. He was suspicious of me as it was, and it wouldn't take much of a leap of logic to believe I was a burglar. "I showed up at the wrong time, I guess. He also believes I shot Fabre and/or am a cop, so…" I left it at that.

"Then how did you know *Benevolence* would be there?"

That was trickier, but I had an explanation ready. "I spotted the name on Ada's ship tracking app the other day, heading to the Mediterranean from the Bosporus." I hoped she wouldn't refute the claim, but she looked like she'd forgotten she hadn't shown it to me. "I recognized the name as a ship that the border and customs raided about a year ago in New York. They found drugs and people in a container. I made an educated, or hopeful, guess that it might be involved in Dobrev's businesses."

Gagne rubbed his face. "I guess it is Dobrev's ship, then. And Dobrev had Melnyk killed. So, there's just him and this Bosco operating on Mediterranean now?"

I nodded. "Though it's only matter of time before Bosco removes Dobrev too."

"We have to find him," Gagne stated.

"Good luck with that," I said grimly. "By the look of it, he's been around for a long time, and he's very successful. And no one's ever suspected him. He'd left by the time we returned, so he's not taking any chances either. With his yacht, he could be hiding anywhere."

"But he knows that you know about him now," Ada pointed out.

My gut tightened. "He left me on Melnyk's yacht to be killed. He might believe that it worked."

"Just in case, you'd best lay low for a while," Bellamy said.

"Oh, I intend to."

The wise thing to do would be to follow rule number three: Ditch everything, adopt a new identity, and relocate to safer waters. But I was starting to realize I didn't want to leave. Against all odds, I'd made friends of the detectives. And I wasn't ready to leave Ada before I'd had a chance to find out if there could be something more between us.

I wouldn't be safe with Bosco out there, and that would risk Ada too. Breaking my own rules could get me killed, but Bosco might find me no matter who I pretended to be. If he was looking for me, I would make it easy for him. But I wasn't going to be a sitting duck for him to find. I would go after him.

For that to happen, I would have to break the most important rule of them all, rule number seven: Don't return to the life of crime. Because sometimes you needed a thief to catch a thief.

I would catch Bosco. And then I would be safe.

# EPILOGUE

## ADA

I EMERGED FROM MY ADVENTURE with no repercussions, personal or professional. I didn't catch a cold—unlike Bellamy who had a man flu to end them all—and the detectives stated in their report that I'd entered *Arctos* with Bellamy to party. My boss even commended me for my actions to save Bellamy and Eliot.

As if Eliot hadn't handled the latter. I wouldn't have known to look for the Jet Ski hatch, and I wouldn't have thought to blow up the other RIB.

We'd spent Sunday talking to authorities, before Gagne and Bellamy returned to Lyon to wrap up their investigation. They had a general idea of who had killed Fabre and Lepine and why, and not much hope locating the exact people who had pulled the trigger.

I stayed in Monaco until Monday. I'd been given the day off and I was too exhausted to travel home. Eliot allowed me to stay in his room and relocated to the detectives' room instead. I was amazed to realize that I wouldn't have minded if we'd shared the room. Maybe it was the near-death experience, maybe it was the shared shower.

I'd most certainly checked what was underneath his well-fitting suits, and had been more than intrigued by the tight, muscled body. I don't know if he'd done the same to me, but he had been a perfect gentleman like he'd promised. More's the pity.

When I woke up on Monday, he had left. There was only a note that said the room was paid for. My disappointment was inordinate.

I had trouble settling back to my routines when I returned home. I took no pleasure in putting on my Ada Reed persona, and I slipped a little. I constantly found myself staring at my computer screen at work without seeing what was on it. Nothing enticed me at home.

I tried calling Eliot a couple of times, but he didn't answer them or my messages. He wasn't home when I went to look and he didn't show up on the self-defense class. I could take a hint, so I stopped bothering him. Laïla didn't help with her constant questions about our adventure and Eliot, and if I was seeing him.

Vaguely, I recognized that I was suffering from some sort of post traumatic episode, but apart from booking an appointment with a counselor at work, there was nothing I could do about it. It would pass.

The only thing that interested me was investigating Salvatore Bosco. It was amazing how little information there was of him freely available, and all of it was good. He was an outstanding citizen of an old Italian family and a businessman. If he hadn't revealed everything to Eliot, I wouldn't have even suspected he was running a criminal organization.

I hoped he wasn't going after Eliot, but I wasn't holding my breath.

Only then did it occur to me that Eliot was probably doing what the detectives had told him and laying low. He would emerge when he felt safe.

That revived me enough from my slump that I checked my other job. On the secure marketplace where people solicited criminal services was a request for a job made for me: cracking a safe at a private residence in Rome. There was no time limit, but the client had provided information about when the house would be empty.

I didn't need it for the money, but it would get me out of my gloom. I didn't hesitate to accept.

The second Saturday in June, I entered a Renaissance villa on Gianicolo, a hill on the west side of the Tiber in Rome, not far from the Vatican. The place was quiet and empty, as I'd known it would be after keeping an eye on the place since previous night, after arriving on a late flight to Rome. I hadn't been able to take a full day off so soon after my previous break.

I'd prepared well beforehand. I'd accessed the blueprints of the house—new ones that showed all the work that had been done to the place, especially the security measures and the location of the safe.

I climbed a trellis to the *loggia*, the second-floor gallery at the back, ignoring the spectacular view down the hill toward the river Tiber and the ancient city on the other side. The alarm on the balcony door was an older model and easy to handle, and the lock was a moment's work to open.

Everything was dark and quiet inside. The study where the safe was located was down a short hallway. The windows faced the neighbor's wall, and even though that place was dark too, I made sure to close the heavy drapes tight, before switching on the desk lamp.

A moment of nostalgia halted me as I remembered my first encounter with Eliot. It had been only a month ago, but it felt like a lifetime had happened since.

The safe was hidden behind an original Tintoretto that I wouldn't have minded stealing for myself in other circumstances. I made a mental note of it though, in case a client put out an order for one.

Alarms were protecting it, but like with the gallery door, they were an older system and could be dealt with by cutting the wiring. The painting turned silently aside like a door, with hinges on one long edge, and I took a good look at the safe. I sighed in relief that it was still the model that the blueprints had indicated. It was one of my favorites.

Easy though it was to open, it wasn't fast. It took five agonizingly long minutes to crack it, during which I kept one ear on my surroundings. When the final bolt dropped, I leaned my forehead on the cool metal door to calm down again. Then I pulled the door open.

It was empty.

The lights in the room were switched on. In panic, I twirled to the door, ready to bolt.

A man was standing at the doorway, dressed in black like me, a smug smile on his handsome face as he pointed a weapon at me. I felt like I was looking at a ghost—which wasn't far from the truth, even if I'd known he wasn't dead.

"Hello, wife. It's been a long time."

I'd spent years trying to find him. But my late husband had found me first.

# ACKNOWLEDGEMENTS

Eliot Reed started his life as Jonny Moreira in *P.I. Tracy Hayes* mystery series as the larger-than-life mafia enforcer. He grew a bit too large for the books, though, and had to be given a chance to go on his own. I'd like to thank you, my readers, for reading and liking the Tracy Hayes books enough to give him the opportunity—and following him here.

Eliot and Ada will return in *The Perfect Hoax*.

# ABOUT THE AUTHOR

Susanna Shore is an independent author. She writes *Two-Natured London* paranormal romance series about vampires and wolf-shifters that roam London, *P.I. Tracy Hayes* series of a Brooklyn waitress turned private investigator, and *House of Magic* paranormal mysteries set in London. She also writes stand-alone thrillers and contemporary romances. When she's not writing, she's reading or—should her husband manage to drag her outdoors—taking long walks.

WWW.SUSANNASHORE.COM

Printed in Great Britain
by Amazon

10658467R00160